WILD NIGHT RISING

What Reviewers Say About Barbara Ann Wright's Work

The Mage and the Monster

"I have truly enjoyed reading the novels in 'The Sisters of Sarras' series by Barbara Ann Wright. …I've been delighted with all three books. The story of Gisele and Vale is a fitting conclusion to this series. It takes the characters and the narrative of the first two books and pulls us into a story that includes danger, adventure, and war. It's also a chance for some, including Gisele and Vale, to find love and acceptance. There are quite a few twists and turns in the plot. This tale will definitely keep you wondering as you read."—Rainbow Reflections

The Scout and the Scoundrel

"The second lesbian fantasy romance in Wright's The Sisters of Sarras trilogy takes to the military for a delightful character-centered story about trust and loyalty. Sarassian Commander Zara del Amanecer is socially awkward and ultra-rational. As punishment for a recent faux pas with a Colonel's daughter, her scouting squad is the first in an experiment in using prisoners as recruits, putting flirty, smart-mouthed thief Veronique 'Roni' Bisset under Zara's command and setting the stage for their opposites-attract romance. …Series fans will not be disappointed." *Publishers Weekly*

"Zara appealed to me immediately because firstly, she appears to be on the autism spectrum, and secondly, neither Wright nor the characters call attention to it. Her preference for solitude, difficulties reading social cues, and struggles to recognize other people's feelings are just part of her character…and her slow burn romance with Veronique (Roni), the thief assigned to her unit as part of an experimental prison reform program, felt comfortably familiar. In the wrong hands, Zara's uncertainty over Roni's flirting could have been played for laughs or pity, but Wright makes it sweet and endearing, putting a fresh spin on the enemies-to-lovers trope."—*Beauty in Ruins: Female Led Fantasy*

The Noble and the Nightingale

"Wright sets up the Sisters of Sarras lesbian fantasy romance trilogy with solid worldbuilding, a delightfully awkward couple who bridge social realms, and an entertaining adventure that leaves plenty of room to grow. …By the end, Wright has established strong personalities for Adella's two sisters and taken the suspense plotline to the brink of war between Sarras and the Firellians, setting up strongly for the next volumes. Readers will be pleased."—*Publishers Weekly*

"This book was a ton of fun. …I think it is very approachable for all types of readers. …I ended up reading this book until 3 [a.m.] because I had to know how everything would unfold and what would happen to all the characters. …This is the kind of story to take you on an adventure and just have fun with. Not only could I not stop reading this book, but it put a big smile on my face. I'm a happy reader."—*Lez Review Books*

Lady of Stone

"Yet another stellar read from Barbara Ann Wright, *Lady of Stone* is a wonderful blend of magical fantasy and lesbian romance that had me eager to find out how it all ends, and yet reluctant to have it end." —*Beauty in Ruins*

Not Your Average Love Spell

"Barbara Ann Wright mixes so much into her story—romance, comedy, drama, action, adventure—that it threatens more than once to collapse under the clash of themes, but those clashes and contrasts only serve to make it stronger and more engaging."—*Beauty in Ruins*

"...a solid little fantasy tale with a lot of really cool elements. ...Wright plays to all the tropes...in a way that keeps the story fresh while preserving the surprises. ...As for the romance, that was surprisingly sweet and amusing, with four women at the heart of the story who are entirely likable. ...The spark of attraction and the emotional connections are undeniable."—*Fem Led Fantasy*

"...a great story filled with magic, wondrous creatures and adventure but what I really enjoyed about the book was the way that the characters grew. ...It is a great thing to read in these trying times and I took hope from it. The story pulls with enough magic to feel like a fully fleshed out fantasy world while keeping our heroes relatable and engaging. ...I give it a full hearted thumbs up and you should definitely check it out."—*Paper Phoenix Ink*

"[*Not Your Average Love Spell*] is an entertaining...romantic fantasy adventure comedy? (I'm not sure how to categorise its Venn diagram of subgenres, either.) Starring an agoraphobic witch; a bright, curious, talkative homunculus; an archivist/scholar with a revolutionary bent; a knight who—at least initially—believes wholeheartedly in her order's mission to stamp out magic; and an invasion of genocidal warriors, *Not Your Average Love Spell* takes its characters on an entertaining ride and delivers all of them a happy ending. (Except for the genocidal warriors. Their happy ending would be terrible for everyone else.)"—*Tor.com*

The Tattered Lands

"Wright's postapocalyptic romance is a fast-paced journey through devastation. ...Plenty of action, surprises, and magic will keep readers turning the pages."—*Publishers Weekly*

House of Fate

"...fast, fun...entertaining. ...*House of Fate* delivers on adventure."
—*Tor.com*

***Lambda Literary Award Finalist*—Coils**

"…Greek myths, gods and monsters and a trip to the Underworld. Sign me up. …This one springs straight into action…a good start, great Greek myth action and a late blooming romance that flowers in the end…"—*Dear Author*

"A unique take on the Greek gods and the afterlife make this a memorable book. The story is fun with just the right amount of camp. Medusa is a hot, if unexpected, love interest. …A truly unexpected ending has us hoping for more stories from this world."—*RT Book Reviews*

Paladins of the Storm Lord

"I loved this. …The world that the Paladins inhabited was fascinating…didn't want to put this down until I knew what happened. I'll be looking for more of Barbara Ann Wright's books."—*Lesbian Romance Reviews*

"*Paladins of the Storm Lord* by Barbara Ann Wright was like an orchestra with all of its pieces creating a symphony. I really truly loved it. I love the intricacy and wide variety of character types. …I just loved practically every character! …Of course my fellow adventure lovers should read *Paladins of the Storm Lord*!"—*Lesbian Review*

Thrall: Beyond Gold and Glory

"In their adventures, the women must wrestle with issues of freedom, loyalty, and justice. The characters were likable, the issues complex, and the battles were exciting. I really enjoyed this book and I highly recommend it."—*All Our Worlds: Diverse Fantastic Fiction*

"This was the first Barbara Ann Wright novel I've read, and I doubt it will be the last. Her dialogue was concise and natural, and she built a fantastical world that I easily imagined from one scene to the next. Lovers of Vikings, monsters and magic won't be disappointed by this one."—*Curve*

The Pyramid Waltz

"…a healthy dose of a very creative, yet believable, world into which the reader will step to find enjoyment and heart-thumping action. It's a fiendishly delightful tale."—*Lambda Literary*

"Chock full of familiar elements that avid fantasy readers will adore…[*The Pyramid Waltz*] adds in a compelling and slowly evolving romance. …Set against a backdrop of political intrigue with the possibility of monsters and mystery at every turn, the two women slowly learn each other, sharing secrets and longing, until a fragile love blossoms between them…"—*USA Today Happily Ever After*

For Want of a Fiend

"This book will keep you turning the page to find out the answers. …Fans of the fantasy genre will really enjoy this installment of the story. We can't wait for the next book."—*Curve*

A Kingdom Lost

"There is only one other time in my life I have uncontrollably shouted out in cheer while reading a book. [*A Kingdom Lost*] made the second. …Over the course of these three books all the characters have blossomed and developed so eloquently. …I simply just thought this whole novel was brilliant."—*Lesbian Review*

The Fiend Queen

"After reading this series Barbara Ann Wright has made my favorite author list. Her writing always seems to sweep me away to another world. The pacing, characters, and language were all perfect. …I am so addicted to Fantasy now. I knew fantasy was one of my favorite genres but it was always hard for me to come by a consistent source of fantasy books. After finishing the series A Pyradisté Adventure I knew that I had found a diamond. I can't wait to read the rest of Barbara Ann Wright's works. …Read it! I am obsessed and I don't know how I will ever want to read a non-fantasy Lesfic ever again. I literally felt drunk off the series. Even after I was done with this book I thought about it constantly for at least two days."—*Lesbian Review*

Visit us at www.boldstrokesbooks.com

By the Author

The Pyradisté Adventures

The Pyramid Waltz

For Want of a Fiend

A Kingdom Lost

The Fiend Queen

Lady of Stone

Thrall: Beyond Gold and Glory

The Godfall Novels

Paladins of the Storm Lord

Widows of the Sun-Moon

Children of the Healer

Inheritors of Chaos

Coils

House of Fate

The Tattered Lands

Not Your Average Love Spell

The Sisters of Sarras

The Noble and the Nightingale

The Scout and the Scoundrel

The Mage and the Monster

Haunted by Myth

Wild Night Rising

Wild Night Rising

by

Barbara Ann Wright

2025

WILD NIGHT RISING

© 2025 By Barbara Ann Wright. All Rights Reserved.

ISBN 13: 978-1-63679-749-6

This Trade Paperback Original Is Published By
Bold Strokes Books, Inc.
P.O. Box 249
Valley Falls, NY 12185

First Edition: August 2025

THIS IS A WORK OF FICTION. NAMES, CHARACTERS, PLACES, AND INCIDENTS ARE THE PRODUCT OF THE AUTHOR'S IMAGINATION OR ARE USED FICTITIOUSLY. ANY RESEMBLANCE TO ACTUAL PERSONS, LIVING OR DEAD, BUSINESS ESTABLISHMENTS, EVENTS, OR LOCALES IS ENTIRELY COINCIDENTAL.

THIS BOOK, OR PARTS THEREOF, MAY NOT BE REPRODUCED IN ANY FORM WITHOUT PERMISSION.

Credits
Editor: Cindy Cresap
Production Design: Susan Ramundo
Cover Design By Inkspiral Design

Acknowledgments

This past year has been one of the most difficult of my entire life: health woes and bad news and the loss of my mom, a blow from which I'll never fully recover. The fact that I'm still here is due to the tireless support of friends like Erin, David, Deb, Natsu, Matt, Angela, Sarah, and all the family I've found in the writer community.

Special thanks to Cindy, Sandy, and Ruth from BSB who've checked on me from time to time and haven't once groused at me about deadlines, all of which were fractured by this book, but I've made it to the finish line.

And thanks to you, the readers, your support has meant the world to me. I hope we continue having adventures together for a long time to come.

Dedication

For Mom. I miss you every day.

Prologue

Gwyn never thought she'd value objects solely by how well they served as a barricade. But when trying to keep out a biker gang led by Tisiphone—Fury of vengeance—and made up of fey, Amazons, and a few Valkyrie, stoutness was a coveted trait.

She lifted an old armoire heavier than a safe and pushed it against the door. "Did you give all the money back?"

Steffan, mayor of their current location in Nowhere, Nebraska, nodded violently, tears trickling down his cheeks as he piled flotsam in front of the windows of his enormous house. "I swear, all of it."

It had taken him a while to admit that the Wild Hunt was on his heels, even after Gwyn had warned him. As She Who Goes Before, she was only supposed to advise the innocent to stay indoors and heighten the fear of the Hunt's prey, maybe remind them to get their affairs in order. But if she caused Tiss to fail in just one mission, the Hunt could be hers to lead again.

Steffan had only believed her when the bodies had started dropping. Anyone who stood in the way of the Hunt was doomed, especially now that it was led by a former Fury. If Steffan had returned all the money, the Hunt should have given up. Atonement was supposed to appease the Furies, even if whoever summoned them didn't quite agree.

"And the money you already pissed away?" she asked.

He leaned on his knees and breathed hard. "I sold everything I could to pay it back."

"What about this house?" There was no doubt the Hunt was still on their way; she could sense them coming. But if Steffan had atoned, and Tiss refused to back off, the Hunt's faith in her would be shaken, weakening her. Maybe that would give Gwyn enough ammunition for a challenge.

Then again, maybe atonement wouldn't work at all, especially since every time she'd tried, the greedy had always held something back. Maybe nothing could make up for some crimes if they didn't repent in their heart.

Steffan wasn't looking at her.

"Well?" she asked, her hope dying.

"I've got to have a roof over my head!"

Gwyn glanced up. It looked like he had maybe four roofs over his head, if this monstrosity was any indication. It stuck out in this small town like a boil on Steffan's lily-white backside. She sighed from her boots as he continued to hustle around, trying to block the windows in the office, the most defensible room in the house.

Not that it would do any good.

When Gwyn shifted the armoire away from the door, Steffan dropped the potted plant he'd been dragging across the floor. "What are you doing?"

"I had high hopes for you, chum. Stolen money should have been easily returned. You could have ruined your reputation, given up your freedom, and saved your life."

"I did. I will. The grand jury is on Tuesday, and my lawyer says—" He choked as she stared. Guilt sat like a fat, ugly toad in his expression before it morphed to anger. "When I get out, I'll need—"

She walked out, ignoring his pleas. She only hoped Tiss and the others hadn't guessed at what she was trying to do here. She couldn't thwart them if she was dead. Better to not let them see her at all.

Clearly, Steffan wasn't the one to help put Gwyn in charge again. And the Hunt would go on killing, a vehicle for vengeance instead of the somewhat benign hunters they had been in the past. Any senseless deaths would be on her head for failing again.

And heads like Steffan's.

He followed her through the mostly empty house, grabbing at her arm, but his strength was nothing to hers. When he tugged on her favorite band T-shirt, she gave him a glare, and that was enough to make him let go, though the pleading continued right up until she marched out the back door.

"Please, please, please," he was saying, bleating like a sheep. The thunder of motorcycles rumbled in the distance.

Gwyn marched toward her Kawasaki Vulcan. The mounts of the Hunt could take almost any shape the rider commanded, and motorcycles fit in so much better than horses these days. She slung her leg over her bike and started it, but the sounds of the approaching Hunt masked the growl.

"Better get inside, chum," she yelled over the noise. "You've got company coming." She slipped on her helmet, kicked Steffan back with one booted foot, and gunned it, her back tire slipping a bit in the gravel drive as she roared around the garage, taking the path near the lake to get to the main road. She paused, one foot on the blacktop as a cloud of dust ran up Steffan's front drive, the bikes of the Wild Hunt growling like demon dogs as they descended on their prey.

She rode away before the screaming started.

CHAPTER ONE

Catching supernatural criminals would have been much easier if Holly's fey ancestry included something a little faster. A cheetah, say. Or a greyhound. Hell, even a field mouse would have added some speed. But, no, somewhere in her lineage, there had been a mermaid or siren or some kind of fish, extremely useful on land.

Except not.

"Move your ass," Renne shouted from the other end of the alley. It wasn't fair. Even though he had shark in his bloodline, he ran much faster than her.

So not only were her ancestors fish, they were slow fish. "What the hell is he?" Holly asked between gasps as she rounded the corner on Renne's heels. The stench of the alley followed her on a gust of humid bayou air. Even in the fall, the air in downtown Houston was thick as soup.

Ahead, their suspect parkoured off the roof of a car in a pay lot.

"Nimble," Renne said, being absolutely no help at all. "I'll go one over, head him off." He dashed down a side street.

Holly pushed on, tapping into her reserves of speed. She might be slower than their suspect, but she was faster than a pure human. She hadn't failed out of the police academy for any physical limitations.

The suspect looked over his shoulder at her and bounced off another car, making the alarm ring into the night. The steady rhythm of the honks felt like fingernails along Holly's spine, another gift of her fey ancestors: a slight allergy to anything too orderly. Memories of the rigors of the police academy still made her break out in hives.

At least working for the Supernatural Collection and Detainment Agency never made her ill.

Except for times like now, when the car alarm sent tingles skittering along the scales that ran down the center of her back and along each leg from her ass to her ankles. She tried to block the rhythmic honking from her mind as she leapt toward a pickup, pushed off the top of a huge tire, and hurled herself over the hood to tackle the suspect just as Renne streaked around the corner of the lot.

The suspect let out a porcine squeal and bucked, but she twisted to stay on top, banging one shin on the asphalt. "Stop struggling. You're under arrest."

Unsurprisingly, he declined, writhing even after Renne planted a palm in the middle of his back. "I place you under the geas of the SCDA, entered into with the elves who rule the plane of chaos in the human year of 2015, the fey year of the Shattered Turret."

A brief green glow outlined them all, and the suspect groaned but stopped resisting, barely scaring up a wiggle when Renne locked a pair of enchanted handcuffs around his wrists.

Holly hauled him to his feet. "For beings of chaos, the elves are awfully particular about the wording of their geas."

Renne grinned, his too-white dentures gleaming even brighter than his pale skin. "No one would ever enter into an agreement with them otherwise."

True. All fey looked for loopholes in deals. She was allowed to say that as a demi-fey herself. Her parents had certainly pushed every boundary in life to get the most stuff from the least effort. The geas served a purpose. There were no supernatural jails, and the elves, the pinnacle of fey-ness—according to them—who lived in the human realm wouldn't give the SCDA carte blanche to kill, not when their quarry might include members of the fey community, especially those with elven ancestry. Banishment to Signal, a city in a more chaotic plane, was the only solution. Until those criminals reached the portal between this world and that, someone had to keep them safe.

Even when suspects like this one stole a lot of money from some very dangerous people. Several members of the agency had suggested leaving this one to said dangerous people, but rough justice was no kind of justice at all. To Holly's eternal gratitude, Renne and their boss, Marcus, agreed with her.

Holly frog-marched the suspect back toward her and Renne's car, sticking to the shadows. Being under the geas always made suspects more docile, lessening the chances of the SCDA attracting the notice of the human police. Holly had no doubt Marcus would send someone to get them out of trouble, but that would involve the use of magic, and an organization that wasn't supposed to exist couldn't show their hand too often. All humans acknowledged a criminal underworld, but few knew about the layers of underworlds under those.

Once the suspect was secure in the back seat, Holly started up their Oldsmobile sedan, thankful it didn't have all the electric gadgets of new cars that seemed to go haywire in her presence, and pulled into the traffic that dotted downtown Houston at any time of day or night.

In the passenger seat, Renne worked his jaw back and forth.

"He land a good punch?" Holly asked.

"Just a tad." He pushed his dentures out and stretched his jaw. His normal, pointed teeth grew quickly to full size, always ready to spring back when not held in by the two plates. He'd have to snap them off later to put the dentures back in and pass as human—they'd just grow in again like a shark's—but on the ride to headquarters, it didn't matter.

Though she did get tired of picking his snapped-off teeth from the ashtray.

Once the suspect was safely locked up in a cell under the ever-watchful eye of a basilisk, Holly and Renne trooped upstairs. He took a moment to fix his dark hair in a window as they passed and straightened his suit jacket. Holly didn't bother. Bits of her hair were always going to escape her ponytail no matter how much hairspray she used, and if she bothered to smooth any wrinkles in her clothes, they'd work their way back in, her natural chaos always ready to rumple her. Her leg hurt but not enough to dull her sense of pride and the rush that came with doing what she'd been born to do.

As Renne preened, Holly's thoughts drifted once again to her parents. What would it be like to lock them in a cell? They'd been neglectful crooks who'd taught her to use the gifts of her heritage to get what she wanted, no matter what the law or society said. She'd known it was wrong then and was doubly sure of that now. Maybe they'd repent under the basilisk's eye.

Renne nudged her as he started for the elevator. "You've got that face again."

"What? I'm riding an arrest high."

"It's your, if I ever get my hands on my folks, face."

She couldn't help smiling even as she shook her head. "Don't get in the way of my dreams, Renne."

"You need better dreams, hun." His Louisiana accent got thicker the longer he spoke with his normal teeth, and she fought her own Texas twang that wanted to emerge in solidarity.

"My dreams are fine, thank you."

"A little imagination wouldn't hurt."

"Uh-huh."

"Big sack o' cash, new digs."

"Yep." Inside the elevator, she pushed the button for the top floor, and the door creaked closed. She only hoped it wouldn't break down in her presence again. She made herself take calming breaths. The less emotional she was, the more likely the technology surrounding her would actually work.

Renne leaned against the wall, scooting down so his lanky frame didn't seem that much taller. "You could always wish for a gorgeous woman on your…fin."

Holly put her hands on her hips. "Look who's talking, shark boy."

He flashed those sharp, nearly triangular teeth and winked, happy enough with getting a rise out of her, it seemed. "I got plenty of lovelies of all genders swimming in my seas, don't you worry."

She practically bolted out the doors when they finally opened. "Keep your seas to yourself." It irked her that he was never as bothered by his piscine characteristics as she was.

Because his were cooler. Even with the dentures.

Nope, stay calm, ride the high.

Marcus Aurkin, chief of the Houston branch of the SCDA, turned from a large computer screen mounted on the wall when Holly and Renne entered the hub of their operation. She didn't need a nod of his massive head to tell her to stay back from the monitor or the much-repaired Roku-PC-cable box setup underneath it. Last time she'd touched it, they'd lost signal for two days, but she thought their IT department—one disgruntled gremlin—was as much to blame as her. Fey with cutting-edge tech were like crabs with golf clubs: they could hold on but couldn't be expected to play nicely.

If only they had the magic of the elves to navigate a world made for humans. Or the capital to hire enough humans to work all this tech.

Or—

Renne nudged her, and she focused on the actual screen, stepping to the side of her chicken house-sized boss in order to see.

It looked like a video call from one of the other offices, judging by the peeling paint and patches of bare cinderblock in the background. Secret crime-fighting agencies didn't have the budget of the FBI, even if some high-level humans in the US government knew about them.

"It isn't just the human mayor they killed," a voice offscreen said before Jules Samson, Marcus's Kansas counterpart, appeared on the screen. "It was anyone who seems to have gotten in their way. The human authorities have labeled them a dangerous gang, though they're busy wasting time on the drug connections of human gangs."

Holly wouldn't have suspected that the Midwest had a lot of gang activity but supposed that made it the perfect place to hide.

"What makes you think they're headed for Houston?" Marcus said slowly, his voice the ultimate bass. Some put the way he spoke together with his massive frame and upturned nose and thought him stupid as well as slow. They usually didn't make that mistake twice.

"Their route out of town, punctuated with bodies. And the occasional corpse along the way. And the fact that they virtually disappear between bodies points to the fact that they either have some kind of invisibility glamour or another way to hide." Samson crossed her thin arms, all angles and bones who could still rip a car door from its hinges. "Why they decided to leave Europe is anyone's guess." She nodded offscreen, and her image was replaced with a map of northern Europe next to one of the US, with green lines crisscrossing the former and headed across the other from NYC to Nebraska, then straight down.

"Old-country BS," Marcus said, a common beef with older fey. If a person had enough fey blood—particularly elven or tainted by gods or mythical monsters—they could live for hundreds, even thousands, of years, and those who'd immigrated from Europe tended to sneer at "old-country" grudges.

"Not if they're targeting humans," Samson said as she reappeared.

"Blood feuds?" Marcus asked. "Handed down into human lines?"

Samson shook her head. "No connection we can find."

Excitement made Holly's bones tingle. A proper mystery, an actual gang, the chance to save who knew how many people? God, she was ready. "Has anyone in the agency tangled with them?" she asked, desperate for more info.

Samson looked up as if listening to the heavens, and Holly realized she couldn't see her, but she answered anyway. "No, all we have are a few sightings from Europe and here. I'm sending you all our info, Marcus."

Holly bit her lip at the slight emphasis on her boss's name. But she wanted to read those files so badly.

"One more odd thing," Samson said. "This gang seems to have an outrider who shows up before the bulk of them. Our informants report that she tries to help the humans who've been at the center of these attacks, though if she's trying to prevent the violence, she's doing a shitty job."

"A dissenter," Renne muttered.

Marcus rumbled, "Hmm," and shook his head. "With an old-country gang, she's probably a herald." He drummed his sausage fingers on a nearby desk. "I've got a few possibles in mind for the group's identity. I'll keep you informed."

Samson nodded as Marcus gestured to Ciarin the gremlin at the IT station, and it seemed to be a bit of a race as to who got to hang up first.

Holly was nearly quivering as she watched Marcus think. If he didn't assign her to this, she'd…

What? Quit? Law enforcement felt as much a part of her blood as her fey heritage. And she'd already proven she couldn't cut it in the human police. She doubted that the federal government or even world agencies would be any better.

"Look through recent surveillance for this herald around here," Marcus said. "Our best bet will be to get ahold of her first."

Ciaran swiveled his small chair to face his tiny custom keyboard. His desktop was held together by duct tape, but he somehow managed to make it work.

"Finn, Ama, check with your informants," Marcus said next. "Especially those from the old countries. Someone's gotta know something."

Finn, who fit in with humans even with his pink hair, opened a drawer on his desk while a file floated in midair toward him, borne by his tiny, winged, invisible partner, Ama.

"Holly, Renne," Marcus said as he turned.

Holly was sure the clock ticked backward as he paused.

"Keep up your patrols, keep your eyes open."

Holly waited for more, but none came. "Really, boss?"

"Ten-four," Renne said as he hooked his hand around Holly's elbow and towed her from the room before she could speak again. "You ain't gonna get nowhere pissing off the boss," he said when they were alone in the tiny break room.

"C'mon, Renne, everyone else works this case while we—"

"Are out doing something instead of sitting on our asses."

Fair point. Still, Holly paced. She came too close to the ancient coffeepot while agitated, and the clock built into the base flickered and died.

Renne nodded to it. "And don't tell me you want to trade places with Ciaran."

"No."

"Or Finn and Ama."

"No." Being relatively new, she didn't have any informants to speak of. "But we could, I don't know, try to meet this gang before they get here."

"How? Head north? Where to? And if they have glamour or some magical way to travel, how would we find them?"

"I don't know." She leaned against the counter in defeat. "I hate when you're right."

"Hating life as often as that isn't good for your heart."

She gave him a dark look. "I was going to thank you for keeping me from making Marcus angry, but never mind."

"You're welcome." He slung a long arm around her shoulders. "Anyway, shift's over for now. It's beer o'clock."

Part of her wanted to argue and say they needed to get back out there, but dawn was only a few hours off, and they did their best hunting at night. She could only hope this gang was headed for bed as well. She wanted to be well rested when she kicked their asses.

CHAPTER TWO

Gwyn slowed on the freeway near dusk and looked at the sprawling skyline of downtown Houston in the distance. How in all of Hades was she supposed to herald the arrival of the Hunt in this mess? A quick internet search had revealed that Houston was home to four million people. And that was just in the city limits.

At least she was sure the target *was* in the city limits, or near downtown. That was where she felt the pull. But no city the Hunt had ever visited had looked like this.

Gods, so many people were going to die.

She drove slowly into the one-way streets of downtown. The fetid breeze over the bayous lent the air a creeping humidity, and with the steel and glass behemoths surrounding her, no fresh air could get through to dispel the miasma, even though it was mid-October. Night was falling, but the heat from the sun wouldn't dissipate fast among the concrete and asphalt.

As Gwyn stopped at a red light, a blast of cold air from an automatic door washed over her, disturbing the whiff of stale garbage from a nearby alley. Not the most welcoming place on earth, though the beckoning lights and sounds from restaurants coming to life after the workday gave the streets a nice burst of chaotic energy.

Of course, with the way she felt, she wouldn't have been happy on a golden beach being massaged by Aphrodite's handmaidens.

She pulled into a metered parking space and gave the meter a charge of pure chaos, shorting it out. When the humans detected such things, they equated it to electromagnetism, though that definition didn't quite fit. She'd welcome any explanation that served to keep her kind a secret. The fey might have been more powerful than humans, but as history had proven time and again, humanity had numbers on their side. An army of ants could overwhelm creatures many times their size.

She tucked her helmet under her arm and shook out her hair. She'd likely survive any motorcycle accident without a lot of damage, but she attracted attention when she rode without protection. Incognito was not only the best for her species; it was the best way to find her prey.

Or even just a quiet drink.

Gwyn let her senses flow outward, looking for the target, of course, but also for anyone with fey blood like elves, fairies, pixies, brownies, and the like, anyone whose power hailed from the chaotic realms, otherwise known as Faerie. Fey had walked these streets recently, their energy crackling in the air. Happy surprise, there was more than one nearby, congregating in the same space. She followed her senses to a sign that said, *The Carnival Lounge*.

It was a bar, if the signage on the windows was to be believed, one announcing that happy hour was in full swing, Tuesdays were trivia nights, and Friday belonged to karaoke. She'd never been so happy that the weekend had already passed.

Inside the scarred wooden door, there was a sharp turn to the left that opened into a bar, but it was the wall on the right that sent her senses into overdrive. A glamour, the mere illusion of a wall instead of a physical one. Gwyn cast a look over her shoulder to make sure no humans were watching, and stepped through. A tingle spread over her shoulders. Someone had put a spell on the illusionary wall to make it repellent to humans, an added layer of protection, though humans would likely never notice. Nor would they stumble into the paranormal room of the Carnival Lounge.

This side of the bar was a mix of classic design like wooden bars and tables; '80s retro, with neon signs and new wave playing on the jukebox; and discotheque, represented by one slowly spinning mirror ball and a sad green light that gave one corner a sickly glow.

It was a perfect chaotic hodgepodge, and some of the tension left her shoulders. Maybe she'd have an easier time finding the summoner of the Hunt than she thought, especially if Houston had a thriving paranormal community. A human couldn't have summoned the Hunt with something they'd found in a bookshop like *Furies for Beginners* or *The Moron's Guide to the Wild Hunt*. It had to be at least a demi-fey, so this seemed like the perfect place to start asking questions.

Gwyn took a stool near the middle of the bar, leaned her elbows on it, and waited for her eyes to adjust to the gloom. The willowy sylph behind the bar slid a lemon drop in front of her. She had to smile. Reading surface thoughts seemed a very useful skill as a bartender. It also made it easier on Gwyn. People expected an old fey like her to either drink mead like a gnome, milk like a brownie, or wine like a high-born elf, but she'd always gone for something fruitier, sweeter, suiting her lower-born elven and fairy heritage.

Now she only had to concoct a way to bring up—

"Summoning a Fury?" the sylph asked, her large green eyes widening so they took up almost half her face. When she moved, her nearly transparent wings caught the light, sending prisms across Gwyn's vision. "People still do that?" She grimaced, showing off her needlelike teeth.

Gwyn tried to smile and calm her thoughts to silence. "Humans don't. But fey? Maybe a high priest or a druid if there are any left?" She tried to fight a sense of urgency now that she'd said it aloud, but she couldn't help thinking of the destruction Tiss would wreak if—

Shit.

The sylph nearly dropped a glass. Her ice-blond hair shifted on her head as if caught in a sudden wind, disturbed by her innate chaos.

"Not if I can stop it," Gwyn said hurriedly. She glanced around, but the other patrons she could finally make out didn't seem to be paying them any mind. A gnome the size of her hand sat on the bar a few places down, but they seemed asleep, chin resting on a whiskey glass. "That's why I need to find the summoner. Or the target." Even unobserved, she felt eyes trained on her back, as if the universe was watching, calling her a betrayer. But wasn't it more of a betrayal to go along a path she didn't agree with, one that meant a lot of people were going to die?

The sylph set the glass down and glanced around as if sensing those invisible eyes, too. "I don't…"

Don't want to get involved? Don't know anyone?

Gwyn made herself sit back and kept her power tight within her. It wouldn't do to give a random bartender a nasty shock. Especially when said bartender could probably deliver quite a shock of her own.

"I don't think I can help." The sylph didn't add what stopped her, but her eyes darted toward the door. "There's the local SCDA, you could try them?"

Gwyn shook her head. "Never heard of them."

The sylph gave her a look that said she was tired of how ignorant fey from the old country could be. "The agency? They catch paranormal criminals?"

Ah, she didn't know this particular agency, but she had known a few groups over the years who'd tried to police the otherworldly community, and there were always human ghost hunters. She'd even heard of a demigoddess who ran a sanctuary for legendary creatures, but she'd never been tempted to go there. She could protect herself, and her people had been around far longer than any branch of "law enforcement."

Back in the day, the Wild Hunt had occasionally punished the wicked, just as Tiss herself had, but they hadn't allowed the collateral damage that Tiss seemed to thrive on now. This new agency was no doubt too busy chasing humans or demi-fey who chose to summon spirits or used dark magic. They'd have no time to help. But Gwyn couldn't afford to ignore any leads. With modern technology, maybe even law enforcement would prove useful. "Where do they do business?"

The sylph shrugged. "You hang around long enough, you'll run into some. They were here this morning for drinks, but I don't know where their headquarters is." She leaned forward slightly, and the faint pearlescent sheen of her skin caught the light, drawing Gwyn's eye as it would anyone with fey blood. She'd often wondered if she could slow the Hunt down with a glitter bomb, but that wouldn't stop the Amazons or Valkyrie who rode alongside them.

And it damn sure wouldn't stop Tiss.

"The people who get hauled in by the SCDA never come out again," the sylph said, raising her pencil-thin eyebrows.

"Not true," the gnome said as they raised their head from the glass. Their eyes were still closed, and their tiny body slumped like they were melting into a puddle of water or booze. "They get banished. They take 'em out and banish 'em." They put a hand to their forehead in mock salute. Their pointy red hat slipped farther over their forehead. "So long, bye-bye. Thanks fer the service."

The sylph glanced at them as if they'd ruined a good horror story. "Shut up, Binks. You don't know shit." Her high-pitched voice turned hard as steel, reminding Gwyn that sylphs might look like Tinkerbell—apart from the teeth—but they frequently starred in legends where they teamed up with pixies and tore people apart.

"I been banished." The gnome opened red eyes that were slitted like a cat's. "I'm a hard villain, me."

A few other patrons chuckled. Binks gave the room a slow glare, then leaned on their glass again like that dash of anger had taken all their energy. "Used to be," they muttered.

Yeah, used to be. There was a lot of that going around in the world of the immortals. Even Tiss wasn't the power she used to be. But she was still a godsdamned menace. "When do they come in?" Gwyn asked. "The SCDA?"

"Closer to dawn, but you might get lucky. Like I said, they were in this morning."

And hopefully, she wouldn't get nabbed just for daring to speak to them. She didn't get along with the law, being pro-chaos herself, but maybe if the agents had a lot of fey blood, it wouldn't be so bad. She took her drink to a table near the window and settled in for a long wait. Maybe she could risk getting her cell phone out. If she kept her innate power low, she could safely use technology, and with any luck—

Something short tore past the window, and a leggy brunette sprinted in hot pursuit. Gwyn leaned forward and caught a glance of the brunette's flapping suit jacket disappearing down the sidewalk while a similarly dressed person across the street kept pace.

Her law-enforcement meter pinged. She turned toward the bar.

"You got lucky," the sylph said.

The gnome laughed, a noise like a nail on corrugated tin. "So long, bye-bye!"

Gwyn ducked out of the bar and sprinted, no doubt in her mind that the three people running down the street in the early evening dark had fey blood, or at least something not wholly human. She had to call on her own preternatural speed and settled into a fast, fluid gait that sent her mind back to chases through forests not yet tamed by human hands, when the world had been divided into fey and prey. And later, when Odin had led the Wild Hunt, and Gwyn had simply been among its ranks, not yet leader and far from being reduced to She Who Goes Before.

In those days, their herald only cautioned humans and animals and lesser fey to make way and hide in their homes or hedgerows because the Hunt was coming through, and anyone outside risked being trampled or dragged along behind.

Smiling, enjoying this chase after finding so little to enjoy of late, Gwyn whooped as she leapt a trash can, earning a few curious looks from the smattering of pedestrians in this small section of downtown.

Her quarry passed down a street lined with apartments and condos, a few houses and businesses scattered through a city that seemed to have few zoning laws. Blocks of businesses turned residential with alarming quickness, and a chase such as theirs might be noticed by humans headed home for the day.

Even that was exciting. And not in the usual ways that might get her killed. She was almost sorry when one of the suit-wearing agents brought down their target with a lunge and a forceful grip on the shoulder, whirling them around. As the two suits pinned their target's arms behind their back, a streetlight brought their features into clarity, and Gwyn paused in a shadow to watch.

The leggy brunette appeared female, lean and powerful, while her even taller partner had darker hair and broader shoulders, probably male, though she'd have to be closer to smell them and couldn't guess at their genders. They were both attractive, though the sinewy toughness and subtle curves of the brunette appealed to her more. That and the determined look on her face as she recited the terms of some kind of contract to her target, whose pointed features, small build, and bushy beard hinted at satyr blood.

When the agents began marching their captive in Gwyn's direction, she faded back a bit, content to watch a little longer, maybe follow these two to their base. A cry came from across the street, and she looked that way, wondering if the satyr-born had an accomplice, but it was two humans. A breeze carried their scent to her just as the larger male raised his hand to the female in a skirt.

"Stop, Holly," the male agent said, holding the arm of the brunette, who pulled toward the confrontation. "We don't have any jurisdiction over—"

"Fuck jurisdiction." The fires of justice seemed to shine from the brunette's eyes, bright as any Valkyrie, but she'd have to fight her partner to get loose.

Gwyn was already moving before the crack of a palm hitting flesh carried over the road, and the female human staggered back. Having a bastion of justice on her side suited Gwyn's plans nicely, and if that bastion owed her a favor, so much the better.

Though people who picked on those weaker than them deserved to have the stuffing knocked out of them anyway.

She twisted the big guy's arm behind him, wincing at the odor of cheap cologne. "If you wanna pick on someone small, chum, try me." He squealed as she drove him up on tiptoe even though he was nearly a foot taller. The female human stood, eyes wide, staring at Gwyn as if she was the goddess Brigitte. "You want to have a poke at him, darlin'? I'll hold him for you."

The human female ran, yelling for a cab that was passing one street over while fumbling with her phone.

"Shame." Gwyn spun the man around and pulled his collar so he had to bend to her level. She let her power flow over his skin, not hurting him but warning that she could. His pupils bloomed, and she could smell his fear as some ancient, primal part of his brain responded to her power as it would a tiger in the wild.

She liked that image. "Yeah, I'm the baddest animal in the jungle, chum, and I'm looking after the women in these parts. You hit that one or any of the others 'round here, and I'll come for your balls." When she let him go, he ran. She hoped her threat worked for at least a little while.

More importantly, the leggy brunette was watching with admiration before looking at her partner in triumph, as if she had caused Gwyn's actions or at least took part in the victory.

Perfect. They were pals already.

Chapter Three

Holly abhorred rough justice, but sometimes, there didn't seem to be any alternative. And no matter how many times Renne told her she couldn't intervene in human crimes, she would never just stand and let one happen, especially the strong preying on the weak like that prick across the street.

Rough justice had prevailed this time.

When the short, well-muscled woman who'd broken up the fight sauntered back across the street like she owned it, Holly's gratitude began to turn like meringue melting in the sun. There was plenty of fey in the newcomer, judging by the chaos she exuded and her cocky manner. She had killer, perfectly arched eyebrows—red to match her thick hair—and her green eyes sparkled in the dark, highlighting the way they turned up at the corner like a cat's.

A pure fey, maybe with a lot of elven blood. Great. She'd no doubt bring some of Marcus's old-country bullshit with her.

"Do I have the pleasure of addressing agents of the SCDA?" the stranger asked, her slight accent landing somewhere between Irish and Nordic.

"No fucking way," Joni the fence said from where Holly and Renne held him between them.

Renne gave him a little shake to shut him up. "And who might you be?" He sounded a little interested, but he seemed a little interested in everybody.

The fey woman bowed. Her tight T-shirt showed off her muscular arms and full breasts, and her pants looked like leather, highlighting the muscles in her thighs, too.

And that dark thing tucked under her arm was a motorcycle helmet.

Holly's senses went on alert, and she wished she could send Renne a telepathic message.

"Gwyn," the fey woman said. "And I have a proposal two officers of the light might be interested in."

Yeah, like they were fucking stupid. "We don't make deals." She bit her lip to keep from adding, "with elves." No reason to broadcast her prejudices against her fellow fey. And making deals with any of them was a bad idea.

"Ah," Gwyn said with a twinkle, "it's not a deal I'm proposing, l—"

"If you're thinking of calling me lass or love, forget it," Holly said.

Gwyn shut her mouth with a snap. Smart.

Renne grinned as if terribly amused by it all. He produced a card from his jacket pocket. "If you've any information you think we need to know, feel free to call." He added a wink that Gwyn didn't seem fazed by.

Holly took the hint to exit, though she did have questions. Like, are you part of a murderous motorcycle gang, ludicrously coincidental as that might have been.

Gwyn stuttered as she moved to follow them. "B…but…" She sighed as if she had the world on her shoulders, and Holly risked another look. It was the most genuine sound Gwyn had made so far. She muttered something like, "Why does nothing go my way?"

Holly pulled Joni and Renne to a halt. "Do you need help?"

With a look of gratitude and hope that was frustratingly covered with more swagger, Gwyn brightened. "As a matter of fact, I do, l… Officer."

Holly rewarded her with a small smile. "Well, since you're not in immediate danger, you can call that number and make an appointment."

"How do you know I'm not in immediate danger?"

"You seem like you can handle yourself."

"I was thinking the same when you captured the goat."

"Satyr, thank you," Joni said. "And I'm only half."

Holly had to shake her head. She'd forgotten he was there. Another strike against Gwyn. Holly couldn't afford to let herself get distracted.

And now Renne was smirking at her, and she couldn't afford to give him more ammunition, either. She was ready to give the spiel about calling the office again when Joni said, "Finally. It's about time."

Something about the way he said it meant he wasn't just relieved that they were done talking. Holly glanced to the side just as Renne mumbled, "Shit."

Two shadowy figures appeared at the end of the street, and Holly's senses prickled, meaning more were nearby and had just stepped within range of what she could feel.

Joni the fence had goons.

Renne drew his gun, being one of the few members of the SCDA who could stand holding so much iron. Holly grabbed her telescoping nightstick off her belt and gave it a flick to extend it to its full length. She stepped in front of Gwyn, tightening her grip on Joni's arm. "Back off," she said, raising her voice as she glanced around, spotting one more goon on a side street by a nail salon. Luckily, all the businesses on the street were already closed; no humans would see them. Unluckily, that also meant there was little light, and the one streetlight closest to the goons stuttered as if affected by magic.

Or subpar maintenance.

"You don't want to do it, boys," Renne said. "It ain't worth your lives."

"Speak for yourself," Joni said. "Get a move on, guys."

The goons weren't moving. At all. The hair on Holly's neck stood up. Were they going to use magic instead of muscle?

"It's a glamour!" Gwyn yanked on Holly's arm, and the force of it brought her to her knees. Joni fell with her, screeching in protest.

Something whistled over their heads, and Renne cried out.

From a gap between a massage place and a CPA, a shadow darted toward Holly, a glint of light in its hand. She blocked with her baton and heard a loud *ting*. The shadow thrust again and again before ducking as if not trying to hit her at all.

They were after Joni.

She swung with a grunt of effort, blocking an attack inches from Joni's nose.

"What the fuck?" he shouted, then cried out again as he was pulled out of harm's way by Gwyn.

The shadowy figure backed off, and Holly pushed to her feet. Renne's gun cracked the quiet of the night. He had his own assailant flitting through the dark, and now that a shot had been fired, someone might call the human police.

"Give us the squealer, and we'll leave you in peace," Holly's opponent said in a surprisingly high-pitched voice. "It's that or pieces."

Okay, they deserved death for that line alone. "He betrayed you, did he?" she asked. Maybe if they heard sirens, they'd flee. She couldn't advance on them and still protect Joni and Gwyn.

"It wasn't me," Joni yelled. "I'd never tell—ah, fuck it. You've gotta protect my ass, SCDA. It's in the geas."

That was true. Holly would have done it anyway, seeing protecting her captives as part of her duty, but the SCDA's deal with the elves stated that the criminal slated for banishment made it to the portal unharmed.

Relatively.

"They can use glamour," Gwyn called.

"Late to the party much?" Holly said with a snarl.

"Talking to your partner. You're fighting air, lad!"

"What?" Renne said as he wheezed. "They're not…what?"

Holly's opponent took another step back. The fake goons vanished, and realization hit Holly like a brick. "Your guy's not real. They're distracting you because you have the—"

Her attacker ran off like a shot, moving so fast, they seemed to leave a blurry outline hanging in midair.

"You might have told me sooner," Renne said, holstering his gun as the sound of sirens echoed in the distance.

"I was busy keeping this one from running." Gwyn had one of Joni's arms in her strong grip. "He's been kicking like a mule."

Holly grabbed his other arm. "Thanks."

Gwyn tipped an imaginary cap and picked up her helmet from the sidewalk. "Always happy to help. Now, if we can get out of here,

I can fill you in on the dangerous group headed for your town that's gonna kill a whole lot of people."

Holly just kept her jaw from dropping. She'd wanted to work on the murderous gang case, but she'd never expected it to just announce itself on the street. "Um, yeah. That'd be…yeah."

"Smooth," Renne muttered.

❖

Gwyn hadn't had to be charming for a long time. Holly had made it a little easier with her sleek hair; striking, angular features; and legs for days, even though she didn't seem the type to be won over by a wink and a smile.

Of course, neither did her hulking boss who felt like fey but had to have some troll mixed in there somewhere. This interview would have been so much better with Holly instead of this lump.

"Let's go through it again," he said, sounding as if his throat was made of rock.

Gwyn sighed. She hadn't had to deal with law enforcement in a *very* long time and had *not* missed the procedural monotony. She'd hoped a police force of fey and other supernatural creatures would have been a little quicker to act and less likely to drone on and on, but alas. She stretched her neck and took a deep breath, trying to find something of comfort in this tiny room that seemed like a broom closet with Marcus sitting across the flimsy table.

"The Wild Hunt—" she said.

"Whom you used to ride with."

"Right. Is now led by Tisiphone, Tiss—"

"A vengeful Fury." He leaned his head on his hand.

"A-plus. They've been responding to various summonses."

"And you have no clue about who made them."

"Would you like to tell the story?" she snapped.

He made a rumbling sound that might have been a laugh or a growl. "Go on."

"Thank you. Anyway, I now serve as She Who Goes Before, warning people of what's coming so the innocent can get out of the way of the Hunt. Or that's the way it's supposed to work." She paused for his contribution, but when he only stared at her in this dingy room with its single table, two chairs, and peeling paint, she took a deep breath. "But—"

"In this age, there are too many people to warn, and no one knows who the summoner or target is, so no one heeds you." He waved toward her vaguely.

She ground her teeth. Maybe he was trying to piss her off so she'd attack him, he could kill her, and tell his bosses the problem was solved. Until the Hunt arrived.

Remember why you're here. Get the Hunt back and save some lives. Only maybe not this asshole. "I'm sure in Tiss's mind, it's just like in the old days when everyone in a village knew who the wronged party and the culprit was. They could stake them out for the Furies, and everyone else would be spared. Or they could hound them out of town. Same difference. But the Hunt is more of a tidal wave than a bullet, and they can sense the target's direction and somehow know them on sight. Until they catch that sight, lots of people get in their way. It can't be helped." She bit her lip, deciding to lay it on a bit thicker. "And I think Tiss has become more unpredictable in recent years. In the past, she'd ride past someone standing out of the way, but now…"

She didn't finish, leaving the truth and letting them infer the lie. Well, mostly a lie. Tiss might go after bystanders if they pissed her off. She certainly wouldn't flinch from it.

"Cities are too big to find the target quickly and get others to safety," Marcus said, still looking as unmovable as granite.

Gwyn was glad she'd framed her mission as only saving lives and not also wanting her old job back. She'd let them come to that conclusion on their own. She was the right person for the job, had a proven track record of keeping the Hunt hidden, waiting for… whatever she was going to do with them when she got them back.

That decision could wait, though a hollow feeling seeped into her chest at having to decide.

"And they'll decimate humans in a city this big," he said with a slow blink. "Unless we can figure out who this target is and get them to right their wrong or figure out who the summoner is and get them to call it off."

"Correct," she said. Gods, he could crack a smile, lift an eyebrow, shoot her the finger, something.

"And how will that keep the Hunt from doing this same thing all over again?"

"I didn't say it was a long-term solution, but it will build mistrust in the rest of the Hunt, and they will oust Tiss as their leader or leave her weak enough to challenge."

"Leaving her and them free to cause whatever havoc they like."

Gwyn fought the urge to put her head in her hands. "I thought you'd be happy to have a heads-up, the germ of a plan. What do you want from me, a five-year warranty? Forms signed in triplicate? A PowerPoint presentation of other options?"

"You seem well-versed in modern lingo."

Oh no, they were not about to pick apart her life. "So you have some prejudices, huh? Think all of us in the old country are still living in fairy mounds and dancing in mushroom rings under the full moon?"

He didn't seem to have a response to that. Halle-fucking-lujah.

"You can either help me or let me go, and I'll try to help your citizens myself." Before he could give her anymore non-expressions, she held up a hand. "You can't arrest me. I've done nothing wrong."

"You're admittedly a member of a murderous paranormal biker gang."

True, but… "Most of us prefer the company of women, too. Gonna add that to your list of prejudices?"

He snorted. "Nice try."

A reaction! Gwyn almost crowed.

A soft knock sounded on the door, followed by what seemed to be a heated discussion in the hall, the voices nearly growling and hissing, clearly two people who no doubt thought they were much quieter than in reality.

If Marcus was irritated by the interruption, he didn't show it. Big surprise. "Come."

Holly opened the door, shaking off her partner's restraining hand to come in. "What if we arrest Tiss and banish her to Signal with the other criminals?"

Gwyn took a note from Marcus's playbook and stayed absolutely still so she didn't shriek with laughter. "She's a Fury."

Holly blinked as if waiting for more.

"Of vengeance. A vengeful Fury."

"Saying it over and over won't make me understand," Holly said, hands on her hips, all her irritation on full display.

"The name says it all," her partner muttered from the hallway.

Holly breathed deep, no doubt in anticipation of biting his head off, but Gwyn jumped in:

"She's incredibly strong and powerful. The only way to defeat her is by challenging her to combat, and no one can succeed in that while she has the trust of the Hunt. Having their power added to hers makes her practically immortal."

"Practically?"

"You'd need the help of a deity. Got one handy?"

Holly sucked her lip, but Gwyn didn't think she'd appreciate being told how adorable it was in front of her boss, who still hadn't commented on the interruption.

"Can we speak to her?" Holly asked.

"Ask her to give herself up? Not a chance. I'm guessing you don't want to try to convince her to go elsewhere." No, not a paladin like this one, who chafed when she wasn't allowed to follow her conscience. It seemed a rare trait in a fey, but maybe Holly was some magical mix of fey and human that resulted in the ultimate do-gooder. She didn't even have a slight point to her ears, the usual giveaway of fey ancestry. Gwyn wondered if she dared ask exactly what her fey traits were.

Holly shook her head. "No, it's clear she has to be stopped, but—"

Marcus gave her an inscrutable look before standing. "I need to make a few calls." He glanced between them with glacial slowness. "Get to work finding this target or the summoner. If that's all we can do at this point, let's damn well get it done."

Holly stood a little straighter, clearly not understanding the enormity of that task, but she seemed to be all in, and that was what Gwyn wanted. No doubt Holly had dreams of disbanding the Hunt or taking all of them down, but she wouldn't have to worry once Gwyn was back in charge. They would never find themselves on opposites sides of a conflict.

In theory.

CHAPTER FOUR

Holly let Renne drag her from the interview room, even though she wasn't done with Gwyn. Not even a little.

"I know you can't stand waiting around," Renne said in the dim, narrow hall.

"Everyone knows that, and yet, it's all I'm asked to do."

"Sometimes, there's nothing else to do."

"Unacceptable." She needed to get her hands on something: evidence, suspects, even a random, unrelated crime.

He sighed and slumped against the wall like a scarecrow that had lost some stuffing. "I pray you're never anyone's birthing coach."

She bristled, but the image of trying to be supportive while waiting for something she had no control over that was *also* dangerous for the person she was trying to support? She had to chuckle through the fear. "I'd be researching online how to do a C-section."

"God help the doctors." He prodded her with his scuffed leather shoe. "Even if the boss lets you question her, you can't make her tell what she doesn't know."

She bit her lip and crossed her arms as she leaned against the opposite wall. "She's hiding something."

"If she's been alive long enough, she's probably hiding lots of things."

"Is that supposed to make me feel better?"

"It's supposed to make you realize you won't be able to get anything else from her, whether she knows it or not."

"But she didn't give us anything!" Holly put her hands on her head and walked in a frustrated circle.

"We know that whoever summoned the Hunt knows old magic. How many people like that can stay hidden for long in this gossipy town? They must be new to Houston."

He was right. A large city could provide anonymity for a while, but the paranormal community, and fey in particular, were a chatty bunch.

"We shake the tree," she said. "Anyone new in town with that kind of power will be making friends."

"Or enemies."

"Or clients." An old-world power coming to town would bring older fey out of the shadows searching for the power left behind in ages long past. "Let's try combing through the files of the human cops. They could have stumbled on something bizarre already and just not know it."

And if that didn't work, she supposed they could always patrol the streets looking for trouble. Dawn wasn't far off, but Holly didn't feel like sleeping. Even the tired look in Renne's dark eyes seemed more edgy than lethargic. Maybe Marcus would let them take Gwyn along, both to keep an eye on her and just in case they came across anything suspicious. It wouldn't do to have to track her down if they got a hot tip.

Those were the *only* two reasons. Renne could tease all he liked, but Holly wasn't interested in someone whose life was so complicated, no matter what she looked like or how strong and capable she was or the little flashes of vulnerability Holly had seen in her eyes.

She stomped off toward her desk before Renne could read her mind and smirk again.

Gwyn supposed she should have been happy. She was doing something besides sitting around waiting for the Hunt to show up or wandering the streets hoping to feel a twinge about who the target might be. But doing a ride along with the SCDA just felt like they were keeping her out of the way.

She'd already told the big boss everything she was prepared to say. So answering the same questions at their grimy headquarters wouldn't do anyone any good. And this way, she got to spend time with Holly, who was a rare sight for any kind of eyes. If only she wasn't so completely straitlaced. Breaking down her rules and watching her come undone might have been fun, but she obviously thought Gwyn wasn't worth her time.

As they sat in the car waiting for Renne to return with three promised coffees, Gwyn gave in to the undeniable urge to poke this particular bear. "Is it all old-country fey you don't like, or am I deserving of special treatment?" she asked, sitting forward, her arms braced against both front seats.

"You should keep your seat belt on," Holly said, not bothering to look over her shoulder or in the rearview mirror. "Renne will be back in a minute."

"Now, see, I don't know you well enough to tell which answer that was." She had the strangest desire to smooth down a cowlick in Holly's ponytail, but that would no doubt be unwelcome in the extreme, and she'd never forced her touch on anyone whose ass she wasn't trying to kick.

Holly sighed. "I don't have any beef with you." She finally looked in the mirror, her dark gaze sharp as a cut diamond. "Or the old-country fey."

"So you're frosty to everyone?"

"That's right." She seemed pleased as she nodded. Maybe she even believed herself.

"But not to your partner."

Holly turned a fraction. "What do you want? You don't seem like the type who needs a nursemaid to hold her hand. If you're looking for someone to f—get close to, Renne would probably oblige."

"He's not my type." And that let out the implication that Holly *was* her type, but she just let it lie.

"So cast a wider net. There are plenty of people in town."

"I'm not pestering you for a date, dar—Holly." She bristled at the idea that she'd have to beg for companionship, but she still wouldn't risk calling Holly a pet name in retaliation.

Holly nodded as if acknowledging the correction. "Then what?"

"We have to work together. Might as well be cordial." But even that desire was fading. She wouldn't beg anyone for anything, least of all friendship.

"Cordial." Holly nodded again, sounding at least a little chagrined. "Sorry, I'm brusque when I'm…focused."

"And when you don't have a lead, I get it. I've been frustrated trying to stop the Hunt for a long time." That surprised her with how much it hurt. Getting Holly to open up was an interesting challenge, sure, but in the end, Gwyn planned to use her to regain leadership of the Hunt. She couldn't afford to open up in return and feel genuine feelings.

"That sounds frustrating as he—ck," Holly said.

Gwyn couldn't help a grin. "You can swear all you like. I won't get offended."

"I'm trying to cut down."

"Renne's suggestion?"

"How did you know?" Holly asked, heavy on the sarcasm.

From the elbow jabs and side-eyes, and the way Renne oozed politeness to cover Holly's "brusqueness," but Gwyn didn't want to give away how observant she could be. "Lucky guess."

Holly's snort said she didn't quite buy that, but she didn't press.

Renne opened the car door as if summoned and passed a tray of coffees to Holly before sliding in. "Y'all hit upon a solution to our dilemma?"

"Which one?" Gwyn asked, then wanted to kick herself for potentially giving away more than she meant.

Luckily, Renne only chuckled. "You been working on world peace and global warming, too?"

"We haven't thought of a way to find the target or the summoner or any old—" Holly mashed her lips together as if keeping the rest of that sentence in, then sipped her coffee before putting the car in gear and pulling into traffic.

"Old-world malarky?" Gwyn guessed. Holly didn't seem old enough for those sorts of prejudices, so she'd probably picked them up from her boss. It still put Gwyn's hackles up, and she almost gave in to some "new" world biases of her own, but she'd long ago stopped thinking of anyone with human blood as a different breed. "Trace us back far enough, and we all have common ancestors," she said after a sip of coffee and a deep, calming breath. "Just like anything else." She couldn't help adding, "Let's not get caught up in history. No group of people, human or fey, has a blameless record."

Holly's shoulders tightened just when Gwyn thought she couldn't get tenser. "But if a group of people is still acting like jackasses, they haven't learned anything from history, have they?"

"You wanna talk jackasses? What about—"

"Them Cowboys?" Renne interrupted loudly. He turned to Holly's confused glance, then looked back at Gwyn. "Oh, was this a private discussion? Perhaps you'd like to be left alone?" He didn't add, "So you can make out," but Gwyn caught the implication that a passionate fight could turn hot-blooded in other ways.

True, Holly looked wonderful with so much color in her cheeks, her chest heaving, but Gwyn preferred that sort of reaction stemming from another source besides anger. "No, thanks," she said. "We're good."

But Holly seemed to feel the need to add, "You're insufferable, Renne."

"Happy to be of service." He began to scroll through his phone, drinking his coffee.

Gwyn was about to ask where they were going, get this investigation back on track when Renne said, "We've got a live one. Figuratively speaking. Ciaran sent over an HPD file on a suspicious death. A security guard killed in an alley." He paused, his thumb moving over the screen.

Gwyn could almost hear the drum roll in his head.

"And?" Holly asked. No doubt she fell for this every time. "What's so suspicious?"

"A witness says the guard was killed by a zombie."

All was silent for a moment, save the *hiss* of the air-conditioner that barely kept apace of the muggy atmosphere.

"Necromancy?" Gwyn asked, turning the idea over in her head. "That's some old magic I haven't witnessed in many an age."

Holly shook her head. "Sounds made-up."

"That's what the cops think," Renne said. "Either the witness was high and has seen too many movies, or the suspect was high on something stronger and was able to batter the guard to death after taking a bullet to the chest."

"They confirmed the shot?" Holly asked, sounding far less certain.

"Um." Renne scrolled a bit more. "Guard's gun was discharged. No bullet found at the scene."

"Blood?" Gwyn asked.

"Just the guard's from what they can tell."

Gwyn sat back. "Maybe the witness was right."

Holly's eyes in the rearview screamed skepticism. "Let's not jump to conclusions. There could be lots of reasons the suspect didn't bleed a lot, even if they were shot. Maybe it only grazed them, maybe they were wearing a vest or lots of clothing that absorbed it, maybe their blood mingled with the guard's—"

"Maybe they're undead and no longer bleed," Gwyn added. When she got another glare, she put up her hands. "Hey, an open mind goes both ways."

"And either way, we have to investigate." Holly sighed, and Gwyn could guess what was going on in her head because it was going on in her own: it was better than doing nothing. "Fine, give me directions. We'll drop Gwyn off and—"

"Can I come?" she asked just as Renne said, "It's nearby."

As if regretting all her life choices, Holly sighed again. "If you both swear to stop trying to get on my nerves, and, Gwyn, you keep from interfering." But she didn't sound violently opposed to the idea, probably because it meant less wasted time.

Gwyn and Renne spoke over each other in enthusiastic assent, and Renne added, "I'll try not to interfere, too, for what it's worth."

Gwyn managed to turn her chuckle into a cough.

"What did I just say?" Holly asked, but even she seemed a little charmed. And why not? If she didn't find him amusing, she would have killed him long before now, it seemed.

Even more importantly, her reaction meant her frosty exterior could be thawed, and that was good news for more than Gwyn's libido.

Down, girl. She couldn't afford to make this situation more complicated with these kinds of feelings. Nor did she want to secure

Holly's help in that way. Holly would be a scary enough opponent if she felt her friendship had been used. Gods help anyone who jilted her.

❖

The witness first, Holly decided. The crime scene had been open for days, and none of them was a forensic expert. They'd check it out, for sure, but Holly wanted to interview the witness, who might open up a bit with people who believed her.

Not that Holly wholeheartedly did. As far as she knew, zombies were fictional, never mind Gwyn's mention of necromancy. But there were non-zombie paranormal reasons why someone could take a bullet and keep going, many ways to appear to get shot but remain fine.

They needed more data. No one could make bricks without clay, as Sherlock Holmes said.

Ruby Sandovar lived in one of the newer condos near I-45 on the south side of downtown, one with a security desk that didn't let visitors roam freely, even with the official badges that the SCDA only showed to members of the non-paranormal community. The official-looking cards listed their titles as "community outreach specialists," a non-specific name that allowed them to attach themselves to any other agency and whose only purpose was to check on the mental or physical health of their interviewees after an incident.

Holly typically let Renne take the lead there.

Ruby let them up and into her condo but seemed to move grudgingly, a too-large sweater wrapped around her like a cloak. When she sat, she crossed her thin arms and legs, ink-dark eyes radiating hostility, her entire posture saying that she expected to be laughed at but damned if she was going to take it anymore.

Renne sat across from her without being invited, facing the impressive view of downtown, but he only focused on Ruby. "Ms. Sandovar, how have you been coping after your frightening ordeal?"

He let his accent through in thick, soothing southern waves, forehead creased with care, too-white smile offering understanding and kindness. Ruby slowly uncurled when no mockery came her way, and Holly was free to scan the bookshelves and photos. Gwyn studied a framed print of magnolia blossoms above the couch.

"The police laughed at me," Ruby said before she ever mentioned the word zombie.

Renne shook his head. "So frustrating. And when you were only trying to be a good citizen."

"Yeah!" She sat up straighter, into it now. "And, I mean, it looked like…I really thought…"

Holly had to force herself not to stare or lean forward.

Ruby sighed hugely and put her head in her hands. "A zombie," she said, voice muffled behind a curtain of dark hair. When no one so much as snorted, she peeked between her fingers.

"That sounds terrifying," Renne said, appropriately wide-eyed.

"It was." Tears sprang to her eyes, and Holly really wished they could assure her that she wasn't crazy, that the unexplainable happened every day, but the agency had rules for a reason. "He got a bullet in the chest. I turned into the alley as this…thing was coming at the guard, and he shot it, but it kept going, and it didn't bleed, and its skin was gray, and one eyeball was just gone, and it didn't make noise, and it smelled really bad." She sobbed the last word, and Gwyn handed her a bottle of water and a box of tissues.

I should have done that. It never occurred to Holly to do those sorts of things. She hadn't even noticed Gwyn leave the room. She was never sure what people wanted in their grief, and she'd lived around humans her whole life. Who knew if Gwyn had?

Holly forced herself to breathe and focus and not get lost in her spiraling thoughts or the anger they often generated. "It attacked the guard?" she asked quietly, interrupting Ruby's sniffling, hoping to distract her and get the interview back on track.

Ruby nodded, folded her tissue and unfolded it, staring at her hands. "It just sort of fell on him, the guard, knocked him down. It beat him over and over." Her voice went hazy, not yet able to process this particular horror. Maybe she'd get lucky and never would. "Even when the guard went still, it kept…" She seemed to shrink, folding into her memories.

Renne shifted, bumping the table, and even that small noise was like a clap in the quiet room.

Ruby blinked, focusing on him as if minutes had passed without her noticing. "Sorry, do y'all want some water or something?"

"We're fine, thank you," he said kindly.

Holly wanted to give him time to work his magic, but she also really wanted to get out of this emotional soup. "After the, um, the guard, uh, expired, the zombie left?"

"I think it heard something," Ruby said, looking into the middle distance. "I don't know. I was distracted by—" She shook her head. "Yeah, that's it. Someone was shouting." She straightened some pillows. "Yeah, that's all. It's fine. I'm fine." She offered them a weak smile.

Renne stood, and Holly was thankful she didn't have to prod him. Gwyn rested a hand on Ruby's shoulder. "Take your time, love. Be kind to yourself."

Holly could almost feel something thaw inside her, a rush in her chest. A social worker had once said something similar after her parents had been arrested yet again. And she had so needed to hear it.

Even if she rarely took that advice.

Renne fished two cards out of his pocket. One had his cell number, in case Ruby remembered anything else, and one was for a network of counselors that he always gave out when they were playing community outreach specialists.

Even with those offers of comfort, Ruby hurried them toward the door, no doubt wanting to be left alone to continue crying her eyes out.

What would she think if the police ever contacted her again, and she mentioned the community officers who never existed? How many more humans were out there wondering who the hell the SCDA really was? Maybe they had their own slew of conspiracy-related websites like the men in black or Bigfoot. Holly waited until she was back in the hall before snorting at the thought of the SCDA being another cryptid.

"The alley?" Renne asked.

"Mm-hmm." She didn't know if an old crime scene could tell them anything, but it was worth a look.

"You convinced about zombies?" Gwyn asked when they were back in the Olds.

Holly sighed as she began to navigate through traffic. Ruby had sounded so sure, and she could have been telling the truth as she'd interpreted it. "I like to reserve judgment."

"Or hate to admit when you're wrong?" Gwyn muttered. She wasn't quiet enough for Holly to think that was meant to go unheard.

"Naw," Renne said before Holly could appropriately bristle. "She always reserves judgment. Except for things that are her idea."

He was lucky she didn't unbuckle his seat belt, brake hard, and send him through the windshield. "Maybe *you two* want to be left alone."

"Just ribbing you, Holls."

She hoped her side-eye conveyed just how unamused she was. "Have either of you considered golems?"

They were satisfyingly quiet for a moment before stomping on her idea at the same time, their comments lost in each other's:

"Not with the missing eyeball."

"Gray skin? Golems are usually—"

"Wouldn't have to call off—"

"Burning eyes—"

"Okay, shut up," Holly cried.

After a moment of silence, Gwyn said, "Do you get lots of golems here?"

No, Holly had never seen or even heard of one here. That was also very old magic. "Okay, I will accept a zombie as a working theory. But Marcus will want proof, and this doesn't sound like it has anything to do with the Hunt."

Even if it did feel good to have something to work on, it wasn't the problem she *most* wanted to solve. But zombies still sounded easier to deal with than Tisiphone. She'd had a few seconds before they'd left to google the Furies. They were some *really* old-world bullshit. One myth said that Furies were the children of the Titans, beings who'd supposedly created the universe, but those were just stories that predated physics and astronomy. Still, Furies were mentioned in myths that were very old indeed. It was hard to get much older, even when dipping into Egyptian or Mesopotamian or Chinese mythology.

"You're right to be skeptical," Gwyn said. "Even I've rarely encountered necromancy. Those powers are inherited. I thought they'd died out long ago."

"Could someone have inherited a zombie?" Renne asked.

"From what I remember, they don't last that long. And they'd need a necromancer to control it." She *tsked*. "Even those who practice blood or demon magic look askance at those who raise the dead. Necromancers are shunned by human and paranormal communities."

Holly nodded. Made sense. It was more than just natural skepticism that made her reluctant to accept the zombie theory. It was…icky. "It's nice to work with someone who has firsthand knowledge," she had to admit.

"Was that a compliment?" Gwyn asked. "Pinch me, Renne. I must be dreaming."

Holly rolled her eyes but smiled all the same. At least Renne didn't comment.

CHAPTER FIVE

Even after Holly's sarcastic response, Gwyn preened from the compliment, light as it was. If such words were going to be as hard to find as diamonds, she was going to treat them as such. And she did have *firsthand knowledge* of necromancy, though it had been at least two hundred years since she'd met a necromancer, and things hadn't gone well for that one. Like many of them, he had been mostly human, his powers inherited. To be a necromancer, all one had to do was trace their bloodline back to one of the death gods and learn from a teacher, no fey blood required.

In the alley, Gwyn sensed a few tendrils of magic wafting in the breeze, but Holly had been right about a city this size throwing off her radar. There were lots of fey here, not to mention other supernatural creatures and probably a human witch or two. She caught hints of magic wherever she went, but no one nearby was cranking out spells right now, and there were no fey next door, save for Holly and Renne.

She also had the same niggling sense she always got when she was close to the target of the Hunt. It mixed with all the other specks of power and sat like an itch on the back of her neck.

"I smell the most blood here," Renne said, standing where the guard had no doubt been bludgeoned to death. "If someone was shot farther down the alley, they didn't bleed all over the place."

Gwyn wasn't sure what kind of fey ancestry he had, but she had no reason to doubt his nose.

"I haven't felt a lot of magic spells," Holly said, "but this place is definitely…twitchy."

"Necromancy is surprisingly orderly," Gwyn said, eager to be of more help, spoiled by the one diamond she'd been given. "There are supposedly rules and precision to the rituals. Most of the practitioners are more human than not."

Holly gave a cute little shiver; no doubt her fey side was one particularly averse to order, more at home in chaos. Gwyn could relate.

"This door is sporting some serious dents," Renne said. He scrolled on his phone. "Maybe our zombie was trying to break in when the guard came around the corner."

"Seems like there'd be easier ways to break in than by beating down a metal door." Gwyn knelt to look at the heavy-duty dents in the rust. "Though it looks like it made some progress. More than the average human could."

"Or the average anything," Renne said. "Maybe someone Marcus's size could do that."

"But an undead machine that doesn't feel pain?" Gwyn added.

Instead of grumbling, Holly looked thoughtful. She scanned the ground, inhaling deeply. That couldn't be fun in a dirty alley. "I think they left something behind." She took out her telescoping baton, prodded into a gap under the brick wall, and flicked something out that skittered to a stop against Gwyn's boot.

Gray and shriveled but oddly familiar. Gwyn's stomach dropped. "Is that…a toe?" She had a strong stomach, but sudden body parts were enough to make her bile simmer. "Oh gods."

"Okay," Holly said matter-of-factly, hands on her hips. "The zombie thing is starting to look more realistic."

"You didn't find the missing eye down there, too, did ya?" Renne asked.

Holly grinned, but Gwyn wasn't there yet. She did not envy them their job. With a swallow, she looked away. "If, um, someone had raised a zombie in this alley, I think I'd still sense that amount of magic, lawful or not."

Holly nodded. "If it involves a ritual, doing it out in the open would attract too much attention." She glanced at either end of the alley. "Someone must have driven the zombie here and taken it away."

"The shouting voice Ruby heard," Renne said. He stooped and picked up the toe.

Gwyn suppressed a groan. "Shouldn't you have gloves or something?"

"The SCDA forensic budget is sorely lacking," he said with a cock-eyed grin. "Nothing for DNA analysis, I'm afraid. But if we find a possible owner, it shouldn't be too difficult to pick him out of a lineup."

Gwyn had a vision of whisking Ruby into a darkened room to peer at a row of waiting feet. *Do you recognize your assailant? Yes, it's the gray desiccated one missing a toe!*

Holly marched to the end of the alley. "Does the police report say anything was found on the traffic cameras? That late at night, they might have gotten lucky."

Renne pulled out his cell. "Not in this report. I'll text Ciaran." He slipped the toe into a jacket pocket.

Gwyn had to catch up with Holly to quiet her protesting stomach. "Not a fan of cell phones?"

"Eh. I have an old one." She pulled out a flip phone. "But I keep it off most of the time. There's a five percent chance I'll brick it on any given day. More if I'm agitated."

Probably up to fifteen or twenty percent, then, but Gwyn didn't mention that. "That must be annoying. You have my sympathy."

Holly stared as if looking for the sarcasm, then said, "Thanks."

Gwyn wanted to make a joke about that, to shatter this moment of genuineness, but she'd lived long enough to know that was her own insecurities looking to sabotage her. Not that the knowledge made it any easier to bear, just to be aware of. And be more anxious about. Ah, sometimes a long life really was a curse. A fairly benign one, but a curse nonetheless.

"If we do find a zombie, what do we do with it? Banish it like the others?" Holly snorted. "I bet the elves would love a mindless undead killer in Signal, their home away from home."

Gwyn searched her memory but found only one solution for the undead. "Best to put it down and focus on the necromancer." She let her senses fly free again but got only the same vague feelings as before and underneath all that, the nagging feeling that the target of the Hunt was *somewhere* in the city. Bloody useless. "What is this Signal place like?" she asked, needing something else to focus on.

"Dunno. Never been."

Gwyn would have looked at her askance before but frowned now. "And how many people have you sent there?"

Holly's head turned slowly, and Gwyn could almost hear the tight tendons creak. "Why?"

"Banishing them to somewhere you've never even seen? How do you know that this Signal isn't just a pile of bodies near the realm of chaos?"

"Why would the elves insist on the *criminals* we catch being safely transported to an interplanar gate just to kill them?"

"What if those criminals just grace the dinner tables of some monster?"

"What are you suggesting we do with them instead?" Holly's personal chaos field whipped around her, though Gwyn doubted anyone but fey would sense it.

"If your ethics are as important to you as they seem, you should find out." Back off, her inner voice said, but all her frustration was gathering now that it had found an outlet, a tiny hole in the dam.

"You think I haven't asked? No one goes through the portal without the elves' permission." Holly took a deep breath and glanced around as if to make sure they were unobserved.

Something Gwyn should have been doing, but she'd been too caught up in her own feelings of powerlessness. At least this realization came with the clarity to force herself to change tracks before she ruined her next best chance of stopping Tiss. Maybe even a friendship, something she hadn't enjoyed in centuries. "I'm sorry. I'm feeling useless, and…it doesn't matter. I'm sorry."

To her infinite surprise, Holly seemed quick to relax and breathe deep. "Yeah, I know that aggravation very well. Okay, apology accepted." She studied Gwyn with alarming acuity. "You've been trying to stop the Hunt for a long time. On your own."

Admitting her failures to herself was one thing. Hearing it from someone else? She felt like she went through all the stages of grief in one moment, ending in speechless embarrassment rather than acceptance. "Well, I'm…I—"

Holly put a cool hand on her forearm. "You have my sympathy, too."

"All right, all right," Gwyn said, giving her hand an awkward pat. "Let's stop before we're bawling in each other's arms."

Holly laughed brightly, glanced behind them at the alley, and stepped back, clearing her throat. Gwyn did not want to turn and face whatever look Renne was giving them.

"Let's see if Ciaran's got anything for us," Holly said.

❖

Holly's every interaction with Gwyn seemed emotionally fraught. She'd never been irritated, touched, angry, and sympathetic in such a short span of time.

Renne watching with amused interest didn't help. He was lucky his more admirable qualities overcame his being the king of not minding his own freaking business. He waved his phone, signaling that Ciaran had found something, another point in his favor. Without him, Holly would have spent much of her time traveling back and forth to get info directly from the office.

"Ciaran says the police spotted an old van stopped here on the night of the murder. They're tracing it through the city."

"God," Holly muttered. "What if the cops have already caught our necromancer? Or the zombie?"

"Problem solved from your end?" Gwyn asked. "It's doubtful that a necromancer would be able to get the ingredients for his rituals in prison, and over time, the zombie will just rot."

"If it's not already in a lab freaking out a coroner," Renne said.

A team higher up the SCDA food chain would have to sort that out. The elves wanted to keep the existence of the paranormal a secret? They could damn well send a team of specialists to steal a zombie and rewrite history, the real men in black.

Elves in black.

Nah, they'd favor bright colors and sequins. Elves didn't speak drab.

Ciaran dug a little deeper and found that the police had tracked the van to an address near the eighth ward, one of those neighborhoods stuck between the "revitalization" parts of downtown and the areas of poverty that had been pushed around the city due to previous development. The van had disappeared after that. The police guessed it was hidden somewhere in the ward or had been destroyed. The list of owners was muddy indeed, with the last known being a dead person. Maybe even the particular dead person they were looking for.

"If whoever picked up our zombie can cast glamour, the van might not have disappeared at all," Holly said. "It could be sitting in someone's driveway, and the human cops would never spot it." This case was looking more promising than she'd dared hope, definitely in their wheelhouse. And now it made even more sense to keep Gwyn with them. She could sense glamour more readily than anyone on the force besides a fairy like Ama.

The idea pleased Holly. Strange. They'd done little but bicker, and having a civilian tagging along still struck her as wrong. But Gwyn was proving an asset. Maybe she wasn't a civilian but a specialist. Yeah, that fit in Holly's brain better. Gwyn was part of an organization that had been engaging in criminal activity, but she was trying to stop it, doing what she could from the inside. Holly could appreciate that. And the Wild Hunt didn't sound like a group that a person simply quit. But if there was a way, it said something that Gwyn hadn't taken it, choosing to keep trying to dethrone Tiss after uncountable failures.

Holly shuddered at that as they piled back in the car, and she drove toward the neighborhood where the van had "disappeared." With fey heritage, Holly might enjoy a slightly longer life than the average human, but she wasn't immortal, doomed to have her failures and shortcomings follow her until the sun went dark.

"You need to drive slower if you want me to sense glamour," Gwyn said from the back seat.

Holly eased back on the gas she'd been using to get away from those terrifying thoughts.

Gwyn hung her head out the window like a dog, frowning at the little neighborhood as if it had personally offended her. That was probably just her concentration face, but Holly had to keep herself from grinning at the sight.

"Stop!" Gwyn said.

Holly carefully avoided slamming on the brakes, slowing and pulling over so they didn't attract attention.

"That one," Gwyn said, pointing to a tidy house with a yard covered in kitschy flamingoes and cement frogs holding sunflowers and an army of gnomes and other statuary. The porch was festooned with macrame plant holders and a large, cheerful scarecrow holding a sign that said, *Welcome, friends!* If they had a doormat, it would no doubt say, *Live, Laugh, Love*.

"Not really necromancy-ish," Renne said.

"Maybe they go all out for Halloween," Holly said. If they didn't, the world would make less sense.

"I'm guessing you guys don't bother with the whole judge and warrant system?" Gwyn asked. She kept rubbing the back of her neck as if the nearby magic was giving her hives.

"No warrants, but we do have a system. Sort of. We have to clear it with Marcus." Holly turned in her seat. "Are you all right?" She didn't feel any different than usual, and she didn't see a van anywhere.

"That glamour is strong." Gwyn shuddered. "I feel like my hair's on fire."

That didn't bode well. "Ever known a necromancer to use glamour?"

"No, that's fey stuff. And most of the fey I know steer clear of death rituals, being immortal and all."

Made sense.

"What's the plan if Marcus says to go in?" Gwyn asked.

You stay here, Holly wanted to say, but she also wanted to put that fight off until the last minute, having no doubt there would *be* a fight.

A scream from the house in question drifted through the car's open windows. Fuck. Holly opened her door and jumped out before her conscious mind even caught up. She paused, but Renne's pleas to wait and Gwyn's cautions were drowned out of her mind by another scream. That one meant business, and she couldn't hesitate if someone needed help. She ran to the door, glad her rational brain thought to pull her baton and try the knob from the side instead of going straight to kicking the door in or standing in the middle of the now open doorway.

Gladder when a bright bolt of energy caught her arm instead of her chest. At least until the pain began.

The impact crackled up her arm to her shoulder, as if someone had plunged her side into a pan of boiling oil. Her foot slipped, the baton clattered from her hand, and she crashed to the porch, her elbow banging on the word *Laugh* on the doormat.

CHAPTER SIX

Gwyn had preternatural speed on her side, but she worked to catch up with Holly's hummingbird reflexes. Maybe the potency of the glamour over the van was rattling her senses.

She was halfway across the lawn when Holly went down. She hid behind a tall garden gnome and hissed at Renne as he sprinted past, gun drawn. He had his back against the side of the house in an instant, but someone could have fired another bolt of magic at him.

Holly groaned and rolled toward him. He dragged her clear of the door with one hand. Her teeth were gritted, her scowl determined, even murderous.

"Hold up," Gwyn called. She scooted behind a small statue of a bulldog on a toadstool and tried to peer inside the open door.

A shadow moved inside right as someone called, "Auntie, wait!"

Gwyn waved Renne and Holly farther from the door.

"Get away from my house," a voice thundered, "and I may spare your lives."

Both Holly and Renne took several steps away, shaking their heads as if confused. There must've been a little something magical to that voice, though it flowed ineffectually over Gwyn.

"Cunning bastards." She launched forward, pulling on all the speed she could muster, and sprinted through the open door. A flash came from her left. "Shit!" She ducked, but it still trailed a line of fire across her forehead, setting her ears to ringing. Her head pounded, senses overloaded as spots danced in her vision.

When her shoulder slammed into the wall, she forced herself to turn and took a stumbling hop toward where the flash had come from. She stayed low and glimpsed another shadow in the dark room.

"There ya fuckin' are." She kicked, aiming for where the legs would be. They cried out and toppled as her shin connected with flesh.

While Gwyn crouched, Holly leapt over her head like Artemis and dove on the fallen person, baton in her left hand. She pinned their shoulders to the ground as another flash began to build.

"Auntie," a voice cried from the other end of the room. "Please, don't." A pale figure stepped into a shaft of light coming from a gap in some curtains.

"Don't move." Renne loomed in the open door, gun pointed at the newcomer.

Gwyn stood, shaky, and breathed deep. The pale man and his auntie reeked of fear. The dim room slowly came into focus, all floral patterns and woven rugs and enough cutesy kitsch to choke a basket of kittens.

Auntie spat and struggled, causing quite a ruckus for someone so tiny. Her looks practically screamed fairy with slight points to her ears and wispy blond hair, though she was around four feet tall. Fairy blood would explain why her glamour was so strong, Gwyn could feel it in her back teeth.

Holly knelt beside Auntie now, the baton still pinning her shoulders. "You're under arrest." Her right arm dangled, but she appeared equally capable with the left.

"You can't have him," Auntie said, a light German accent coming through as her volume lowered.

"Please, don't hurt her," the pale man said, his accent even more pronounced. He was all angles and bones, his lank white hair just long enough to brush his shoulders.

Gwyn didn't sense fairy magic from him, but if he was blood kin to someone with as much fairy blood as his auntie, he had to have something. As he took another step, Gwyn sensed another sort of magic, but with Auntie so close and the glamour and the ache in her head, she couldn't place it. She tensed, ready in case he tried anything.

"It's me you want," the pale man said. "Arrest me."

"Sunny, no," Auntie said.

"My aunt is only trying to protect me, but I knew someone would come. I tried to go out to meet you, but she screamed at me to stop. I'm the criminal here."

"Stop, Sunny. Say nothing!"

"I killed someone. I am a murderer."

Auntie went as limp as if someone had pulled her plug. "Sunny."

Holly leaned back, reaching under her jacket and pulling out a pair of handcuffs. Gwyn shuffled toward her, ready to help, though the pain was still making spots dance in her eyes when she moved. And something else was nagging for her attention now, too, maybe this Sunny lad's magic. Great, how much power were these two packing?

"No," Sunny said before Holly could cuff the aunt. "Take me, not her."

"We're taking you both. She assaulted me," Holly said crisply.

"No, that…was me," Sunny said.

Holly paused. The aunt pushed up on her arms and said something in German. It had been a long time since Gwyn had spoken it, but it sounded like a plea. Sunny answered in kind.

Holly seemed torn.

"I killed that man in the alley. Take me." Sunny held his wrists out for the cuffs.

Gwyn rubbed her temples to stop her head from spinning as little lights danced in her periphery. When Holly looked at Renne, he shrugged. With a sigh, Holly went to cuff Sunny first. Gwyn kept an eye on Auntie in case she pulled more magic from her sleeve. With the way Gwyn's senses were reeling, they had to have something else.

"I place you under the geas of the SCDA," Holly said.

The new magic felt too familiar. *Damn that glamour.* She couldn't put her finger on it.

"Entered into with the elves who rule the plane of chaos in the human year of 2015…"

A magic Gwyn had felt not long before. "Wait."

"The fey year of the Shattered Turret." Holly glanced up, the cuffs clicking closed. "What?"

Gwyn felt the geas settle around Sunny, lighting him and Holly in a brief green glow, more magic added to Gwyn's senses, but she fought through all the background noise to a familiar buzz.

She'd never had to fight through glamour to sense it before.

The weight of the universe settled atop her. "Everyone," she said breathlessly, "meet the latest target of the Hunt, now under the protection of the SCDA."

And if they couldn't make him repent, Tiss was going to kill everyone in the agency as the geas compelled them to protect him.

Fuck.

❖

Holly froze, though she didn't feel that surprised. If anything, their necromancer being the target of the Hunt seemed inevitable. Because of fucking course. She should have seen this coming, lamenting just this once that she'd ditched her "gift" of prophecy a long time ago.

But this wasn't the time to dwell on that.

The woman who'd only been identified as Auntie struggled to her feet, firing questions about who they were, who the Hunt was, what was going to happen, all mixed with excuses and threats that contrasted nicely with her pleas for them to be understanding and sympathetic.

"Enough," Holly said. "Everyone's coming to the office." They probably wouldn't sentence the aunt to be banished, not yet, but she had some explaining to do.

Auntie seemed ready and eager. The real suspect, Sunny, argued about how there was no reason to take his aunt. Renne spoke to them slowly in his drawl, and they seemed to relax a bit for the walk to the car. Maybe he had siren in his ancestry to go with the shark.

He sat in the back seat with the suspect in the middle. Gwyn nodded at Holly from the passenger seat. "How's the arm?"

"The feeling's coming back. Your head?"

Gwyn touched the red streak near her temple that looked like a burn mark. "Same. Look"—she glanced toward the back seat—"I'm sorry I didn't say anything sooner. I didn't…with the glamour…"

"Forget it." Would it have been better to know beforehand that the suspect was the target of the Hunt? Maybe. But it wouldn't have changed anything. Holly still would have taken him into custody. And the geas was part of that. By his own admission, he was a murderer. And whether he repented and appeased the Hunt didn't matter. He was Signal-bound.

And now Holly was firmly part of the Hunt dilemma at least. The target was her suspect. She'd placed the geas. All the SCDA was responsible, but she was the front line.

She almost licked her lips as anticipation burned in her belly.

"You seem kinda excited," Gwyn said quietly. Renne was still soothing the two in the back as Holly began to drive. "Am I wrong? Are we not as fucked as I thought?"

"Oh no, we are completely. It's just…" How could she explain without sounding like a self-absorbed asshole? "I'll make sure everyone stays safe."

Gwyn lifted an eyebrow. "Does that include yourself? Because that look in your eye says you're hungry for a fight, lo—Holly. If you want a simple rumble, I'll be happy to take you out back of the shop, but if you're thinking of taking on Tiss, I beg you, think again. I'd hate for the next time I see you to be at your funeral."

Holly dearly wanted to argue, to remind both Gwyn and herself that she was trained and determined, dangerous if provoked, but the little she'd managed to read about the Furies came charging back through her head. Still. "A rumble, huh?"

"It's just what the doctor ordered sometimes." She winked.

Holly chuckled as she shook her head and rested her throbbing arm in her lap. "There will be no rumbling." Of any kind, she wanted to add, but that came too close to admitting that an attraction could develop here. Perhaps. Someday.

"Shame," Gwyn said.

Holly let that go. For now.

At the office, they put the suspect and the aunt, who was a suspect herself in Holly's eyes, in separate rooms. The aunt had told them that the van was parked in the driveway under a powerful glamour. Holly hadn't even sensed it. They had to send Ama, their fairy officer, to help collect it since she was the only one who could see through that spell.

The suspect told them that the "risen," their zombie, was in the van, but that they shouldn't be disturbed because it was inactive. Holly shuddered. Sure. Who would be disturbed by a dead body in a warm car? No, it needed to be up and moving around to get a reaction, surely.

Except not.

At least her arm was now just numb instead of feeling full of bees, and she didn't buy that the necromancer had done it. She warned Marcus about those bursts of energy and whatever trick the aunt had tried with her voice. That last power hadn't worked on Gwyn at all, so Marcus asked her to linger in the hall outside the interview rooms while Holly and Renne finished their debrief. It seemed odd that he'd put any trust in Gwyn before Holly realized that the task got her out of earshot for the moment, too.

"You think she's telling the truth about him being the target?" Marcus asked.

"Why lie?" Holly said.

Renne shrugged. "The aunt seems pretty powerful. Maybe she was doing something to mess with Gwyn's senses until she was almost on top of him."

"Is that why you think Gwyn might be lying?" Holly asked. "Because she didn't know that Sunny was the target of the Hunt until the last minute?"

"Until the geas was in place," Marcus said. "Guaranteeing we have to help her or at least keep her close."

"Why does it matter?" Holly fought to keep the annoyance out of her voice. "We know the Hunt is real, and we have to do something about them whether it's with Gwyn or not."

"No one's disputing that," Renne said in his mollifying tone.

Marcus was staring at the wall with his usual glacial intensity. Holly had to wonder what he would look like if he was ever truly pissed.

"I need to get on a call with the other branch heads." Now he sounded a bit tired. Bureaucracy might have been the ultimate test of patience. He pointed at them with a finger the size of a summer sausage. "Once we confirm ID on those two, get Ciaran and comb through any records we can find on them. See if you can find any connection to the paranormal communities here. Also, find out if the dead guard had any paranormal connections of his own. Someone sicced a Fury on this necromancer, and if we find out who, we're that much closer to getting them to stop."

"What about the suspect interview?" Holly asked.

His finger swung to her alone. "Leave that to Ama until we get a full handle on their abilities. A fairy should be immune to any kind of compulsion, and they can't glamour their way past her."

Or Gwyn in the hall, but she didn't want to say that aloud. She was having a hard enough time admitting to herself that they should keep Gwyn around a little longer. She didn't need other people knowing it as well.

"What are you thinking?" Renne said after Marcus hulked away.

"Nothing. Following orders." She sat at her desk to wait on the confirmed IDs.

"That is not your strictly following orders face."

"It's my normal face."

"Exactly."

She put her feet on the open lower drawer and tried to school her expression. "How's this?"

With a skeptical look, he sat on the edge of her desk. "Very convincing." He worked his jaw back and forth before pulling his dentures out.

Holly fished in her middle drawer for a bottle of aspirin and passed it over. He'd had those dentures in for almost twenty-four hours. His gums had to be killing him.

He shook a couple pills in his mouth as his natural teeth filled in. "Thanks," he said after a swallow of water from the bottle on her desk. "Now, tell me what you're thinking because no one's ever looked eager to do paperwork." He held up a hand before she could argue. "Not even paperwork that might provide answers to our current dilemma."

"I dunno, Renne, this just feels…important. I'm glad to be part of something important."

"You mean you don't think keeping the streets safe from paranormal criminals is important?"

His tone was clearly teasing, but she found it hard to disagree. "Yeah, but this is *important* important."

"Ah yes, the official designation."

She fired a rubber band at him. "Stop peeing in my corn flakes."

"I would never." His eyes widened, but he backed off his interrogation pose and sat in his chair across from her. "Does any of your current mood relate to our new fey friend?"

"Stop."

"Hmm?"

"*Renne.*"

"Why such a warning tone to a casual inquiry?"

"If you're so interested, you ask her out."

"I'm not the one she's been flirting with all day."

A nice ego boost, perhaps, but there was no way. Still, if she gave Renne a little, maybe he'd drop it. "She's cute but not that cute."

"To ask out?"

"To fracture protocol for."

He snorted, but at least he seemed less interested as he started to tidy his desk. "You fracture protocol for jaywalkers."

"Just because I draw different lines than you doesn't mean I don't have them."

"Touché. Some things are worth drawing new ones for."

She sat back, a thousand responses and protestations warring within her, but one raised its head above the rest. "You're lacking your own companionship at the moment, aren't you?"

He rocked back as if she'd just admitted to wearing cactus underwear. "I'll have you know—"

"Yeah, yeah, one syllable from you, and they're stacked up around the block, but there's no one right now, is there? That's why you're so interested in getting me to hook up." She narrowed her eyes. "Not just that. You want me to cross lines because you want company in your own rule-breaking?"

He swallowed.

"No, you want permission to cross."

With a snort, he turned away. "When did you become a detective supreme?"

"Aha."

"Though that sounds like something from the taco truck, detective with extra guac."

"Now who's deflecting?" After a moment of silence, she leaned back and laced her hands behind her head. "Who is it? Ama?"

"Too small."

"Ciaran?"

He frowned as he thought. "That'd be too weird as well as too small."

It would, but she couldn't let him derail her. "Marcus?"

"That'd just take too long."

She'd saved her best guess for last because he'd been her first guess, and she'd wanted to hear Renne's responses to the others, but they only had one coworker left: Ama's male partner with the pink hair and unknown fey background. "Finn?"

"Will you just drop it?"

Aha, but she kept that inside. "I will if you will."

"Deal."

She felt a little bad for him, even when the IDs arrived, and they had to get to work. *If* she had a minor attraction to Gwyn, it wouldn't matter once this case was over. Gwyn would leave, her obligation to the Hunt over after Tiss was out of the picture. Renne would be stuck working with Finn for a while, seeing him every day, and dating coworkers was a bad idea. Besides the fact that the office vibe might turn weird, or that breakups could get messy, what if one was promoted over the other? Jealousy, the upsetting of the power dynamic, and favoritism might—

A thought from before popped that bubble and rose to the top. Why had she assumed Gwyn would leave the Hunt after Tiss was defeated? She seemed to hate her job as a herald and what the Hunt had become, but after Tiss was gone, it could become something different.

Holly had wondered if the entire Hunt should be arrested, but it didn't sound like they could ignore Tiss's orders just like Gwyn couldn't. But unlike Gwyn, the rest of the Hunt was in favor of Tiss.

Gwyn hoped to change that, for the Hunt to lose confidence in their leader.

So they'd be ripe for a new one?

She shook her head. Gwyn would have mentioned that. Surely.

Chapter Seven

After the identities of their "suspects" were confirmed, Marcus agreed to let Gwyn sit in on the interview. It had taken a bit of cajoling. And for reasons Gwyn didn't quite understand, Holly and Renne were assigned to conduct said interview. Maybe because it had been their case to begin with. Maybe because they knew the most about the Hunt after working with Gwyn. Or maybe their combo punch of Holly's intensity and Renne's calm energy made them a formidable team when it came to getting information.

All of that paled in comparison to the most ludicrous fact of their case so far: "Your name is actually Sunny?" Gwyn asked.

He fiddled with the edge of the table. He was very pale under the light. And even with the white hair, he couldn't be more than twenty-five. He was trim, with an angular face and a German accent, though his English sounded fine. "Yes."

"And you come from a long line of necromancers?"

"Yes."

"*Sunny* the *necromancer*."

He seemed more nervous, hazel eyes darting around the room. "Y…yes."

Holly cleared her throat and gave Gwyn some serious side-eye, no doubt reminding her of who was supposed to be leading this discussion. "Mr. Klein—"

"Sunny is fine."

She gave him a long stare. "Mr. Klein, you admit to killing the security guard at—"

"Well, Melissa killed him."

"Melissa?"

"My risen." At their blank looks, he said more quietly, "The undead. I mentioned her before."

"The zombie?" Gwyn asked.

His cheeks went very pink. "We don't use such a word."

"Your…risen is named Melissa?" Renne asked.

"Not in life, I'm sure, but I like to name them again in death." Whatever he saw in Gwyn's expression seemed to make him fidget again, and he went pink all the way to his ears.

Holly looked as disturbed as Gwyn felt. "Why?" Holly shook her head and put a hand up. "I mean, why kill the guard?"

"I didn't mean to." His eyes went watery, and he breathed deeply. "We were trying to get in the door of a coffee shop, and he, the guard, came by. I didn't think anyone would…" His voice shuddered before he swallowed. "I thought that, even if someone was around, they would run or hide, not attack Melissa, but he shot her, and it's part of their programming to defend themselves." His words got faster, tumbling over each other until they bled together, and Gwyn had trouble parsing them with his accent.

Renne leaned forward, pushing a paper cup of water. "Take a deep breath, Sunny, and start at the beginning."

He obeyed, and after a sip of water, he told his tale in fits and starts. His aunt had cancer, a rare affliction for someone with as much fey blood as she seemed to have, but it happened. And through a combination of shitty insurance and bad luck, treatment had eaten all their savings, and she still needed more.

Hence, Sunny's plan to commit a series of robberies with Melissa as his accomplice, someone who could beat down alley doors and never demanded a cut of the takings. The coffee shop had been their first attempt after an acquaintance had mentioned how much cash the owner left in the place overnight because he hated going to the bank after a long shift.

"We didn't know that all the shops nearby had hired a security guard to make his rounds in the alleys," Sunny said.

"And you didn't think anyone, guard or not, would attack a zom—Melissa," Gwyn said.

"Why would they? Why didn't he run? Has he never seen a movie? I…" Sunny sighed from his toes. "Did he have a family?"

Holly shuffled some papers instead of answering. That undoubtedly meant yes. "Do you know if anyone's been trying to find you? Besides us and the police?"

He seemed thoughtful. "Do you mean the Wild Hunt?"

Gwyn jolted as if the universe had poked her spine with a pin. She'd mentioned the Hunt in his house, but she hadn't really expected him to remember, especially since he hadn't seemed curious, only shocked by everything happening.

"What do you know about the Wild Hunt?" Holly asked. "Did someone threaten to call them down on you?"

"No." At their collective stares, he swallowed hard. "I summoned them."

The world went quiet. Gwyn had never met a summoner before. Sunny felt like the *target*. Maybe they felt the same to her senses? "On who? The guard's family?"

"No." He sat back, aghast. "On me. I killed the guard. My aunt's magic kept me in the house, kept me from going to the police. I found the Wild Hunt in one of her books, so…"

"You summoned them?" Renne asked.

"On yourself?" Holly added.

"Yes." At more silence, Sunny added, "To pay for my crime." He said it slowly, as if they were toddlers who needed to be taught the price of murder.

Gwyn had never known such silence. Her heart seemed to still; the world held its breath. She had to lick her lips with a dust-like tongue. "They'll kill you."

"Yes," he said again, face as confused as if she'd lapsed into her mother tongue. "I deserve—"

Gwyn slammed her hands on the table, the sound like a gunshot in the small room. Holly leaped to her feet. Renne reached for a gun that wasn't there.

A red mist took over Gwyn's vision as the sound of her fury came rushing in to fill the silence. She wanted to scream, but her throat was full of gravel, and she didn't recognize her own voice.

"Fool, bloody unconscionable fool, you don't get it. They'll kill you, aye. But, oh, how they'll kill you."

Chaotic energy crackled from her fingertips, and the fluorescent lights flickered like mad, hundreds of years of frustration boiling out of Gwyn like infection from a wound. "They'll rip you apart, boy, so fast you'll see your own innards before you die, and that's if Tiss is in a merciful mood." She leaned forward as Sunny went even paler, as if the Hunt had already started on him. "But she has never taken pity on a murderer. That's her particular area of expertise."

"Gwyn," Holly said quietly.

"No," she said, not letting go of Sunny's gaze. "He needs to know what his stupidity has wrought. Have you ever seen someone flayed, my lad? How about quartered after being drawn and hanged? No, not in this day and age, but Tiss isn't from your day, and your gut can imagine what your eyes haven't seen, can't it?"

"Gwyn," Holly said again as Renne said, "Perhaps—"

But Gwyn growled, her magic shuddering over her, taking her from herald to hunter inside. Sunny reeked of fear but not enough to pay for his idiocy or her frustration. "You'll not only see your organs but every muscle, bone, and sinew, a proper preview of hell before she finally lets you go there." She dug her thumbs into the table, and the metal yielded like tallow in the hot sun. "I've seen it take *days*."

"That's enough," Holly boomed, the command in her tone finally breaking the spell Gwyn had cast over herself as much as Sunny.

She breathed deep and turned. Holly had her own soft glow, her light of justice, more greens and gold in her dark eyes.

"Enough," Holly said again, still offering a warning before she acted where many goddesses would not. She was too beautiful and formidable in her anger to deny.

Shame rolled over Gwyn in a wave, carrying the further embarrassment of tears, and she leapt up, stepping over her cheap metal chair as it clanged to the floor. She didn't stop moving until she was in the private parking lot out back and kneeling amidst the old cars and broken asphalt and hardy weeds.

She wept and tried not to vomit, so alone for so long. Every hope dashed, every plan thwarted, and her latest ray of hope had damned *himself*.

"Gwyn?" Holly's voice, soft and uncertain, the kind someone would use with an injured animal.

As a current slave to her emotions, that was what Gwyn felt like. She twisted, remembering Holly's discomfort with Ruby's tears and dreaded having to reassure someone when she only wanted comfort.

But Holly's eyes held only sympathy. True, she stood with one foot cocked to the side as if ready to flee at the first sign of an incoming hug, but she was there.

"He did it to himself," Gwyn managed to get out. Gods, she felt like an open wound. "I can't…" What? Feel like this? Be this open? Afford to get caught up in herself right then?

"I know." Holly leaned on a car, her shoulders square as if she'd face any sorrow head-on. At least for a little while. "Just when you think you've encountered the pinnacle of stupidity, along comes another challenger."

Gwyn barked a laugh she didn't feel. "His very damned existence is throwing all my efforts back in my face." She sat cross-legged, playing with a shard of broken glass by her foot. "If he hadn't been such a moron, I might've had more time between summonings, might've been able to figure out—"

Holly's hand landed on hers, and she realized she'd been digging the point of the glass into her finger. The pain was a slight comfort, even though it hadn't broken the skin. No matter what, she was a tough old fey, though she let Holly take the glass and slip it in her pocket like the true protector she was.

Gwyn wanted to spill her entire plan, admit that disbanding or defeating the Hunt wasn't her goal, but it had been so long since such tender sympathy had been aimed at her. She couldn't have cast it aside for anything, maybe even Tiss's defeat.

"This could be the break you've been looking for," Holly said after a few moments of silence. "We've got the summoner and the target. Even if he can't or won't call off the Hunt, surely we can figure something out with our resources and your know-how."

It was nice being part of a team again. Gwyn wanted to save Holly the pain of what would surely feel like a betrayal, but Holly clearly wasn't going anywhere, geas or no geas, and the closer Gwyn stayed, the safer Holly would be.

"You're right," Gwyn said, wiping her cheeks and the sweat on her forehead. "Is it always this muggy here in the fall?"

Holly glanced around with both frustration and fondness. "I think of September in Houston as August Part Two. Sometimes, an October like this one is part three." She shrugged. "Who knows, it could be the other side of chilly come Halloween. Or warm on Thanksgiving." Another shrug. "Or both."

"Chaos weather, very fey."

Holly's smile brightened the night. "I have a lot of love-hate feelings when it comes to my home state."

Didn't they all? Especially at the speed with which the world changed now. Except for the things that stayed frustratingly the same. Like stupid people.

Gwyn stood and brushed the dirt from her pants. "I need a shower, a bed, and some time to think. Are there any hotels nearby that fall between the categories of 'sharing with bugs' and 'costing a kidney'?" She had money to spare, but she didn't like to throw it around.

"You can stay with me." Holly looked shocked even as she said it, as if she'd been possessed for those five words, but now the ghost had abandoned her.

Gwyn was so touched, the tears floated back to the surface, though she kept them under. "Really?"

A beat of silence stretched before they both spoke over each other:

"If you don't want—"

"Wouldn't want to impose—"

"I wouldn't have offered if I didn't mean—"

"It would make things easier."

The words left the night feeling more humid than ever.

Gwyn hadn't felt this nervous about spending the night with a woman since the first time, and sex wasn't even happening now.

Or maybe?

"No," she said aloud.

"No?" Holly's face twisted as if it couldn't decide between disappointed and relieved.

"No, I mean, yes, I'd…" She took a deep breath. "Thank you. I gratefully accept." She thought fast. "Refusing an offer at first is an…old-country thing, but I realized you might not know that." She clasped her lips shut before she could babble any further.

Holly nodded and seemed to settle on relieved, but that could have been because Gwyn had stopped talking. "Well, I'll go make arrangements for our prisoners, check in with Marcus, and be right back with Renne." She turned away and back. "We carpool. We don't live together or anything." Her cheeks darkened, the difference evident even in the dim light.

She fled before Gwyn had even finished saying, "Okay." She didn't know if that had been a reassurance that Holly and Renne weren't dating or what. She'd already guessed that, but the idea that Holly shared her nerves made her stomach twist in a pleasant, thoroughly unwelcome way.

As Holly marched back inside the SCDA office, she wondered what the hell she was supposed to do now. *Gwyn* was going to be in her *house*. Holly's mouth had completely opened without her permission. She'd seen a sad person and pictured her alone in a hotel room, and it had seemed like a recipe for suicide or something.

Yes, that was it. She was doing a public service, a good deed, the kind of thing she excelled at. It had nothing to do with the fact that Gwyn's vulnerability had moved her more than any show of bravado ever could. Or that Gwyn's plight made Holly want to hold her, comfort her. She never did such things because she either didn't think of them or didn't know when or if they'd be welcome. But the urge to hug Gwyn had been so strong, she'd had to lean on her hands.

Because she could not get involved like that. Gwyn was at best an informant and at worst a suspect. This case wouldn't end with Tiss's defeat or capture. The Hunt would have to be disbanded, its history investigated. What if Holly discovered something that implicated Gwyn? Even if she didn't, no old-world fey would just decide to remain wherever she'd ended up. Their relationship, whatever it might be, had an expiration date.

She grabbed Renne from upstairs, wishing she'd told Gwyn not to mention her invitation to him. She did not need his teasing. Maybe she could run him through the parking lot, grab Gwyn, and keep them both talking.

But creaking downward in the elevator, she blurted, "I asked Gwyn to stay the night with me." She could feel the rotation of the air as he slowly turned his head, but she didn't look.

"I see."

"Just tell me why it's a bad idea, and help me think of a way out of it."

When he didn't answer, she had to look. He'd crossed his arms and leaned on the wall. "Not something you normally need my help with."

"Renne." She tried to inject a warning in the word, but it came out embarrassingly weak.

"You got yourself in this pickle, you can get yourself out."

Holly shook her head. "Now you abandon me."

"Or don't." He shrugged. "See what your time together brings."

It *had* been a while. She shook her head. "I can't afford to get distracted from the task at hand. Lives are at stake."

His eyes went wide. "I was talking about getting information about the task at hand. Why, Holly, where is your mind going?"

She could feel the flush on her neck like the heat of a thousand suns. "I hate you." The elevator doors sliding open gave her a perfect exit, and she didn't have to watch his smirk or hear his annoyingly soothing chuckle.

When Holly spotted Gwyn standing by the car with her head dipped bashfully, all her irritation fled. Yes, she might be able to get some information, but that didn't have to be all. A relationship, even a casual one, wasn't possible, but a friendship? A contact? Who knew how or when their worlds might intersect again? Holly might need more info about old-world fey, and Gwyn might need…

Well, after a little time together, Holly would find out.

Her apartment was a one-bedroom, but she kept an air mattress for the occasional overnight guest. A high school friend had stayed with her to look for work once, and Renne's complex had gotten fumigated another time. Sadly, the guest list ended there, but she was still happy she'd kept the damned mattress as Gwyn helped her move the small coffee table in front of the TV to clear some room.

"One chair," Gwyn said about Holly's recliner, an obvious comment about her lack of a social life.

"Uh-uh." She pointed to the two-top dinette table next to her compact kitchen. Too late, she realized that the one chair sitting there backed up Gwyn's observation instead of disputing it. "The other dining chair is in my bedroom. I use it to get to the top shelf in my closet." Her cheeks and neck burned again. That was all Renne's fault. "The point is, there are three chairs," she finished hurriedly.

"Right. My mistake." Gwyn set her motorcycle helmet on the coffee table and helped Holly lay out the air bed.

As it inflated, Holly pointed at the short hallway. "Bathroom's on the right. Washer and dryer are behind that sliding door if you…" She trailed off as she realized for the first time that Gwyn had no luggage. "Um."

Gwyn blinked at her before she slowly grinned. "You don't know many full fey, do you?" Before Holly could object, Gwyn raised her hands. "Not a dig, I promise. Just explaining. The more fey blood someone has, the greater their ties to Faerie, the realm of chaos. A full fey can even touch it. Like so." She drew a line through the air, and it crackled like a staticky blanket.

Holly's scales burned and the hair on her nape and arms stood up as the line flared bright, then flickered like a kaleidoscope. She squinted, gasping as the very air parted, and Gwyn's arm disappeared up to the elbow. A rushing sound built around them, hundreds or thousands of voices, a river of life, drawing Holly forward.

A dark red backpack was thrust into her arms, breaking the spell. Gwyn shut the tear with a wave. "Sorry," she said, taking back the bag. "You were getting a bit close. I should have warned you to stay back."

Holly pointed, the air nearly gone from her lungs. "That… was…"

"The chaos realm," Gwyn said. "Or Faerie, whatever you wanna call it. It's not exactly pure chaos, that's…" She trailed off and peered at Holly's face. "Damn, I really should have warned you. Was that the first time you've felt it?"

Holly let herself be led to her dinette table and didn't even protest when Gwyn brought her a glass of water.

"Here's the quick FAQ," Gwyn said. "Lots of full fey have these hidey holes in Faerie for their belongings. We don't share the specific locations. Some of us have sticky fingers."

Like my parents. Holly drank deeply.

"A person can't travel through the tears. They aren't big enough. Not just size-wise but energy-wise as well. If you tried to get through, the tear would cut you off about halfway, and I mean that literally. Then, the hollow tree I use as my hiding spot would be full of…well, you get the idea. The only way to cross over is through a proper gate. And none but full-blood fey should ever cross over there anyway."

Holly's head snapped up. "But we send people to Signal all the time who aren't fully fey."

"This Signal place sounds like a waystation, a city between this world and Faerie. Or maybe between this realm and one of pure chaos, a place even full fey shouldn't go." She gestured at where the tear had been. "Your crooks will probably be safe in Signal, no matter the shit I gave you earlier." She grinned.

Holly's head was still spinning. "I was so…drawn to it."

Gwyn rested a hand on her shoulder, the warmth a comfort. "It's a fascinating place. I mean that in every sense."

A thousand questions piled up behind Holly's lips, but one rushed past the others. "If you can do magic like that, and you haven't been able to stop the Hunt—" The rest wouldn't come out. She did not admit defeat. Even hypothetically.

"Ah, lass," Gwyn said as she began to pace, hands on top of her head. "Sorry, Holly. Old habits. I can hide my bag in the realm of the fey and use the occasional jolt of chaos, but the days when we could tear great holes in reality or change our shapes or steer the fate of kings is long past. The Hunt can travel back and forth to Faerie but only to pass through. They can't linger. The last of the great magic lies with the elves, pure-born down to their bones, and I doubt there are many left. They're responsible for that geas that says you must protect those to be banished, yeah?"

"And for the banishment at all."

"Ever met one?"

She shook her head. "You?"

"Not for donkey's years." When Holly stared, she added. "A very long time."

Holly swallowed. "Maybe they can help with Tiss."

"Ha. But will they? They don't give a shit about human life."

"What about yours? Mine? The entire SCDA and anyone else who gets in the Hunt's way? If they care about criminals—"

"They care enough to make you dance to their tune but not enough to scoop those criminals up themselves. I can't explain why they do what they do. I only know that those who are still alive congregate around the portals. Where is the portal to Signal, anyway?"

Holly snorted. "The most chaotic place in North America, Las Vegas."

Gwyn shook her head. "I've heard of it, but I don't know much about it."

At last, something Holly could educate Gwyn about. She went to her recliner and gestured for Gwyn to sit on the now inflated air bed and lean back against the coffee table while Holly grabbed the TV remote. "Now, where to start…"

Chapter Eight

As exhausted as she was, Gwyn had barely been able to tear her eyes off the screen for *Bugsy*, *Ocean's Eleven*, and several episodes of *CSI*.

She polished off the last of the frozen pizzas Holly had made as the credits of an episode rolled. "No wonder the elves like Vegas. But if that casino owner had been elven, Mr. Ocean and his eleven would have been molding in their graves."

"Lucky for them."

"Do you know which casino the elves own?"

"The Avalon." Holly scrunched up her face in an adorable way that Gwyn could not afford to be so taken by. "I've never seen it highlighted in a movie or show, though it must be there in the shots of the Strip."

"No doubt a mild spell to avoid unnecessary human attention. Those with fey blood are probably drawn to it like flies." She yawned and lay back. "They'll be getting plenty of cash, don't you doubt."

Holly stood and stretched, another move Gwyn couldn't focus on, though it was much more than adorable. The muscles she had to have under that suit…

"Guess we'll save *Miss Congeniality 2* for another time," Holly said. Their eyes met, and some of Gwyn's thoughts must have shown because Holly's mouth parted slightly, a glint of interest passing over her features. It made her seem very trusting.

And young.

Even in the charged air, Gwyn managed to turn away, feeling as low as a slug. "Anyway, thanks for the food and films, but I should hit the hay."

"Right. I…good night." Holly nearly ran for her bedroom, proving that Gwyn could feel even lower. "Towels are under the sink." A sheet, blanket, and pillow flew from the hall as if Holly had thrown them through her own hole between realms. She clearly couldn't get away from Gwyn and her naked lust quickly enough.

Gwyn made her bed, both literally and not, and forced herself to lie in it. She focused on what Holly's expression would look like once Gwyn admitted that she was taking over the Hunt. Angry, betrayed. Gwyn would keep that thought in her head to quiet any other ideas. She wouldn't add jilted or heartbroken to that list, by Freya. She'd assure Holly that there'd be no more killing. She'd take the Hunt back home and…

Well, she'd cross that bridge anon. For now, she couldn't afford to lose focus, no matter how close temptation lay. Just on the other side of that door. Warm. In soft sheets.

With a growl, she punched her pillow a few times before grabbing her bag and marching into the bathroom for a cold shower.

Holly put her hands over her face. God, what was wrong with her? Gwyn had to be thinking that Holly had never had an overnight guest, let alone a date.

The movies had seemed to go over well; the pizza had been a hit. And Gwyn was a good conversationalist, a font of knowledge about fey and the paranormal world in general. The fact that she could tear a hole in the veil between worlds was something Holly was still trying to find a label for. She was waffling between freaking cool and absolutely terrifying.

Her attitude about anything happening between them had been *no fucking way*, then *maybe friends*, but after the movies, they'd had a *moment.* Desire had shone in Gwyn's eyes as Holly had stretched, and it had been nice to be wanted, let alone by someone so strong and capable and smart, who'd been alive long enough to have countless lovers. But had Holly played it cool and casual? Had she acted mature in a, we can take it or leave it, sort of way?

No, at the first sign of possible rejection, she'd bolted. And Gwyn's turning away might not have been a "never." Just a "not right now." But it had to be never now that Holly had run like a scared middle-schooler at her first dance.

Ignore it, she told herself. Focus on the case. Tomorrow, she'd pretend nothing had happened.

Hurriedly, she changed into a T-shirt. She hadn't brushed her teeth, but there was no way she was going out there now. She took the mints from her jacket pocket and sat in bed to crunch a few. Problem solved. Now, if she could only fall asleep without reliving her humiliation over and over.

Fat chance.

When she finally fell asleep, it was to fitful dreams of the Hunt descending on a town and tearing it to pieces, the images so vivid, she could smell the blood and exhaust, hear the growl of motorcycle engines. They chased her through terror she could almost taste.

She sat up, her arms up to ward off the strike of a boot before realizing she was safe in bed. She breathed deeply, trying to rid herself of the fear that prickled her insides like electric shocks and hummed along her limbs.

Just a dream. It had to be. She did *not* have visions anymore.

Flashes came back to her as most of the dream faded. The setting had been strange, not the skyscrapers of downtown or the houses of the suburbs or the giant malls she would have recognized. These were lines of wooden buildings and dirt streets, something out of the Old West before they'd changed into the uneven blacktop of country roads. Funny, after last night's TV marathon, she should have dreamed of Vegas.

Unless it *was* one of those dreams.

No, no way. The Old West vibe proved that it wasn't. She hadn't had a vision in years, had finally rid herself of them after her last bout of therapy. She fumbled on her nightstand for her phone. With her blackout curtains, she could never tell what time it was. Barely ten a.m. In her usual workday, she would have still been asleep, but everything was topsy-turvy with the Hunt. Marcus would expect them at work soon since they'd gone home well before their usual time of dawn. He never seemed to need sleep. As slow as he was, maybe he was always rested.

Holly texted Renne, asking if he was awake before she tried to psych herself up to go out and see if Gwyn was up, too.

Ignore it. Pretend. Denial is not just a river in Egypt.

She stood just as her phone vibrated. A text from Marcus to her and Renne, as if her thoughts had summoned him:

The Hunt hit the Kansas office.

Jules Samson flashed in Holly's memory. It was only a few days since she had seen Marcus's Kansas counterpart on that video call. She'd seemed to have her shit together, capable and unstoppable.

Holly fired off, *Where?* Just as Renne asked, *How bad?*

Right, right, welfare before logistics. Her ears burned in embarrassment. She fought not to hold her breath while she waited for Marcus's slow-ass reply:

Don't have a complete body count yet.

"Holy shit," Holly whispered. One body was too many. She sank on the foot of her bed as Marcus's next text appeared:

Dodge City.

A town where part of it still looked like the Old West.

Holly sprang to her feet. A freaking vision. God, they were supposed to be gone for good. As much as she usually wished she was faster or stronger or otherwise further empowered to catch criminals, she wanted to dump prophecy from her repertoire.

Fuck, she thought she had dumped it.

When she'd first started at the SCDA, she'd told Marcus and Renne about the flashes of the present or future. Marcus had tried to find a way to use them, but visions were useless. She couldn't summon them or control them or even tell when they'd occurred. And because she experienced them from the point of view of someone there, she couldn't even tell who they were happening to.

And like the Dodge City one, they often made her watch some heinous shit she could have gone her life without seeing.

A knock sounded at her door. "Everything all right?" Gwyn called from the hall. "That's a lot of swearing." When Holly didn't answer at once, Gwyn added, "Unless you're swearing in your sleep, lov—Holly."

She hadn't realized she was swearing at all. She practically threw open the door. Her pulse raced, her breath catching at the sight of Gwyn in her apartment, a sight that was awfully comforting after so little time knowing each other and such an awkward parting last night. Confusion mixed with the comforted feelings, and Holly's hand tingled as she heard a small *fzzt*.

She'd bricked her phone.

Again.

She pushed that aggravation down and hurriedly explained what had happened in Dodge City. Gwyn went quiet, her mouth a thin, bloodless line. When she marched back into the living room, Holly shut her door and changed, flushing when she realized Gwyn had seen her in only a T-shirt, though hopefully, Gwyn hadn't noticed that she wore nothing underneath.

Gwyn's first thought upon seeing the other side of that bedroom door had been that Holly clearly wasn't wearing anything under her oversized, thigh-length T-shirt. Her nipples had stood out against the thin fabric, and as she'd paced during her tale, there had been several peeks of cheek.

And now Gwyn knew at least some of Holly's fey traits. She had a line of blue scales down her bum and the backs of both legs and who knew where else. Luckily, the tale itself had required Gwyn to speak through her surprise and admiration.

By the end, her mind had been turned far from sex.

The Hunt had shown themselves to the Kansas branch of the SCDA. That, or the agents had forced them to appear somehow. Either way, a price had been paid.

For no crime whatsoever.

Gwyn scowled as she changed from sweats into jeans and a dark T-shirt. How could the other members of the Hunt continue to go along with Tiss's wanton destruction? It couldn't just be loyalty to their leader, though that was the explanation she'd gotten the few times she'd asked, before Tiss had punished her into never asking again.

That scar, one of many, still ached on very cold days.

Once Gwyn took her power back, she'd repay Tiss for that and every death, adding these most recent ones to the tab. The Hunt couldn't keep supporting Tiss if she failed as a leader, not if that was the only reason they obeyed her in the first place.

"Ready?" Holly asked as she came into the room in her slacks and button-up and blazer, her dark hair in a ponytail and not a hint of barely concealed nudity.

"Ready." Gwyn had already deposited her bag back in Faerie. When Holly threw her phone in the trash on the way out the door, Gwyn guessed what had happened. "Did you tell Renne we're coming before your phone died?"

"He'll guess. He'll be ready."

Comforting. Dependable. Partners in sync. A crushing weight sat on Gwyn's chest, a jealous yearning so raw, she had to catch her breath.

"You okay?" Holly asked, pausing in her justice march toward the car, brows knitted for Gwyn, even in the midst of this emergency.

Tell her the truth.

Wise words, her mother's ancient, long-vanished voice. Holly might have room in her life for one more partner, even if they were never more than friends.

But this latest chance to thwart Tiss felt like Gwyn's greatest chance in a century, and losing Holly meant losing access to Sunny. She couldn't risk the SCDA freezing her out. Not yet. "I'm fine." Even across eons and planes of existence, she could feel her mother's disappointment.

Renne was waiting for them outside his apartment complex and was uncharacteristically silent on the journey to the office. Gwyn kept her mouth shut, but she knew what was waiting for them there. Sharing news of the Hunt's brutality was new, but the pictures that the survivors had managed to get of the Hunt approaching, the stories, the sobbing? Gwyn had seen it all before, listened to it echoing in her ears nearly every night.

Having a video was also new.

Shot from near the ground, it started with a road cutting through two fields, the dark line stretching toward an old-timey town in the distance. The sound of heavy, pained breathing was nearly as loud as the purr of an idling Harley in the background.

"Oh God," a voice said behind the shot, the camera shaking as it tilted toward the thuds of boots on asphalt.

Gwyn clenched a fist as Tiss loomed over the camera. It had been a long time since Gwyn had seen that tall, muscular form that was well showcased in leathers. Her blue-black hair was swept back under a red bandana, no helmet for her, and her tanned skin was without flaw. She slipped off dark sunglasses to reveal boundless depths in her black eyes. Her strong features and razor-sharp cheekbones might have been handsome if they weren't so unreachable, as devoid of sympathy as a block of stone.

She crouched, and the camera owner whimpered. Everyone in the SCDA office gasped, and the image on the main screen flickered. Holly took a step back from it. Gwyn followed, fighting the urge to look away from the screen and take Holly's hand.

Tiss studied the camera without emotion. These deaths didn't rate her fury. They were merely inconvenient roadblocks, as pitiable as toll booths. She ran a hand across the camera lens. "The toys of humans," she said, her voice even, melodic, some might say. Her human form had always been captivating despite its coldness. "How quickly they change."

The camera operator's coughs came in fits and starts, and Gwyn couldn't help imagining a broken rib, a punctured lung, their lifeblood suffocating them. "I'm…fey."

Tiss's eyes flickered right, reflected light the only heat there. "Maybe that will save you." Her tone said she didn't care either way, and she stood slowly before her boot smashed down on the camera just as calmly, and the image died.

"That's the last communication we got from the chief," a voice said over the darkness. Someone in the SCDA office had shown them the footage over a video call, but they didn't appear onscreen, maybe hesitant to show their grief. "I'm the only one up and around. Everyone else is either hurt or…" The voice shuddered. "The chief sent me on some bullshit errand so I'm not…"

"Civilian casualties?" Marcus asked, and even his businesslike solidity sounded soft after Tiss.

"I don't know. Twenty? There weren't that many people there early in the morning. We scrambled to get ready when the Hunt headed this way. Why did they stop here? Now? What did they get from this?"

Marcus looked at Gwyn.

"Hard to say," she managed after a swallow. Her mouth felt like sandpaper and sawdust. "Something about the place might have sparked some memories in one of the riders, and they stopped to have a look? The Hunt goes everywhere together."

"So they had to kill everyone to do a goddamn tour?" Holly asked. Her expression practically screamed, "And you're one of them."

"Maybe someone tried to get them to leave. And if the SCDA showed up to challenge them…I don't know. I'm not in charge." She just stopped herself from saying, "but I will be." Crossing her arms, she reined in her emotions. "This is what I'm trying to stop. Tiss is out of control. If someone tells her to leave or hell, even go around, she goes through them. She's lucky she's managed to evade a full-scale confrontation with the human authorities so far."

"The chief was already down," the voice said through the speakers. "Why kill her?"

It would sound so unsatisfactory to say that was simply what Tiss did, but she had gotten worse over the years. Not for the first time, Gwyn had the terrifying thought that Tiss's great age had finally caught up to her, a hint of immortal senility that left killing as the only thing she could remember how to do.

Because if it could happen to someone as powerful as her…

"She seemed fascinated by the camera," Marcus said into the silence. "Does she have a phone?"

Gwyn nearly laughed without humor, imagining Tiss playing *Candy Crush* or texting. "No. I get the area of the next target telepathically from the magic of the Hunt itself. She no doubt gets it the same way."

"Rest up, Agent," Marcus said to the nameless voice. "Help is on the way." He made a cutting motion, and the background hum Gwyn hadn't noticed till now went silent.

Chapter Nine

Holly bit her thumbnail and pulled, tearing past the quick into the nailbed. It was a good kind of pain, much more honest than the churn of emotion in her guts.

The whole office was quiet except for the soft rumble of Ciaran's computer and the slow thump as Marcus drummed his fingers on the wall. Holly burned to interrupt his thoughts and demand action. Even a discussion would be welcome. Hell, a companywide team building exercise sounded like heaven. Anything but standing here while the Kansas office had been slaughtered.

And she'd had to watch that awful boot coming down twice, once in that video and in her dream.

Vision.

Fuck, she was going to have to tell Marcus. And he was again going to ask if they could use it at all, even though he had to know the answer was no.

"Come on," Renne said quietly. "Let's take a walk."

As if that would help, but it was better than standing there waiting for an order.

"Tell Gwyn not to leave the building," Marcus said.

Holly glanced around. She hadn't even noticed Gwyn had left the room, her every feeling in turmoil. She followed Renne into the hall. Gwyn leaned against the wall, looking a bit pale under her tan. She'd been nothing but helpful—if a little distracting—but she was also one of *them*, the very gang who'd laid waste to the Kansas office and who knew how many civilians.

Ease up. She's on our side.

"I know how you're feeling," Gwyn said quietly as she fell in step with them. "I've felt the same for centuries."

Another reason not to bite her head off.

Holly reached the door to the stairwell instead of waiting for the elevator and took the stairs to the roof two at a time. The air up above wasn't exactly fresh, with the exhaust and bayous nearby, but it helped clear her mind.

"Why didn't the Kansas office see them coming from farther out?" Renne asked, ever the one to ask questions when Holly was too blinded by anger.

"They can dip into Faerie as they travel. The magic of the Hunt is one of the few powers that can still pass through planar barriers. Sometimes, there are shortcuts there. The distances are…wonky." Gwyn held her hands up. "They can travel unseen but keep an eye on what's happening on this plane. Since I became the herald, I can't travel that way. I have to leg it with the rest of you."

Wait, *since* she became herald? What had she been before?

Gwyn's gaze was far away. Holly waited for more.

"Back when Odin led the Hunt, we chased creatures like white stags and dragons that could travel between realms. The herald warned nearby human villages that the Hunt was coming through, and people needed to stay inside or risk being trampled. Or if Odin was drunk, he'd pick a human off the streets and take them for the ride of their life." She smiled as if remembering the good old days, though being manhandled by a drunken god didn't sound like much fun.

"But the humans got used to Odin's patterns, and they started leaving criminals out in the hope that we'd run them over. Kept the townsfolk's hands unbloodied."

So Gwyn had been a *member* of the Hunt at one time. Holly squeezed her thumb to make the pain pulse. How could she have done that? How could anyone?

"Then, there seemed to be more staked-out people in our path each time, and we come to find out that the humans aren't just leaving criminals but so-called heretics or lunatics or even people who just never fit in. As time went on, they left those whom the local lord disliked or those whose land he wanted. That took the fun out of it for Odin. And he turned the Hunt over to…others."

"Tiss," Renne supplied.

"Not at once. We…sat idle for a time, hunting nothing. But we had a reputation as avenging angels by then. Or that was how Tiss saw us. She'd been purposeless for a long time when she found us. The other Furies were dead." She licked her lips. "I didn't want her in charge. I challenged her early on." She rubbed her side, staring at nothing. "She let me live to be herald, though it was a while before I could walk again, let alone ride."

Holly's heart went out to her automatically. It didn't do what she wanted most of the time. "Were you the only one who challenged her?"

Gwyn shook her head. "I'm the only one who lived. The example, you see. Now she's down to those members who support her, though that'll change if she fails."

But Gwyn couldn't really *know* that. So much of what she had been doing seemed to hinge on guesswork, but much of the realm of the old-world fey seemed like that, rumor and legend and fairy tales. Her fey side felt comforted by the chaos, but her human one would have loved a rulebook.

Renne pulled his phone out of his pocket. "Text from Marcus. I'll be back."

Holly moved to follow him, but Renne's eyes cut to Gwyn. She hoped like hell that he was urging her to get more info and not further some ridiculous fantasy of them getting together.

Gwyn was staring over the city. Holly moved up beside her, wanting to touch her but not knowing how, her business and personal sides at war just as much as her fey and human ones. "Was it just the once that you challenged Tiss?" They might as well lance all the pain while they were at it.

"No." Gwyn touched another place on her side near her hip. Just how many scars did she carry?

Holly had the strangest desire to touch them, soothe them, the feeling muddily between comforting and sexual; everything in her was a battleground today. "I'm sorry," she said. When that seemed inadequate, she added, "That sucks."

Smooth, as Renne would have said.

But it earned her a smile. "Thanks. And I'm sorry about your Kansas mates. I'm really looking forward to the day when I won't have to apologize for Tiss ever again."

"What she's doing isn't your fault."

"If I hadn't lost—"

"I'm sure you did your best."

"If I'd been stronger—"

"That's not something you can help."

"Damn it, woman, stop having answers for everything, and let me wallow in my inadequacies!" Gwyn looked livid for a moment before she collapsed into laughter that was tinged with hysteria. She sank to the dirty floor of the roof.

Holly joined her, strangely calmed by that relatable flash of anger. Every part of her understood that, at least. She put a hand on Gwyn's shoulder blade and felt a rush when Gwyn leaned into her. It was such a heady experience, giving someone the touch they needed, as if she'd guessed the right answer to the million dollar question.

"I can't imagine," Holly said, struggling for a way to finish that thought when it came to Gwyn. "Your entire life."

Gwyn glanced over her shoulder with a chuckle. "It's been a long one. But I can't imagine a short one, how humans keep from having one eye always on the clock."

"We make do."

"Ah, but you're not wholly human. Odds are, you'll live a long time."

If they got rid of Tiss, sure, but Holly couldn't say that, didn't want to pop their bubble just yet. "Have you always…mingled with humans?" she asked, desperate to hold on to the present just one moment longer. *Eyes on the clock, right.*

"They're fun to watch. But they caught on early that it's best to steer clear of the fey. It's why most of the stories about us are dark." She shrugged. "Though we weren't the only reason to stay out of the woods at night. Jenny Greenteeth didn't deserve her entire rap."

Holly's mind rocketed to one of the few good memories of her parents: sharing tales of the old fey, including Jenny the river hag. "She didn't drown children?"

"Oh, she did." Gwyn held one finger up like a lawyer driving a point home. "But not as many as the stories say."

Holly had to laugh, drowned children notwithstanding.

"You modern folks have that great term…" Gwyn snapped her fingers, clearly searching for the right words. "Uncanny valley."

Holly frowned. "The creepy look of robots and stuff?"

"Aye, but you didn't get that instinct from computerized people. Humans evolved it because of us, that unsettling feeling of confronting something that looks human but isn't." She winked, her eyes shining almost as bright as a cat's in the dark.

Holly couldn't suppress a shiver, imagining what it must have been like for her human ancestors out after dark with nothing but torches or lanterns to combat the heavy shadows. If they met a cloaked figure with a too-wide smile who claimed to have lost their way…

Count their fingers, count their teeth.

She imagined their terror when that count turned out wrong or the hair on their necks had stood up because something was off, something sinister.

"You all right?" Gwyn's hand on her knee nearly made her leap out of her skin. "Whoa, easy."

"Sorry, sorry." She shook off the feeling. "You, um, you don't give me uncanny valley feelings."

Gwyn winked again, and damn, it did different things to her this time. Where had all her helpful embarrassment gone? "We've evolved, too."

God, Holly hoped Jenny Greenteeth wasn't running a candy shop somewhere with the witch from Hansel and Gretel. She had enough people to catch right now.

Gwyn was so close to giving in to the urge to pull Holly into her lap. It seemed a strange notion for a very unromantic situation, but Gwyn suspected it was more about comfort than sex. It had been too long since anyone had even tried to understand her, since she'd been able to consider sharing her burdens, and the ache with which she needed more tenderness was so intense, she felt it in her bones.

And if it took a turn for the romantic, that couldn't be the worst thing in the world. In spite of all the reasons they needed to remain professional, Holly was obviously a little interested.

If only Gwyn wasn't hiding so much about her life. If only she wasn't going to get Holly killed. Unlike before, when such thoughts had made Gwyn turn away, it only made her want to hug Holly *more*.

Selfish, dangerous, wicked thoughts.

When Renne reappeared to summon them downstairs, Gwyn nearly blessed him and all his ancestors.

Marcus waited for them in the same room where they'd gotten news of the Kansas office. "I've spoken to the agency higher-ups. They want us to break the geas and hand the necromancer over to the Hunt."

Gwyn's heart stood still. *Now* he was in a hurry? "They're giving in?"

"They can't do that," Holly shouted. "I swore an oath."

When the entire office began muttering and whispering, Renne held his hands up as if trying to calm a bucking horse. "Wait, wait, has anyone ever broken a geas? What happens to them?"

Marcus brought his hand down on a rickety desk, and it collapsed into kindling and twisted metal. Quiet descended like a hammer. "I'll take the heat with the elves," he said calmly. "Me and no one else." He pointed at Gwyn. "How do we contact the Hunt and tell them we're surrendering the prisoner?"

Her head spun. Holly had turned apoplectic red, and Renne had a hand to his mouth like he wanted to throw up. This couldn't be happening, not when Gwyn was so close. A target and a summoner in one person? That was a first, and there had to be something there she could use.

Holly grabbed her arm, comfort and support and all but a pledge of allegiance pouring from her stubborn gaze. She was clearly all in, ready to quit her job and lay down her life.

Tiss would kill her with no more thought than she'd give to swatting a fly.

Holly deserved so much more. Gwyn could still find a way to stop the Hunt alone. Always alone. What were long lives for if not lost causes? She shook off Holly's grip, keeping her eyes on Marcus. "I'll take him and head north, keeping to back roads and unpopulated areas. They'll find us."

Holly made a noise between a gasp and a wail, a sound that should have accompanied the word betrayal in the dictionary.

Better heartbroken than dead.

"No," Holly said. "We can figure this out."

Marcus kept his level gaze on Gwyn. Maybe he couldn't bear to look at Holly, either.

"Surely, there's some way—" Renne started.

Marcus began to move out of the room. "Gwyn, you have an hour to make that punk necromancer reverse the hell he's brought down on us all, then you're gone. Try to keep anyone else from dying."

Except for him, if that was what the elves required for breaking a geas. Even if the SCDA took Sunny out back and shot him, that would still mean failing in their pledge.

Gwyn turned down the hall, hoping like hell that Holly wouldn't grab her or beg her to reconsider or—

"I had a vision," Holly shouted.

Gwyn had to turn, confusion driving out all other thought.

Holly's expression seemed torn between determined and petrified. "I saw the Hunt in an Old West town, saw Tiss kill the head of the Kansas office." She went a bit pale and swallowed as if trying to keep her coffee down. "I haven't had one in a while, a vision, so having one now must mean something, right?" She looked from Marcus to Gwyn. "Right?"

"How long ago?" Marcus asked.

She hesitated, and her darting eyes practically screamed, I am thinking about lying. But that seemed as contrary to her nature as armed robbery. "Just before it happened."

That was about as useful as a Band-Aid over a bullet hole, but this knowledge was another perk Gwyn had never had in her quest to stop Tiss, so she had to consider it. "You're a seer?"

Holly managed to look even more disgusted. "Um, I guess? It doesn't really, I mean, it's not exactly helpful." Her eyes went wide and desperate. "Unless it is?"

"We've discussed this before," Marcus said. "It changes nothing." He nodded at Gwyn. "One hour." He turned slowly, no doubt his version of pivoting on his heel, and left.

Gwyn started down the opposite hall toward where Sunny was being held, not surprised when Holly followed. The urge to both put her off and quiz her about this seer business was tearing Gwyn in half.

"Holly," Renne said behind them.

She flung an arm out like a mother who'd braked too hard. "I will *not* accept this."

"You may have to, love," Gwyn said, using the nickname on purpose, but whether to draw Holly in or push her further way, she couldn't say.

"No, no fucking way."

"Holly," Renne said again.

"I said no!"

"Shut up and listen," he said, staccato and angry. "I'm with you."

That took a bit of the wind out of her sails. More fool her.

"You both heard your boss," Gwyn said, but she didn't sound nearly as determined as she needed to be. "You can't just risk…" Trailing off, she called herself a fool. She needed them to risk whatever they could, use whatever they had, to help her stop Tiss. That was the very reason she was here. "Tell me about these visions." If she knew for a fact that they were rubbish, that might stiffen her spine.

"I…I've had them all my life." Holly's face twisted up as if she was admitting to a lifelong habit of wetting the bed. "They've never been, they've never *seemed*, useful. I have a hard time telling them from dreams, and they're usually, um…"

"Right before the events or during them," Renne finished for her.

Gwyn had never heard of a seer quite like that. "Have they ever happened when you were awake?" Holly shook her head. "Not even when you were trying to make one manifest?"

With another hard swallow, Holly glanced at Renne, again looking like she really wanted to lie but couldn't.

"You've never tried," Gwyn guessed. "You have a gift, and you've never—"

"It's not a gift! It's stupid and useless, like knowing the lotto numbers right before the drawing. It's just frustrating." She'd curled her hands into fists but relaxed them now as if rethinking her outburst, surely realizing she'd just given Gwyn another reason to walk away.

Gwyn tried to put her recrimination aside. New information was always a reason to celebrate. "Well, you've got an hour to try now."

When Holly just stared, mouth slightly open, Renne stepped up beside her. "How?" he asked.

"I'm not a seer. I can't guide you. Surely, you know one in town."

Another of those blank stares. It seemed Holly had done her level best to ignore not only her gift but any like it.

"I'll see who I can find," Renne said, taking off toward the main room of the office.

Gwyn stepped away, too, but Holly said, "Don't go," and she wasn't talking to Renne.

"I only have an hour. I have to figure out a way to cancel his summoning, if a way to do so even exists. Or maybe since he's the summoner, it will be easier to atone?" She sighed. That wouldn't be true if Sunny was as hard on himself as most kind-hearted people seemed to be.

"Oh, I thought for a minute you were just gonna…" Holly gestured weakly at the door at the end of the hall.

Gwyn barked a laugh, still full of despair. "I'll take all the time I'm given."

"You're not alone."

That was the laugh of the century. "Holly, love—"

"Don't start calling me bullshit pet names. I let you get away with one, but that's all. Renne and I are in this with you."

"Your job—"

"Fuck my job." But she lowered her voice a bit as she said it. "I swore an oath, me. That means something and not because of any elves sitting on their asses in some tower in Las Vegas. If you won't work with me, I'll follow you, and I'll stand against Tiss."

"You'll die. That's as certain as the sunrise."

"At least I won't have to live with regrets."

Gwyn shook her head, snorting. "Ah, the stupidity of youth. Don't trade your life so cheaply."

"Wanting to protect people isn't cheap," Holly said through clenched teeth.

"It is when you stand in the path of a hurricane with nothing more than an umbrella."

Holly stabbed her finger toward where Sunny was waiting. "Then find something better for me to use. Because I'll be facing down the storm whether you like it or not." She marched away.

Gwyn sagged against the wall for a moment. Well, she'd wanted an avenging angel, a true warrior. She supposed she couldn't complain now that she'd gotten one.

CHAPTER TEN

Holly wanted to strangle someone. Tiss, Marcus, the elves. She wasn't picky.

"Can't believe they're doing this," she muttered as she paced in the hall. "Who just gives up? Saves our people but dooms the rest? Fucking cowards." She clenched a fist to bring her volume down. Renne would have reminded her that nothing good would come of getting herself thrown out of the office before they figured this shit out. She ground her teeth, temper boiling.

Nope, she needed to hear *him* say it.

She marched back to the main office, expecting whispering and pointing or everyone toeing Marcus's line, but they were all leaning over keyboards or combing through files. Paper rained from a file cabinet as invisible Ama no doubt riffled the drawers.

Holly stumbled to a halt, the anger knocked out of her. "What the f—"

Renne rushed over from their desks. "We're looking up all the seers in the city. Pretty good list so far."

"You…you're doing all this for me?"

He gave her a flat look. "To stop the Hunt and save people." His voice low, he cast a glance toward the hall where Marcus had gone. "Self-centered much?" But he winked, and any little sting she felt vanished.

It was almost enough to make her forget that they were hanging all their hopes on her shitty "gift."

❖

When Gwyn came in the room, Sunny stood so fast, he would have knocked the bed over if it hadn't been bolted to the floor.

She nodded. "Finally understanding the danger you're in, lad?"

His red-rimmed eyes stood out against his pale skin like blood on snow. "I deserve to pay, but what you said about seeing my own… insides." He trembled, tears snaking down his face and shaking loose from his chin.

Yeah, she probably shouldn't have mentioned that bit, but it had gotten the job done. And it was so true. She revisited it often in her nightmares. Unluckily for him, it was time to share some more hard truth. "The SCDA is cutting you loose. I'm to take you to Tiss, leave you at her mercy."

His eyes rolled back like a Victorian heroine's, but he was awake when he collapsed on the bed.

It was a powerful stick to whack him with, but now it was time for the carrot. "Unless…"

"Yes?" he said, sitting up, desperate as a drowning man.

"Tell me the rite you used to summon Tiss so we can figure out how to call her off." She held up a hand before he could babble about paying for his crime. "You'll still have to face the SCDA's justice and be banished, but your insides will remain where they are."

After a lick of his lips, he spoke a few sentences in German, something about hoping for forgiveness, maybe from a god or two. "I found a book," he said in English.

He described an old Gaelic rite he'd unearthed in his aunt's library. Gwyn had heard something similar before: chanting, pleas, burning brazier, a bit of blood.

"Your blood?" she asked.

He nodded.

That was good. The SCDA had released the aunt, but they could call her. If she hauled ass down here with that book, maybe they could use Sunny's blood again to cancel the summons. "Anything else?" she asked.

"One last entreaty."

She nodded, not really listening as he recited it. If she had to guess at which book, it must have been—

"What?" She looked up, her attention snagged by something he'd said.

"The last words, 'in the name of the family—'"

Her heart dropped past her toes. "You made the plea to summon Tiss and the Hunt on behalf of the guard's family?"

He hesitated as if fearful of his own answer. "Yes?"

"Fuck's sake, lad." If the entreaty was in their name, *they'd* have to cancel it. She could hear it now:

Pardon the intrusion while you're grieving, everyone, but this is the necromancer who summoned the zombie that killed your loved one. Would you mind giving us a little blood and repeating these words to call off a Fury of vengeance? Ta.

She didn't even know where to start listing the problems with that.

"That's an issue, isn't it?" Sunny asked softly.

"Aye, Sherlock, that it is." Despair clawed up her throat, but she kept it at bay, thinking fast. "Okay, what about atonement?" Murder made that tricky. There was little someone could do to make up for the fact that someone else was dead, especially in the time they had left. Maybe if she spun it a bit? "You didn't mean to kill anyone, yeah?"

He nodded, swallowing roughly.

"And the zom—uh…"

"Melissa."

"Right, Melissa was just defending herself."

Another nod, but his head began to turn, as if he saw where she was going and didn't want to face it.

But they had to try. "I know that doesn't change the outcome, but it should lessen your guilt."

He wouldn't look at her now; this was someone who'd called the Hunt on himself, after all. Guilt seemed a huge part of his DNA.

"You can make up for it," she said, trying not to let hysteria in. "Some money for the family to—" But he had no money, hence the heist plot. And there was no time to get a job or befriend the family and help around the house. "If we come up with a plan, will that do it for you?"

His mouth worked as if he couldn't get the words out, and he lifted a hand, dropping it uselessly. Even with the Hunt bearing down on them, he couldn't say yes. Hell, even if he said the words, that didn't mean he'd feel them. He couldn't change who he was at the cellular level. The noble necromancer was going to die in the worst way, and he might take Holly with him.

Even if Marcus broke the geas and absorbed that punishment, Holly had made it clear that she and Renne wouldn't abandon Sunny without a fight.

Unless he disappeared first.

Gwyn leapt up and checked the hall to make sure Holly had gone. She needed to act before she could rethink this plan. Sunny was doomed, but he didn't have to take anyone else with him.

❖

Holly looked at her watch again. Half an hour. Thirty fucking minutes before Gwyn had to leave the SCDA office, and Holly was stuck in the waiting room of a palm-reading tarot card flipper.

There were enough blinking neon signs and glittery, rainbow-colored chakra charts to satisfy the most sparkle-loving fey, but they were grating on her human side something fierce. She stood to pace again between the sofa where Renne sat reading a magazine and the unoccupied chairs on the other side of the small room. She got too close to a pink lamp shaped like a palm, all the lines lit up, and it flickered and died.

"I never realized how many types of crystals there are," Renne said behind his magazine.

"Mm."

"And they all have different spiritual properties."

"Mm-hmm."

"Protection, healing…different rocks to soothe every part of the body. I wonder if they have one for the gums."

"Renne." She growled his name, and the light-up business card holder on the side table blinked out with a *fzzt*.

"Holly," he said calmly, laying the magazine in his lap. "Madame Lavoie is the closest psychic to the office who also happens to be a fey and a genuine seer."

"I know."

"And we are here to ask for help."

"I know."

"So we cannot go barging into her sanctum when she already has a client."

"I know, I know, I know."

"Then sit down."

She raised her wrist and tapped her watch.

"I am well aware of the time." He patted the cushion next to him.

She perched on the very edge of a chair, unable to stop her legs going like pistons. *Madame* Lavoie indeed. She couldn't have been giving real advice as a seer, or the line to see her would have been around the block. Either her gift was as useless as Holly's or she was a fraud, no matter what the SCDA's files said about her heritage.

But Gwyn hadn't called to reveal a better idea. This could be their last hope.

Fucking great.

Finally, the bead curtain to the next room parted with a clatter. Holly leapt to her feet, barely keeping herself from rushing the crying woman who came out. Another followed her, a short woman in a huge blue caftan who patted the shoulder of the first.

"Thank you, Madame Lavoie," the sniffling woman said.

"Of course, my dear." She had an eastern European accent as fake as all the charms and necklaces around her wrists and neck. "Plenty of water today and a light meal for dinner. These readings pack an emotional punch that can upset your digestive system."

The teary-eyed woman threw her arms around Madame Lavoie, and Holly's digestive system was in danger, too. "Thank you, thank you."

"My pleasure." Madame Lavoie escorted her out before turning to Holly and Renne with a smile that dropped as soon as she took a second look at them. "Oh, it's some of you," she said, all traces of accent gone. "What can I do to help the fine officers of the SCDA?"

At least she could spot a cop, but most criminals could. Before Holly could blurt out their story, Renne glided in front of her. "Madame," he said, giving a little half bow. "I'm Renne. This is my partner, Holly. We'd like your help on a case."

Her eyes narrowed in suspicion, but she stepped a little closer, no doubt drawn to his charm. "You never have before."

"We've never needed someone to train a seer before."

She inhaled sharply, hesitating before stepping back through the bead curtain, gesturing for them to follow. The dimly lit room beyond held a table covered with velvet shawls and shelves bearing a variety of crystals, both in ball form and natural, sparkling from every corner. When she switched on the overhead light, the magical facade gave way to salt lamps and simple rocks.

Madame Lavoie sank into a chair before taking the charm-covered scarf from her light green hair. "Seer work is tricky," she said, gesturing to the chairs on the other side of the table. "Training someone is even trickier."

Renne prodded Holly to take the closer chair, and she managed to sit on the edge of it, too, but she couldn't keep from crossing her arms. "We have half an hour, *Madame*."

Madame Lavoie blinked large blue eyes before bursting into laughter, her plump cheeks turning red behind her tanned skin.

"What's so funny?" Holly barked.

"Why, your joke, *dear*. Especially if you're the seer in question. A skeptical hothead who loathes her gifts? A half hour? Add those together and you get impossibilities that I will not be attempting in this lifetime." She shooed them toward the curtain.

Holly blinked, not expecting to be read so easily, but she didn't move.

Madame Lavoie's eyebrows rose. "No, I didn't use my gifts. I don't have to with most of my clients. I can read their posture, their expressions, and most people already know the answers to their questions, they just need to hear them aloud." She leaned forward. "So let me repeat, there is no way in hell I can train you in half an hour." After a pointed look at the curtain, she leaned back in her chair.

Holly's estimation went up a notch, and she uncrossed her arms. "There are lots of lives at stake."

"Then I'll try to take a look for you, but the farther the seer is from the problem, the harder it is to see its future."

"That's why I need to learn. I'm right on top of the problem."

"It looks to me like it's far out in front of you."

Before Holly could retort, Renne cleared his throat again. "We're not asking for the full course," he said. "Just a way to bring on Holly's visions sooner. They happen too close to the events to do anything about them."

"So you not only want to see the future, you want to change it?" Madame Lavoie sighed. "You must be young."

Holly wanted so badly to retort, fed up with the condescension of old fey, but she decided to take a page from Renne's book and keep her cool, at least a little. "Young enough that we still have to try."

Madam Lavoie stared again before standing and sighing as if some people would never learn. Holly gripped her chair but managed to stay quiet, willing to put up with quite a bit of bullshit if it led to what she wanted. She expected Madame Lavoie to pull out a manual or some kind of spirit chart, but she slid out a small drawer in a cabinet full of them and switched on an electric kettle in the corner. It boiled within moments, and Holly finally realized what was going on when Madame Lavoie mixed some leaves from the drawer into a paper cup of hot water.

"Oh no," Holly said, standing. "I'm not drinking whatever LSD you have there."

Madame Lavoie snorted. "I don't know what LSD would do to one of our kind, but this concoction wouldn't affect a human at all. A fey seer, on the other hand…" She set the cup in front of Holly. "You'll get visions, more than you ever wanted. Whether they'll be of the right things and whether they'll be anything you can change?" She shrugged. "You'll have to learn to guide them yourself."

When Holly made no move to take the cup, Madame Lavoie sighed again. "You want a fast way to bring on visions? You want to save people? And you want to do it all quickly?" She nodded at the cup. "It's not going to hurt. You won't get sick or have a hangover." She put some of the leaves in a bag and handed them to Renne. "There, if you have to use them again. That's about three doses, maybe four at a stretch. Use only a teaspoon at a time, mind. On the house. Just remember this if my little establishment attracts the SCDA's attention for other reasons."

She waved them toward the bead curtain again before heading toward a door in the back of the room. "Oh, and come back if you want a proper lesson," she said to Holly. "Just bring a better attitude. And a lot of money." She closed the door behind her as she left.

Holly stood, tempted to run after her and demand another option, but something told her that wouldn't be a good idea. Who knew what other tricks Madame Lavoie had up her sleeves? Probably at least one to deal with rowdy customers, and Holly didn't want to find out what that was, even if it would have been nice to let some of this tension out.

"Come on," Renne said, taking the cup and leading Holly to the car. To her surprise, he got behind the wheel, and when she settled in the passenger seat, he passed her the cup. "Drink."

She stared at it, feeling petulant.

He gestured at her watch. "Twenty minutes left. Drink."

Fuck. She tested the tea, and it tasted as bitter and awful as she expected, but at least it had cooled enough to drink. She gulped it down in a few swallows, wincing at the dull, weedy aftertaste and the heat. A slight feeling of lightness came over her, as if she was bobbing around in a pool, and she waited for the world to go swirly or to be sucked down a long tunnel, hurtling toward vision after vision.

Nothing.

"What happens now?" She glanced at Renne, but he was gone, Gwyn in his place.

"I think I'm falling for you," Gwyn said.

Holly took a sharp breath, wanting to speak but having no idea what to say.

CHAPTER ELEVEN

Gwyn tried not to snap at Sunny, not with the agonizing death he had in front of him, but he had been so slow to follow her out of the SCDA building, and now he held on to her timidly from the back of her bike, as if afraid of being too forward. It was worse than if he'd clung to her like a drowning rat.

She wove between cars coming out of downtown Houston and winced every time his grip tightened on her waist, then loosened immediately. It was impossible to hear his apologies behind the helmet she'd given him, but she could imagine them all the same.

He'd tried to refuse the helmet when she'd first offered. "No, no, I could not possibly. You should wear—"

"Just put the fucking thing on," she'd said with a snarl, and he'd jerked it out of her hands and shoved it on his head in a way that would have been comical if she hadn't been taking him to his death. Why had she given it to him? So he'd be fit and healthy for Tiss?

She tried not to think as she focused on the road. Any thoughts would eventually lead to Holly, and she couldn't afford—

With a grunt, she swept the rest of that stupid thought under the rug where it belonged.

When she snaked between cars to make a freeway change, Sunny's grip tightened, his fingers curling, a clear comment on her driving. She whipped around a slower car and into an exit lane just ahead of a Jersey wall and thought she caught a small whimper. After roaring to a stop in a fast food parking lot, she killed the engine, yanked him from the bike, and pulled his helmet off.

He was practically quivering, his eyes round with fear. Even though he stood nearly a foot taller, she could have thrown him across the parking lot, and he wouldn't have been able to stop her. That thought calmed her more than his expression. He didn't deserve to be pummeled or terrified, not at her hands. She wasn't Tiss.

Life would have been so much easier if she was.

You still can be.

She didn't know which of the many voices from her past that was, but she shook her head as if someone had spoken aloud. "I can't." Surrendering wasn't part of her.

Even if that's what you're doing right now?

"Pardon?" Sunny said, yelling over the sounds of traffic.

"I said, are you hungry?" She jerked a thumb over her shoulder at the chicken place.

He frowned a little as if he might be ill, but after another glance at her face, he nodded quickly. "Oh, yeah, yeah, if you are."

She hustled him inside so fast, she nearly carried him.

It wasn't until she was making her way through a plate of chicken she didn't want and couldn't even taste that she spoke again. He was picking at a single biscuit and hadn't made eye contact since the parking lot.

"Are you a vegetarian or something?" she asked.

He glanced around the table as if searching for an answer that wouldn't piss her off more. It was practically a shout in the affirmative. Damn, was nothing about this going to be simple?

"Want some mac and cheese?" She didn't wait for him to answer, just stomped back up to the counter and got it for him to pick at along with his biscuit. If he was vegan, he was fucked in here.

But he muttered his thanks and ate quickly, finally looking at her afterward with the hopeful smile of a toddler who'd finished his veggies and expected dessert.

"Sunny," she said, holding her temper by the slimmest of strings. "You can't…"

What? Be scared of motorcycles? Endear himself to her? Face his upcoming death like a brave little soldier? Would this all have been easier if he screamed and fought? One punch and he'd go down like a rag doll, and she could plop the helmet on his head, tie his wrists around her waist under a jacket, and make it look like he'd fallen asleep behind her.

It was possible he didn't know where she was taking him, that he was still under the illusion that she was helping him. She hadn't admitted anything, after all, just hustled him out the door of the SCDA and onto her bike without looking back.

Oh, fuck, did that make this better or a thousand times worse?

Worse, definitely.

And he was still staring, his smile faltering, no doubt wondering what he'd done to make her so angry. He had no idea what was going on, just blindly trusting her like the absolute fool she'd always known him to be.

Gods, could she do this? Save Holly's life at the risk of her own sanity?

Holly's life was worth that and more. Crusaders like her had to live on and leave dirty shit like this to old fey like Gwyn. One more scar on her soul wouldn't matter. She glanced again at Sunny's now doubtful face. *Make that several scars.*

"What is it?" he asked. "That I can't do?"

"Eat so quickly. You'll get indigestion."

Hit him now when he doesn't know what's coming, make sure he's unconscious when he meets his fate.

It was the least she could do.

But her fists wouldn't work when she led him out the door and handed him the helmet again. She would hand him over for Holly's sake, but she wouldn't become Tiss for anyone.

She put the quandary of when to reveal Sunny's fate in the column of "future problems" and slung one leg over the bike as he climbed up behind her. Just before she started it and pulled out of her parking spot, her phone vibrated in her jacket pocket.

Renne. Or maybe Holly, since she'd bricked her phone.

It didn't matter. Gwyn's absence had no doubt been noted. She glanced at the time. She still had a few minutes left on her hour, but they must have found whatever they were looking for and raced to tell her. She didn't need three guesses about what they'd ask.

She rejected the call and put her phone away before starting her bike and pulling into traffic.

Holly and Renne might not panic at first. No, they'd assume she'd thought of something to help stop Tiss and had acted without telling them. Well, she had. It just wasn't something they'd accept.

They'd get over that.

Sunny won't.

Gwyn tightened her grip on the handlebars, everything in her wanting to wrap the bike around a guardrail. It wouldn't kill her, and it would be a nice, quick death for Sunny. Holly might even believe it had been an accident.

Gwyn had a flash of memory, forty years ago, a coastal road in Ireland. She had been trying to help a target make amends when he'd fallen to his death. That should have made the Hunt move on, but Tiss had been too close, hidden in a storm, and laid waste to a small fishing village. These days, she didn't often bother with disguises. She'd probably burn Houston down just for the hell of it.

"I'm sorry," Gwyn said, the words lost in the rushing wind and growling engine. Sunny's nervous grip on her waist didn't make her madder than a wet hen anymore. He was going to his grave—even if he didn't know it yet—he could act how he liked.

Her phone vibrated again. How could she still feel it over the rumble of the bike? Maybe it wasn't the phone but her own guilty heart. Or maybe Renne was calling over and over because something was very wrong with him and Holly.

Well, all the better for them if Gwyn lured Tiss away.

Unless it was something she could help with.

No, nothing was more important than dethroning Tiss. Alone. As she was always meant to be.

And deny the comfort they'd shared, the understanding, the laughs, the bit of heat?

Stop and answer your godsdamned phone.

She growled. Sunny's grip slackened as if he felt the sound echoing through her. She told all the voices inside her to shut their mouths and kept driving. Sunny's awkward grip would return soon enough.

❖

Holly was saved from having to reply to Gwyn's startling revelation by the fact that she couldn't speak no matter how hard she tried. Panic settled over her like a shroud as she tried to move and couldn't, could only scream in her mind while Gwyn stared at her expectantly.

When Gwyn's face and the car began to morph into other people, other places, relief flooded her.

It's a dream.

Her fear evaporated just like all those times she'd dreamed of being in her childhood home again, then realized she never had to go back.

Faces and snippets of conversations went flooding past, and she forced herself to pay attention. These were the freaking visions she'd been trying to bring on, and if she didn't get something useful, she had wasted her whole hour waiting on a seer and tripping balls in the company car.

"You can't win." That was Tiss staring at her with those dead doll eyes.

Holly abandoned her efforts to say screw you and focused on the room over Tiss's shoulder. Dimly lit. Concrete walls. Parking garage?

"It's enough that I'm still fighting," came out of her mouth, but it was Gwyn's voice, and someone took her hand.

The vision faded like water swirling down a drain and became a roadside diner, then a pack of motorcycles on a black line of highway through the desert. She saw Sunny's determined face, then Renne laughing, his sharp teeth gleaming in the sun.

A body lay facedown on the ground. Dark jacket. Could have been Renne, could have been anyone, but they weren't moving, the sandy soil beneath them wet.

Again, she tried to look up, look around, but the sight was already fading. She swore in frustration, combing every scene for clues from bodies she couldn't move. Gwyn's thick hair moved away from her down the sidewalk on what could only be the Vegas Strip, but it was such a fleeting glimpse before moving on to someone Holly didn't even know.

Oh, you useless piece of shit gift, just show me Gwyn.

No, I said Gwyn.

Gwyn!

Her vision snapped into stillness, as if she'd finally hit the right channel. It was the back of Gwyn's head again, but she was driving her motorcycle. Holly's view was dark, but it was clearly daytime, the sun shining on the cars around them. She was looking through sunglasses.

Or a helmet.

Gwyn was weaving through traffic that screamed Houston, and Holly caught a glimpse of an exit sign as her host turned their head. They were heading north out of town. But when would this happen? Was it Holly on the back of the bike or someone else?

Show me Renne.

The vision wavered for a moment but solidified again as if to say it liked this channel.

Renne!

Her head was starting to pound, but the vision finally shifted to Renne leaning out the window of the Olds, soothing smile in place. "No, ma'am, we don't need an ambulance. This happens all the time."

The host glanced over his shoulder to where Holly was slumped in the passenger seat, eyes shut, mouth open, very dignified.

Probably what she looked like right now.

So this was now? Gwyn was heading out of town now? Then, the person on the back of her bike could only be Sunny.

Son of a bitch.

"Son of a bitch," her vision self yelled drunkenly, and the host body recoiled.

Holly focused inward again and clawed for reality like she would out of a particularly unpleasant dream. *Wake up now. Now. Now!*

Her real eyes fluttered open to see the car dash. Her neck was stiff, her head heavy, a dull throb beating behind her eyes. "It's okay," she managed, but her speech slurred, and her tongue felt like it had been replaced by a small furry animal. *No hangover, my ass.*

Renne said, "Thanks for checking in," and closed his window on a passerby before turning to her. He held the back of a receipt covered in his unruly scrawl. "You all right? I wrote down everything you said. Except 'son of a bitch.' Whom or what was that directed toward?"

She waved at the street. "Gwyn. She took Sunny. Go. Drive." She told him the exit she'd seen, and he put his foot down. Gwyn didn't have that much of a head start. They could catch her. They had to. Tiss was not getting another life if Holly could help it.

"Of all the times to be a martyr," Renne said as he dialed his cell phone. "And she's not even martyring herself."

"She's thinking about everyone else who might die. That's gotta be it." She couldn't bear any other thought.

Renne grunted. "She sure as hell didn't consider what might happen to you if Marcus can't shift the punishment for breaking the geas onto himself."

She waved that away. "I'm sure she thought of me a little."

I think I'm falling for you.

He gave her an incredulous look over his sunglasses. "You've sure changed your tune."

"It doesn't matter," she said, hating the heat in her cheeks. "Because Tiss isn't going to get her hands on Sunny."

Renne wisely kept quiet as he executed his own dance through traffic, all while dialing again and again. Holly had never prayed harder for congestion or construction to keep Gwyn in town. Whether she had been thinking of Holly or not, she was going to have to answer for this betrayal. They would just have to see if Gwyn could still fall for someone who'd thoroughly kicked her ass.

Chapter Twelve

By the time Gwyn cleared the numerous traffic snarls of Houston and was well into the suburbs, she was ready to tear someone's throat out. She would have even given herself fair odds against Tiss. Or at least one of the Amazons. She didn't know if traffic made one brave or just unafraid of hell.

But even as she was able to really open up the throttle, melancholy overtook her. All her arguments to herself about fleeing with Sunny still made sense, sure, but that didn't stop her sorrow, and she knew she'd see Holly's face in her dreams for a long time to come. She didn't think she'd ever disappointed herself so much in her life. And likely everyone else, too.

When a car honked behind her, she switched lanes, not caring what their beef was. She caught a glimpse of a gray Oldsmobile passing her and felt a jolt of sadness. It looked just like Holly's car.

It even had Holly in it, glaring out the passenger window like Freya on the hunt.

Wait.

Gwyn looked again, swerving, and Sunny clutched at her like a wet cat. By Odin's bloody bones, it was Holly, gesturing for Gwyn to exit, the Olds drifting toward Gwyn's lane like a threat. She had thought her emotions a confusing jumble before, but they were a lullaby compared to the symphony of joy, guilt, fear, relief, and anxiety tumbling through her now.

She had to exit. Anything else was inconceivable.

In the parking lot of a Waffle Hut, Holly was out of the car before a full stop, her face as venomous as a cobra, but the sight of her was like sweet music.

"What the fuck are you smiling at?" Holly shouted as Gwyn killed the engine and dismounted. "You said you would wait the hour, that we would think of something to do about Tiss together."

"I know."

"You lied to my face."

"I tried—"

"You kidnapped someone under my protection."

"I couldn't—"

"Shut the fuck up while I'm yelling at you." She pulled her cuffs from her belt, a very real threat.

Gwyn tried to stop smiling. When Holly did nothing but glare, shoulders heaving, Gwyn was tempted to prod her to yell again. Silence was only letting the guilt slip in. "I'm sorry."

"Not good enough. What was your stupid plan?" She stabbed a finger at Sunny. "Were you just going to hand him over? Make a martyr of yourself? Or both of you?"

"What?" Sunny asked, helmet in hand.

Renne had moved over to him without Gwyn noticing, the slippery bastard. He laid a hand on Sunny's arm and guided him toward the Olds.

"You can't take him," Gwyn said. "I'm happy to see you, though you might not believe that, but my reasons for taking him are still sound. Tiss will kill you, Holly. She'll kill the entire SCDA if you stand between her and her quarry. Marcus was right to tell me to go."

"Bullshit."

Gwyn's anger flared. "Gods, you're so naive."

"You came to us for help in the first place!"

"And I shouldn't have," Gwyn roared. "I wanted the help, but I'd forgotten what it's like to have people to care about."

Holly took a step back as if pushed by an invisible hand. Even Renne and Sunny paused, looking bewildered.

With a shaky breath, Gwyn brought herself under control. "You remember what I told him about how he'll die?" She thrust her chin at Sunny. "Well, that goes for you, too. She might not subject you to her full vengeance, but that doesn't mean you'll survive. She will break you in half." Her voice cracked.

Was that just from the image of Holly and all the SCDA lying dead at Tiss's feet or all the deaths Gwyn had been unable to prevent? Maybe everything. As wonderful as meeting Holly had been, it had also opened a deep wound.

She had something to lose again.

"I'm not afraid of dying," Holly said.

"Really? Because I'm terrified of seeing it."

With a frown, Holly looked away, gnawing her lip as if agonizing over what to say. Finally, she shook her head. "No, no, we can figure this out. And if we have to break the geas somehow, we do it on our own terms without anyone dying."

"Holly, how can I make you see—"

"I know! I may not have seen anyone flayed or quartered or whatever, but it's my life to risk." She jabbed a finger at Sunny again. "She's not going to get you."

He looked from her to Gwyn to Renne. "Thank you."

Relief warred with despair in Gwyn's stomach, and she saw Tiss's face in her mind, her placid expression as she crushed someone's skull in her bare hand, as she broke someone's spine over her knee, and as she drove a knife into Gwyn's ribs. Though that last one had made Tiss shudder as if in ecstasy. "I'll fight you if I have to," she said quietly. "To save you."

Holly's eyes widened, her brows up as if the idea surprised and excited her. "You're offering me the same rumble from earlier?" she asked, throwing Gwyn's words back at her, but this wasn't the same.

Could she fight Holly for her own good? Her feet didn't seem inclined to move.

She'd just have to get Holly to attack first.

"I used to lead the Hunt, and after I dethrone Tiss, I will again."

Even with the roar of the freeway, Gwyn would have been able to hear the last of Holly's belief in her shatter. She didn't gasp or gape or launch into the tirade Gwyn wanted. She only huffed without humor and stuck her tongue behind her bottom lip and nodded as if everything made sense. "You're under arrest."

Fuck, she should have known. She took a step back. "Marcus ordered me to go."

"He was wrong."

"As is this." Gwyn put the bike between them as Holly advanced. She wanted a fight, sure, but if Holly put the geas on her, it would become infinitely harder to protect everyone. "Damn it, why can't you just fight me without trying to make it about the law?"

"It's about justice," Holly said, hissing. "For everyone who's been killed." She growled when Gwyn kept fleeing around the bike. "How many people did you kill as leader of the Hunt?"

"None. That's not what we did." She kept ahead of her, trying to think. If she kicked Holly's legs out from under her, that would buy her a few seconds. She could grab Sunny from where Renne had placed him in the car. Or maybe just steal the car? Sunny would be more controllable in there. If she incapacitated Holly and Renne…

Gods, what if she killed them? She had well and truly fucked this mission ten times over. "I did what I thought was right," she said, letting her anger at Tiss and this whole bloody business flood over her.

"When?" Holly asked. "When you played me to get your murder club back? When you nearly cried in my arms? When you flirted with me?"

"No, it wasn't like that. I never meant—"

Holly leaned over the bike like a striking serpent, close enough that Gwyn could see the flecks in her eyes. "Don't you dare say you never meant to hurt me. You knew exactly what you were doing, tried to get under my skin."

Gwyn wanted to bite back. They weren't lovers, had never been more than acquaintances, colleagues, really. But she knew that was nonsense. There were few relationships closer than comrades in arms, and part of her had been hoping for lovers from the moment they'd set eyes on each other.

"You're right, love," she said, letting all the things she'd wanted to feel into that pet name. "About almost everything. The Hunt won't kill again under me, and any little affection I expressed for you was absolutely genuine. I'll cop to using you at the start. I was desperate, a failure for too long. But…it was nice to have a partner for a little while."

If Holly felt any sympathy, it was hidden behind a sneer. She stayed still for so long, Gwyn wondered if she was thinking up another ten accusations to throw in her face.

Then, the cuffs clicked over Gwyn's wrists.

❖

Holly paused before reciting the geas. Gwyn deserved to pay for her lies, but they were not a crime. And Marcus had ordered her to leave with Sunny, so there wasn't a crime there, either. That left her former leadership of the Wild Hunt.

But as yet, there was no proof that she'd murdered anyone.

Damn.

"Don't say it," Gwyn said breathlessly. She'd frozen, but if she decided to fight, well, the enchanted cuffs had never had to subdue a fey as old and powerful as her.

Still.

"I'm not going to put you under the geas," Holly fought to say through clenched teeth. A spark of hope flickered in Gwyn's eyes. Oh, hell no. "I already decided not to before you said anything."

"Holly?" Renne called. "May I see you for a moment?"

She grabbed the keys to the bike before heading over to the car, calling, "Don't move," over her shoulder. Gwyn leaned against her bike, wisely not saying a word.

"What's the plan here?" Renne asked softly.

Sunny poked his head out of the open rear door. "I would like to know as well."

Renne gave him a strained smile. "Sorry, son, too many cooks spoil the broth." He waved Sunny in and shut the door before turning to Holly again.

"You heard her confession," she said.

He nodded.

"And you know what she did."

Another nod.

Her irritation rose. "So?"

He blinked at her, clearly waiting.

She sighed hugely and paced in a circle with her hands on her hips. "I was hoping you'd have an idea, and I could act like I'd thought of it first, and it was obvious."

His smile was sad, and she wished she could indulge in his commiseration, but there wasn't time. And she damn sure wasn't going to let Gwyn see her be anything but angry.

"Whether we use her or not," Renne said, pointing over his shoulder at Gwyn, "we've still got to stop Tiss."

She nodded. "It may cost us our jobs." Not to mention their lives, but that was another thing she'd be damned before she'd say aloud.

He shrugged. "My guess is, we won't be the only ones. Marcus doesn't destroy the furniture because he's *happy* with the decisions of the big bosses."

"Think we should go back?"

After a deep breath and a long look into the middle distance, he crossed his arms. "He told Gwyn to leave. Whatever he's planning, if anything, he doesn't need her or Sunny for it. I'm guessing *we're* not letting her out of our sight?"

"We can't give her the opportunity to kidnap him again." And the rage seething in her had to be answered for somehow. She clenched her fists. "No one asks for my help, eats my pizza, and acts like she understands me, all while lying to my face, and gets away with it."

He frowned. "What pizza?"

"Fuck, Renne, focus."

"Right," he said, looking at her as if she was the one having a hard time following the plot. "We do need to learn everything Gwyn hasn't told us about Tiss if we're going to stay ahead of her, let alone win a fight against her."

That set Holly's skin ablaze. She did not *need* Gwyn for anything. Every little moment they'd shared ached in her memory like a burn scar.

"I meant, *I* need to learn," he said, raising his hands. "You don't have to talk to her again unless you want to."

She cooled a little, thanking whatever gods might be listening that he was here. "Good. Right. Thanks. Now all we need is a next move."

Sunny knocked gently on the car window. "I have heard everything you said because the windows are not soundproof." He spoke loudly and slowly but didn't open the door. "Perhaps I could add something to the broth and not spoil it?" He had a hopeful smile.

Renne snorted and opened the door. "Well, since we are discussing the possible end of your life, we can make an exception."

Sunny gave a nervous, pathetic chuckle. "Gwyn wants Tiss to fail in her duty, yes? This will weaken her enough to defeat her, and no matter who's in charge of the Hunt afterward, her evil will be over."

"Right," Renne said.

"And I would also like to live." Another of those painful laughs. "But I can't call off the Hunt, and I still must face justice for the sake of the geas and my own conscience." He paused again, and Holly's heart went out to him. She'd never met a truly penitent criminal before and wished there was a lighter punishment for him.

"So," Sunny said, looking from one of them to the other. "Banish me."

Holly glanced at Renne. "You've already been sentenced, Sunny."

"No, put me through the portal to Signal. Then, the geas will be fulfilled, and Tiss will be thwarted."

Holly's ears filled with the sound of her pulse. Could it all be so absurdly simple? "Gwyn," she shouted, suspending her vow never to speak to her again. "Can Tiss enter Signal?"

Gwyn straightened and seemed as if she might step toward them but paused, maybe remembering Holly's order not to move. Smart. A bit. "If it's controlled by elves, no one will get in without their permission."

"Would they grant it to her?" Renne asked.

"They don't give anything away for free, and I doubt she has anything to offer. If they want vengeance, they usually take it themselves."

And Marcus always said that no powerful, old-world entities liked someone else peeing in their sandbox.

It was all coming together in her mind. They just needed to get to Vegas.

Without strangling Gwyn.

If possible.

CHAPTER THIRTEEN

Holly's steps toward Gwyn seemed hesitant, just like before when it felt like she was sneaking up on an animal caught in a trap. Or an odious beastie she wanted little contact with. It was hard not to snap at her. Nothing Gwyn had done had evil intentions behind it. Selfish, maybe, but at the end lay the greater good.

Or hell, if that old saying about a road paved with good intentions was true.

She held up her cuffed wrists. They barely impacted her magic, but she needed to be at her best if they now intended to race Tiss. Still, Holly gripped the key and eyed the cuffs as if contemplating leaving them in place.

Enough nonsense.

Gwyn jerked her hands apart, shattering the chain with ease. While Holly gawked, Gwyn snapped the bracelets off her wrists. "You weren't really relying on them, were ya?" she said, trying to get under Holly's skin a little. Her tolerance for being held under suspicion was pretty low after she'd been trying her damndest to protect people for centuries.

Holly recovered enough to roll her eyes and let the key clatter to the ground. "You owe me a new pair of cuffs."

"How about the pink fuzzy kind?"

Holly snarled, the jibe a bridge too far.

"Sorry," Gwyn said hurriedly. She let her lingering guilt rise up again. "It's in my nature to be flip, especially when I'm feeling vulnerable. It's either that or be crabby, like I've mentioned before."

And like before, Holly seemed able to let little things go once she had an apology.

Well, some things.

Holly gestured for Gwyn to precede her to the car, a reminder that she wouldn't be turning her back on Gwyn or forgiving her betrayal anytime soon.

Renne was pecking around on his phone. "There's a flight to Vegas tonight with four seats," he said, keeping them on track.

Gwyn shook her head. "Being in the air won't save us from the Hunt." She nodded toward her bike. "The bikes may look normal, but they're as fey as we are. The mounts of the Hunt can look like just about anything and move anywhere, even through the sky."

"Yours can fly?" Renne asked right as Holly said, "But if we stay ahead of her…"

"No," Gwyn said to Renne. "As the herald, my only perk is not having to get gas or oil changes." She turned to Holly. "Tiss can sense if I've reached her target, and if she senses us moving as fast as a plane, she will pick up the pace. I tried it once." She shivered at the memory of one of her former targets piloting a small plane with her in the passenger seat. They were trying to get out of Tiss's reach, but a bank of roiling clouds had rolled right over them.

She'd thought it a storm until she'd caught a hint of chrome and the glowing eye of a hellish steed through the thick water vapor. The Hunt hadn't attacked the plane, merely forced it down, waiting until Gwyn and the target finally emerged. Gwyn had escaped with the thick scar across her right thigh from a wound that had nearly cost her a leg.

"You all right?" Holly asked, her voice caught between concerned and annoyed.

Gwyn realized she was rubbing her leg and staring into space. "So no planes."

"Why doesn't she always come for her target as fast as she can?" Renne asked.

With another sigh, Gwyn fought not to snap. When were they going to get it? "It's the Wild Hunt, lad, not the Wild Sprint. Tiss likes the chase, the terror." Sunny looked a little green, so she stopped elaborating. "The point is, no planes."

"If she knows you're with the target and not either standing still or moving toward her," Holly said softly, "she'll know you're trying to get in her way."

"She already knows, no doubt is keeping count of all the scars she's given me."

Holly grimaced. "I'm really starting to hate her."

Gwyn was touched until she realized Holly would have been appalled on anyone's behalf who'd lived under Tiss's heel.

"We've got a few hours of daylight left," Renne said. "We'd better make the most of them."

"Right," Holly and Gwyn said at the same time. Holly gave her a sharp glance, and Gwyn felt a little dash of guilt before snarling. She would not start feeling sorry for every little thing that ticked Holly off. She'd be sorry for the rest of her life.

Instead, she stepped around her and gestured for Sunny to get back on the bike.

"Whoa," Holly said. "What do you think you're doing?"

"Taking the target to Vegas to lead Tiss on this merry chase we've cooked up."

Holly brayed a laugh. "So you can try to ditch us at the first opportunity? I don't think so."

"Doesn't the fact that I've agreed to this mad scheme earn me a little trust?" She regretted that as Holly went a tad purple. "Right, forget it. But I need to stay close in case the Hunt catches up."

"Why? You haven't been able to win against them so far."

That hurt.

By the way Holly blanched, she knew she'd gone too far, but the words were still out there, poisonous as death cap mushrooms. And by the way Holly's lips mashed together in a thin white line, no apology was forthcoming.

Gwyn felt all her failures in her bones, aching like her scars, but she couldn't let her feelings out here in front of people who were depending on her.

Whether they liked it or not. "Guess I'll just have to keep up with ya," she said as she walked to her bike. "At least I'll come in handy if you run out of gas."

"You could ride with us," Renne said. "We need to stop for provisions anyway. Might as well go together."

She gave him a grateful smile. "Nah, can't leave my steed. We're not what we used to be, but all our miles we've ridden together." Her bike wasn't sentient, but it had been good company all the same, likely the only one she'd have when death finally caught up to her.

Unless she counted Tiss. Because she was not going to shuffle off without seeing Tiss in her grave. Hell, they'd probably go together. At least then, Gwyn would be spared trying to think up something for the Hunt to do next.

She started her bike and put her helmet on. Best to focus on the battle ahead and put away any silly dreams.

"Ouch," Renne said as he pulled into traffic.

Holly didn't look at him, staring out the window and anywhere but at Gwyn riding nearby. "Don't start with me."

"Just remember to get your knife back out of her chest."

He wasn't wrong, and she'd indulge a smidge of guilt for her words. But… "Did you miss the part where she's been lying to us about everything?"

"I did not."

"Don't tell me you even understand why she did it."

"I do," Sunny said from the back seat. When Holly pinned him with a glare, he held his hands up. "It's not my place to say you should forgive her, but it's easy to understand her. Desperation can make us do anything."

Like summon a zombie to break into a coffee shop because of medical bills. Yeah, she could see *his* desperation, at least.

"What is your aunt going to do now, Sunny?" Renne asked.

Holly bit her lip. She should have asked, liked to think she'd been about to.

Sunny shrugged. "Your boss let me see her before he sent her home. She said not to worry."

Fat chance. Everyone worried about sick loved ones unless they had a heart of marble.

"She has many friends. She said they'd think of something."

Holly had questions about if there were any magical cures, how old his aunt was; no doubt a great store of knowledge would be snuffed out by her death. But she didn't want to lead him farther down that road of thought.

That left her mind open to thoughts of Gwyn. Holly had felt for her, her centuries of loneliness, her perseverance, her dedication in spite of the many scars Tiss had seemingly given her. Had Holly really expected her to be open and upfront about her entire life from the beginning of their…acquaintanceship? After all, *she* hadn't mentioned her stupid visions. They all had their secrets. "Okay, maybe I can see Gwyn not telling us about taking over the Hunt. I can't really imagine her turning it into a murder squad. But taking Sunny and trying to leave?"

"Desperation," Sunny said again.

"You do know she was going to hand you over, right? And her chances against Tiss are better if she has allies."

"People to lose," Renne said.

Holly's cheeks burned at the idea that Gwyn might care that deeply, but damn, she had *seen* it. "Doesn't matter," she said to both of them and herself. "No one tells me when I can or can't risk myself."

Renne sighed, and she knew what he was thinking: that she always risked herself. But only when it was something important.

"Well, she has to accept it now," Sunny said. "You have my word that if she tries to abduct me again, I will get away and call for you."

It was hard not to snort, thinking of him putting up a fight against Gwyn. Her strength wasn't a lie. The way she'd broken those cuffs…

"Thank you, Sunny," Renne said. "Very helpful."

A stop for provisions at a department store meant another discussion of what exactly they needed. Marcus had been calling Renne over and over, but he only answered the phone to deliver a short message about what they had planned, just so the office wouldn't worry. He hung up before Marcus could respond.

"There goes my 401K," he said in the parking lot. "He knows what we're doing but not where we are, so he shouldn't be able to get in our way."

"He fired you?" Holly asked.

"Not yet."

But he might. Holly's stomach sank. This would be yet another foray into law enforcement that she'd failed out of, this one by breaking the rules. Maybe her parents had been partially right. Their kind wasn't cut out to obey. At least she was breaking the rules for the right reasons. Maybe she'd have to become a law unto herself, only more like a superhero than a Fury.

Though Tiss did ride with Amazons, the baddest of badasses.

Maybe taking over the Hunt wasn't such a bad idea.

Holly shook her head. Her and rough justice on the same side? Preposterous.

"I don't know if we should risk going back to town," Renne said. "Even if Marcus agrees with our rebellious plan, he may have to arrest us if we're under his nose, at least for the sake of the higher-ups, and he'd have to send Sunny to the Hunt."

"So we'll need clothes and stuff." Holly put her hands on her head. "And cash." She rarely used cards since she risked shorting out the machines in the middle of a transaction. But her funds were not all that plentiful at the moment.

Gwyn waved a lazy hand, her former swagger in place like a suit of armor. Holly felt like she'd been catapulted back to when they'd first met, and even through her anger, she mourned the connection they'd shared. "I've got you covered in that department," Gwyn said. "I am as blessed in cash as I am deficient in other areas."

Okay, maybe they hadn't completely reset to how they'd acted when they'd first met. Gwyn was clearly smarting from Holly's last remark.

As Renne led Sunny toward the store, he gave Holly a look over his shoulder that said, "We have to work together. Fix it."

She seethed. This was not all on her to mend, but she would do her *one* part. "I didn't mean it."

"What?"

"Don't even. I'm sorry, okay? But only for that. Everything else I said was justified."

Gwyn hung her head, nodding. "Okay, and I deserved it. I shouldn't have tried to cut you out. I panicked." She chuckled tiredly.

"I haven't really panicked in a long time. It just flowed over me like the tide, and I was moving before I even thought. I scared poor Sunny to death and tried to feed him chicken to make up for it. And he's a vegetarian and all."

"Poor Sunny." And the admission of fear soothed Holly a little. "Everyone panics. I can see that."

"Not everyone. Not Tiss." Gwyn's gaze turned as serious as a heart attack. "I was wrong not to let you make the decision about whether to risk your life, but I was not wrong about how dangerous she is."

"I do get it," Holly said, trying to control her temper. "Why do you think I'm not barreling toward her with guns blazing? I *have* been listening, and I'm *still* all in, okay?"

Gwyn nodded, even though she looked like she'd swallowed a lemon, just not a whole one anymore. "It's also not like me to worry so much. Ever since I met you, I've been feeling lots of things that I thought I'd left behind."

I think I'm falling for you.

Holly fought the memories of her vision and was about to snap, anything to keep herself firmly on the angry road she was on, but other flashes followed hard: she'd seen Vegas, desert…

And a body.

She shared it all with Gwyn as they went inside the store, trying to discern what might happen in their future based on her memories and Renne's receipt of notes. They were packing up the car when Gwyn asked, "Do you have any more of that tea? It would be helpful to know where Tiss is right now."

Taking another trip to freaking La-La Land was the last thing Holly wanted, but if it would help.

And she was the only one who could do it.

Ugh.

Maybe she was starting to pine a bit for the days when she'd been desperate to be involved in a big case instead of up to her neck in one.

Nah, this was still way better, tripping balls and all.

❖

Holly stared at the cup of hot water and dissolving leaves that would "open the gateway to her gift," or so Renne had tried to put it. Just a fancy way of saying she was about to be off her face. Again. In front of everyone.

She'd insisted on being in the car. At least then, they could be on their way without waiting for her to fully recover or having to wrestle her barely conscious body into the seat. Not that they'd have to wrestle. Renne or Gwyn could easily lift her, but she didn't like the idea of being so helpless in front of everyone. It was bad enough they were all packed into the stationary Olds, but as Renne had pointed out, it was best they were all listening in case she said something that one of them recognized.

"Is it very unpleasant?" Sunny asked nervously.

"The tea or the experience?" she said.

"Um, either?"

She shrugged. "The aftertaste lingers after the shock of the visions wears off, but in the moment, it's a tie." With a grimace, she swirled the contents of the cup one more time and gulped them down.

Now, everyone was really staring, Renne and Gwyn out of the corner of her eye from the front and back, and she could feel Sunny behind her. Funnily enough, she felt more comfortable that her prisoner was seeing her like this than Gwyn. Maybe because she knew she could take Sunny in a fight, even drugged to the gills.

How far back had her ancestors shed their gills? Were they mermaids? Sirens? Some other kind of fish people she'd never heard of? She tried to remember all the old fairy tales her parents had told her, all the books she'd checked out from the school library, the wanderings on the internet. Naiads, nymphs, nereids, so many N names. How did fish people tell each other apart?

She lifted a hand out of the water without thinking and watched the drops roll down her arm. When the hell had she gotten in the water? Arms slid around her waist and clasped her lovingly, and she tried to turn, but she was caught by the fact that she wasn't in control of this body.

Visions. Right.

And as fun as it might have been to make out with whoever this was, she had a job to do.

Tiss, show me Tiss.

Again, it felt like turning a rusty handle. The visions seemed to be drawn either to some subconscious thoughts, or they had a mind of their own, but the vision of the water bubbled and spread like melting film, and finally firmed up on a parking lot, rows of cars stretching out in front of her.

Her host gripped the steering wheel they sat behind. “I don’t believe this,” they mumbled, seemingly to no one in particular. They craned to see past the car in front of them. Not a parking lot. A traffic jam and a bad one. All around, people were popping out of their cars like groundhogs to see what was the matter.

Her host followed, eyes tracking a plume of smoke from a rise in the freeway up ahead. Was that where Tiss was? Holly had been hoping to see through the eyes of one of the gang, but maybe their fey nature prevented that somehow.

Tiss, show me Tiss.

The vision stayed stubbornly the same as her host pulled out a cell phone and told someone they were going to be late. Unless they were calling Tiss, Holly had no idea what any of this had to do with a vengeful Fury.

Tiss, goddamn it.

The vision pulsed around the edges as if saying, I heard you the first time, and pain drifted through Holly’s temples, though her host seemed not to notice.

“They’re saying what?” her host said into the phone. “Hello?” They looked up, forcing Holly’s eyes to the distance where that plume of smoke had become a curtain that writhed like a living thing, a monster of roiling black, tongues of orange flame dancing beneath it.

It was coming this way.

A crash jerked her attention to the right. Someone was backing his car into another while people screamed, but no one was going anywhere, not in this snarl. Back ahead, people were tumbling down the embankment or running on the shoulder.

The fire beast was coming for them, spreading across all lanes in both directions, leaping from car to car like the plague.

Her host backpedaled, phone clutched in one hand, their breath coming in gasps as they stuttered into a run, the searing flames on their back impossibly quick, and amidst the crackle and roar of fire, she caught the growl of an engine and an equine shriek.

"Holly!"

She sat up, her heart pounding, her back stinging from the bite of the flames.

Renne held her shoulders, his eyes wide, and she could almost smell the fear of everyone else in the car.

Her car. The Olds. She was safe.

Holly took a deep breath, trying to quell her panic, the pain in her back only a memory, a last peek of someone who'd been swallowed by agony. "There was a freeway," she started.

"We know," Gwyn said softly. "You were talking the entire time, describing everything you could see, even the exit signs. We know where you were."

Wow, she didn't even remember that. Her subconscious was on the ball, at least. She swallowed to keep her voice from breaking. "Where was it?"

"Dallas," Renne said, waving his phone. "If that's Tiss, I wonder when—"

"My God," Sunny said quietly in German. He handed a phone up to the front seat. "Gwyn asked me to look at the news, and…" He said a few more words in his native tongue.

Holly took the phone with shaky hands. Breaking news and video, a massive wall of fire obliterating cars and people in a swath down a Dallas freeway during a traffic jam, people already speculating amidst the horror. Had it been an exploding tanker? Some kind of rapidly burning chemical? Some compared it to a sign from God. But they were wrong.

Holly pushed the phone away. She couldn't bear to watch the videos or see the pictures flooding in. "Why did she do this?" she whispered.

"The traffic," Gwyn said between her teeth.

Holly turned so fast, her head spun. "She doesn't need the roads, you said. She could have gone around or through Faerie or even overhead, why touch down in the mortal world right there and do this?" She wanted to shove the phone in Gwyn's face and demand she answer for all those lives lost, but Gwyn's furious expression said it wasn't necessary.

"I don't know. And it doesn't matter. Because we're going to fucking stop her."

It was exactly the right thing to say. Holly's nerve stiffened with her resolve. "Right."

Renne nodded at her, and she didn't bother to look at Sunny. It wasn't like he had a choice, and they were his only chance of surviving someone who burned people to death just because they were in her way.

"We're going to fucking stop her," Holly said, "even if we have to put her in the ground."

Chapter Fourteen

Gwyn let Holly's resolve carry her out of the car and onto her bike. It was all fine and well to vow to put Tiss in the ground, but that was impossible while she still had the power of the Hunt behind her. Once Sunny was safely in Signal, Tiss would have failed, and her power would be less, the Hunt's faith in her shaken. Only then could Gwyn hope to vanquish her.

Alone. No matter what Holly thought.

Gwyn pulled into traffic behind Renne, following him as they zipped out of town. Las Vegas was a long way from Houston, but they were going to drive hell for leather, and maybe they'd find a few ways to slow Tiss down along the way.

Or at least keep her out of the most populated areas in Texas.

The video of that firestorm along the freeway was burned into Gwyn's mind. She'd seen Tiss among those flames as clear as day, but from everyone else's reactions, most of humanity would be unaware. Tiss could still be stealthy when she wanted, it seemed, only Gwyn had been fey enough to see her. She supposed that worked in their favor. The last thing they needed was a tide of humans fleeing the city to get in their way. And maybe the lack of panic would keep them out of Tiss's way, too.

Still, they needed a way to slow Tiss down if they were going to stay ahead of her. Gwyn racked her brain as she rode, alternating between frustration and how good it felt to be sinking her teeth into a problem like this again. New ways to maybe thwart Tiss didn't come along very often. She tried not to let the fact that she had yet to find one that worked get her down.

They stayed well south of Dallas as they headed for New Mexico. It wasn't until they stopped for a late dinner around Lubbock that she'd finally hit on a solution. "Ley lines," she said over the table.

Renne and Holly just looked at each other, but Sunny perked up. "You're going to use a magical ritual?" he asked.

At continuing blank looks from Holly and Renne, Gwyn sighed. "Don't they teach the old magics anymore?"

"We try to avoid magic of any kind," Renne said.

Holly nodded. "We tend to chase people for doing that."

"You guys need to hang out with some fey who aren't cops or criminals," Gwyn said. "Ley lines are lines of power that run all over the world, and in some places, they cross over from one plane to the next. Tiss may be able to cross from one realm to another via the Hunt's magic, but she still has to travel. She can't just fold space like a wormhole."

"You know what wormholes are?" Holly asked with an arched brow.

Gwyn fought her irritation. "Ah, no, I'm usually too busy cleaning out my cave and dancing naked under the full moon for luck."

Holly frowned. "Don't get snippy with me. You didn't know much about Las Vegas, so why can't I be surprised that you know what a wormhole is?"

"Just because I'm not up-to-date on American cities doesn't mean I don't read at all."

Renne cleared his throat loudly. "So ley lines?"

Even while mildly insulted, Gwyn was glad to be back to arguing good-naturedly with Holly. Anything was better than bitter recriminations or chilly silence. She almost wished Renne hadn't interrupted. "Right, ley lines cross all realms, even Faerie, so Tiss will have to cross some on her way to find us. We can set a trap for her on one of these lines that should slow her down."

"What if she doesn't cross where the trap is?" Renne asked.

"It shouldn't matter," Sunny said with a smile, seeming ecstatic to be included in the planning. "If something is attuned to her, it should find her anywhere along the line."

Gwyn jerked a thumb at where he sat next to her. "See what happens when you read?"

Holly snorted, but her twitching lip said she was somewhat happy about their return to casual animosity, too. "I'll put *Fury Trapping for Dummies* on my library list."

"Sounds like a cracking read if it does exist. If it doesn't, let's write it."

That got a smile from Holly, though Renne stayed disturbingly sober. He pulled up some information on his phone about Furies. "I can't find any weaknesses," he said. "Not like a fey."

Gwyn shrugged. "I don't know that she has any. But the Hunt is fey. It's the power of the mounts we can slow, pure fey magic. Iron across a ley line might slow them down since the bikes aren't really metal." She rubbed her lips. "But it won't be as simple as sprinkling iron filings across the road at a ley line point."

They all named some other fey weaknesses: rowan branches, red thread, the power of order. Sunny's enthusiasm seemed to dwindle, and he doodled on the back of his paper placemat, muttering to himself in German until their food came.

When they all began to dig in, he slid the placemat to the middle of the table. "Something like this?" he asked.

Gwyn looked over the lines and numbers and what looked like mathematical formulas. She recognized the surrounding roads and what seemed to be ley lines covering them, all in the different colors of crayons that rested on every table. "What the hell?"

"I had to peek at the Google Maps to get the freeways right, but I remember all my main ley lines. Since Tiss is coming from the east, this is where a spell would need to be attached, and we'd need these conditions." He rattled off ingredients and vectors and something about angles of the wind. By the time he was done, Renne and Holly looked as flabbergasted as Gwyn felt.

"If you're going to cast ritual magic, ask a ritual magic caster," Sunny said, his cheeks pink. "Necromancy has lots of precise points. Get one wrong, and you have catastrophe."

Holly pushed the placemat away and shook her head. "That hurts my eyes even to look at it."

Gwyn nodded in sympathy. "Order magic."

"You can do all that?" Renne said, pointing at the paper and looking at Sunny in wonder.

"Oh, yeah, it shouldn't be too hard. I'll need some essence from Gwyn's…mount. And it would help if you have something of Tiss's. And of course, I need to know what you want to happen to her. Well, to her ride."

"Could you kill it?" Holly asked.

Gwyn shook her head. "They're not really alive. But slow them down? Probably. They're weak to running water."

Holly snorted. "I don't think we can reroute a river."

"No," Sunny said, making some adjustments to his placemat. "But maybe if we used some pouring water in the ritual?" He nibbled his lip as he worked.

Gwyn nearly hugged him. Where had this kid been all her life? She should have sought help from a ritual caster years ago, but like many who came by their magic naturally, she never really thought about them.

"How about we separate them?" Renne asked. "If they're stronger together."

Another great idea. As everyone fell to discussing things once more, Gwyn reveled in it. Comrades. Partners. Friends, if she could still call them that since one was the target of the Hunt who was going to be banished at the end of their adventure. And the other two, well, she'd nearly fucked up their relationship for good with her panic.

She let herself soak that in for a moment, too. She needed a grand gesture by way of apology, especially for Holly. No matter how Holly had thought of the two of them at the outset, they'd been building a connection; it had to be why she was so angry, and Renne was so calm. Other than the fact that those seemed to be their natural states.

"I'm sorry," she said during a lull in the discussion. "Truly." She was talking to all of them but forced herself to look at Holly. "I know I already apologized, but it's worth saying again. No matter what happens, I'll always be indebted to you for your help. And I'm so sorry I tried to cut myself off from it." She pulled a silver ring with a moonstone off her pinkie finger. "Among the fey, exchanging a token is a way of saying, I'm in your debt, but it also means we're connected." She slid it across the table between Renne and Holly, but she hoped they knew which of them it was really for. “This was my mother’s.”

Holly shook her head rapidly, her expression seeming torn between forgiveness and embarrassment. “I can’t—”

Gwyn wiggled her fingers. She wore a ring on every other one most days. “Don’t worry. I’ve lots of jewelry from her. It’s not that exciting of a token.” She tried to keep it light, knowing that was the only way Holly would take the ring, but she also hoped Holly saw the meaning of it in her eyes. “Please. It’s more than a debt to be repaid. It’s also a thank-you.”

For once, she wished Holly had grown up among some old-world fey; she would have known how big a deal this was to refuse. Gwyn supposed there was no ideal place between old-world knowledge and a young perspective unsullied by time.

“Thank you,” Renne said.

Gwyn’s stomach dropped when he reached for the ring, but he pushed it closer to Holly, giving Gwyn a wink. She’d have to give him something nice, too, if they all survived this.

“Thanks,” Holly said, her voice thick, but she picked up the ring and seemed as if she might put it in her pocket before she jammed it onto her right ring finger, her hands more slender despite the fact that she was taller. Her gaze roved about the table as if searching for a safe harbor before she glanced at Gwyn and gave her a smile as full as it was brief. “Thank you.”

Sunny was looking between them with a delighted grin. He said something in German that sounded like, “I can see you two together,” but tapped the ley line map he’d been drawing and launched back into the plan.

The silver ring seemed to burn on Holly’s finger, and it had nothing to do with any fey sensitivity. She rarely wore jewelry and couldn’t help squeezing her fingers together to feel the cool metal.

No woman had ever given her jewelry before.

No, she couldn’t let that go to her head. As Gwyn had said, it was a thank-you, a fey IOU that no doubt had its origins in the mists of time.

Still.

She clenched her hand into a fist. No, there was no still. She was angry. Gwyn had lied to her, kept things from her, and tried to ditch her. She had every right to stay angry, apologies and rings be damned.

Still.

She fought the urge to sigh and focused on the conversation. They had a plan, and that felt wonderful, and she had a part to play in it. Or she would if she just paid attention.

"Do you have anything that belonged to Tiss?" Renne asked.

Gwyn nibbled her thumb, and something stirred in Holly's core. Her sex drive clearly hadn't gotten the memo that she was trying to be angry. Or maybe it had just been won over by the jewelry. Shameless. "She doesn't exactly trust me to hold her wallet," Gwyn said. "We haven't actually been face-to-face in years." She rubbed her shoulder as if it pained her, and Holly had a sudden mental image of giving her a massage.

Stop.

"She's given me plenty of scars," Gwyn said, snorting. "I don't suppose that would work."

"Cutting off your scars?" Renne said, his eyebrows nearly to his hairline.

"Very Shakespeare," Holly added.

But Sunny was rubbing his chin. "Using blood in magic is powerful. Did she give you any scars with her bare hands?"

"A few," Gwyn said with a shiver.

"I suppose some of her essence could linger. She's a powerful entity, yes?"

"Very."

Holly's heart went out to her again. Remembering Gwyn's circumstances softened her more than a ring ever could. She told herself again to keep her mind on the task at hand. "Did you ever make her bleed?" she asked. "If you were both cut at the same time, maybe some of her…essence is in your blood."

Renne ducked his head. "Gross. Like a fey STD."

"But one we could definitely use," Sunny said.

Gwyn was looking out the windows, but her gaze seemed focused on the past. "There was one time, when she found us, our first fight, before she had the might of the Hunt behind her." She shook her head slowly. "I underestimated what she could do, but I got one good hit in. I can confirm that she does bleed, and I won't underestimate her again."

Holly would have been spoiling for a rematch, too. "Will mingled blood work?" she asked Sunny.

He shrugged. "Setting a trap for a Fury who leads a fey motorcycle gang is new territory for me. But I promise to do my best."

Excitement bubbled in Holly's stomach, but hard on the heels of it came a yawn. "I don't suppose Tiss stops to sleep? Renne and I can take turns driving, but…"

Gwyn smiled. "Worried about me?"

Holly liked it much better when she was acting shy or damaged, but she couldn't say that. "Is that a yes, or what?"

"She doesn't sleep," Gwyn said, "but most of the Hunt has to. They'll have to stop."

"Thank goodness," Renne said with a stretch. "Because it's quite a drive to Vegas, and something tells me we'll need our wits about us the whole way." He motioned for the check, and after Gwyn paid and they left, they found a nearby hotel that had two rooms available.

Now all that was left to decide was who was going to sleep where.

Holly and Renne in one room and Gwyn and Sunny in the other made the most sense. Holly wanted to be suspicious about giving Gwyn the opportunity to run off with Sunny again, but the ring sat heavy on her finger whenever her mind drifted that way. It wasn't likely, and besides, Gwyn had to know Holly could find her again.

Still, when Holly and Renne were getting their bags of new clothes from the car, he looked at her and raised an eyebrow.

"Don't even," she told him.

"It might be your last opportunity before the grand finale of our little adventure."

"Why would I want to complicate things?"

"Might clear your mind."

"Renne." Holly sighed and rested her arm on the roof of the car. A thousand excuses lined up in her head. She was still a little angry. They needed sleep. There were already too many variables in this plan to create further complications. And also… "What if she doesn't want to?"

She wanted to say, what if she doesn't want *me*, but she remembered that look in Gwyn's eye at her apartment. There had been definite interest there.

But she had also turned away.

"She's been glancing over here ever since you and I walked over." He nodded toward where Gwyn and Sunny were talking near the bike. Gwyn had already retrieved her bag from Faerie, so everyone was waiting on Holly and Renne.

"So?" she asked.

He shrugged. "Then don't plan to sleep with her. Just talk to her, iron out all the complicated feelings you won't admit to."

She glared at him, hating when he was right. "Why can't I just talk to you?"

"I can't give you closure in this." He slung his bag over his shoulder and grinned at her. "And I'm not the one you want to make out with."

She nearly threw her bag at him, starting to loathe him as much as she loved him.

Holly kept her eyes in front of her as they marched to the elevators and down the hall to where their rooms were across from each other. No one said a word, not even when Holly gave the second key to Renne and gestured for him and Sunny to go in the opposite room from her and Gwyn.

Holly dumped her bag on one of the queen beds and turned to find Gwyn setting her own bag down and staring at the bed so hard, Holly expected it to crack under the weight. Her slightly pointed ears had gone a bit red, and the effect was so cute, Holly nearly chuckled. Instead, she sat on the end of the bed and took a deep breath. "Right. Let's do this."

Gwyn's eyes went wide as she stared. "Um." She laughed nervously. "Just like that? No honeyed words? No kissing?"

Holly's cheeks burned as realization dawned. "No! That's not what I…" She rubbed her forehead. "Talk. Let's talk."

"Oh. Sorry." Gwyn perched on the end of her bed, her neck now as red as her ears. "I thought…sorry."

"I'm not that bad at seduction."

"Of course not. I'm just, well, I was thinking…" She swallowed, and the color creeping onto her cheeks said just what she was thinking.

So she *did* want to. Holly felt a tremendous sense of relief that she wasn't proud of, but still, it was nice to be wanted. "We really should talk first."

"First?"

"God." Holly barked a laugh. "This whole conversation is going to be fraught with innuendo and double entendre and both of us reading things into it that shouldn't be read."

Gwyn laughed, too, and some of the pressure in the room lightened. "No doubt. I'll try my best to behave. We're just talking."

"Right." But now silence descended, and Holly couldn't think of a word to say. "After I take a shower." She grabbed her bag and ran for the bathroom before there could be any question as to whether that was an invitation. But as she was about to lock the door, she paused, wondering if it would be so bad if Gwyn did join her.

She snatched her hand back. She couldn't ask, not after all that rigmarole. They had to talk first. They'd agreed.

But she still didn't lock the door.

CHAPTER FIFTEEN

As soon as the bathroom door closed, Gwyn stood. Then sat. And stood again.

"For fuck's sake," she muttered. She paced, hands on her hips. They were just there to talk. And even if that did lead to more, she had more than a millennia of experience to draw on. There was absolutely no reason she should have been nervous about pleasing a beautiful woman in bed.

And Holly *was* beautiful. And passionate. Loyal. Committed to what she knew was right. Brave. Great legs.

All of that should have had Gwyn salivating in anticipation, not pacing like someone facing a firing squad. Their relationship was already complicated; she didn't have to worry about making it more so. And Holly now knew the truth about Gwyn's past. Maybe this was an elaborate setup to make her suffer. Holly would turn her on, then exile her to her own bed with a cold shoulder.

No, that was stupid. Gwyn had clearly spent too many nights with overly mischievous and cruel fey.

Maybe that was it. She'd never met anyone quite like Holly, let alone had the opportunity to be intimate with them. She didn't want to lose Holly, either as a comrade or a friend. Or more.

Odin's bones, it sucked having something to lose. But she was quickly forgetting how to be alone.

Damn.

The bathroom door opened, and she nearly leapt to the ceiling. She whipped around to see Holly emerge from a billowing cloud of steam wearing a T-shirt like the one she'd had on in her apartment, but she was also wearing shorts this time.

Pity.

Her eyes were wide, body angled slightly to the side as if the wrong word would send her running. Affection rushed through Gwyn. If anyone deserved to have tons of self-confidence, it was Holly, but the lack just made Gwyn want to hold her.

Words first. "You're absolutely gorgeous."

Holly blushed and looked down, pushing a wet strand of hair behind her ear as she smiled. She was still wearing the ring. "You use that line on everyone?"

"I've never said it before." Gwyn took a step toward her. "And I'd never use a line on you." She hoped Holly could feel her desire, not only physically but to know everything about her and keep them by each other's side.

Holly stared at her lips and licked her own. "Thanks."

Gwyn brushed Holly's wet hair back and rested her palm against her pink cheek. "Do you want to talk or…"

One side of Holly's mouth quirked up. She leaned close instead, one hand landing on Gwyn's hip as she brushed their lips together.

Trying not to pounce, Gwyn leaned in, taking the invitation and more than happy to drive. The tables would no doubt turn soon enough, and she was here for that, too. She opened her mouth against Holly's, bringing her tongue into play and gratified beyond words when Holly moaned into her mouth.

Holly backed her toward the bed, kissing her all the way, and still managed to say, "We still need to talk."

Gwyn stopped, her core on fire to keep going, but she would wait if that was what Holly wanted. For years if necessary. Holly was worth it.

After a glance into Gwyn's eyes, Holly chuckled. Pledge to wait or not, some of her disappointment must have shown. "Later," Holly said softly, kissing her again. "After we make out. A lot."

❖

Holly woke to a phone ringing like mad, but she hesitated to reach for it. She was more likely to brick it first thing in the morning.

Hadn't she bricked it already?

And why was she pressed against something warm and pliable that smelled heavenly?

Like a livestream, the past few days blew through her mind, ending with visions of the night before: her and Gwyn talking late into the night, a lot of making out before Gwyn had gone to shower. Then, more talking. And kissing. They must have nodded off in the same bed.

Holly froze, taking stock of where her limbs were. Gwyn's back was pressed against her front. Their legs were tangled together, and Holly's arm rested over Gwyn's side.

And her hand was pressed to Gwyn's very sexy abs.

Her very sexy *bare* abs.

She could feel the swell of Gwyn's breasts against her thumb.

Oh God. Gwyn's shirt must have ridden up somehow, or maybe she'd taken it off in her sleep. Had Holly taken it off? Had she ever taken off someone's shirt in her sleep? She searched her memory, but no one had ever affected her like Gwyn. Even now, struggling with embarrassment and the fatigue that followed a night of too many stupid emotions, a part of her wanted to kiss Gwyn awake and shift her hand upward. Or downward. That part of her wasn't picky.

She knew just which part it was, too.

Gwyn stirred, and Holly's panic spiked. She kept herself frozen, desperate to see what Gwyn would do, happy to let her lead, another new experience for her, but she trusted Gwyn to make a decision that was best for both of them, at least in this situation.

Yet another new feeling for the books.

"Mm, morning," Gwyn muttered. She snuggled backward a bit, making Holly twitch. Gwyn chuckled, the sound like heaven. She took Holly's hand that had gone wandering in the night and gave it a squeeze. "Were you dreamin', or did you wake up with naughty thoughts?"

"S…sorry," Holly said, gently taking her hand back. "It went AWOL."

"No, no, permission granted." Gwyn rolled over. In the sliver of light coming between the thick curtains, her hair was as wild as if she'd tossed and turned all night. Maybe Holly had disturbed it with this chaos field Gwyn had told her about the night before. "I mean, we had our big talk, and now there's this big bed we haven't taken full advantage of."

Holly swallowed as all her parts told her to go for it, drowning out her fear.

That phone vibrated again. Gwyn's phone.

With a sigh, she reached for it and answered. "Yeah, Renne… okay, yeah, we're on our way." She hung up and turned on the bedside lamp before sitting up against the headboard "They're heading down to breakfast." She tucked a strand of Holly's hair behind her ear. "Good morning again."

The look and tone somewhat made up for the fact that the bed would continue to not have full advantage taken of it. Gwyn's shirt had fallen back over her stomach, but she was still sexy as hell as she got up and went to the bathroom. She was all lean muscle that would have put any Instagram model to shame, even with the scars that crossed her flesh here and there. She moved like a leopard or a goddess. Hell, she might even be able to claim a goddess as one of her ancestors. Holly had that same flash from her former vision, Gwyn staring her down and saying, "I think I'm falling for you."

That such a woman could fall for her…

"Did any of your former bedmates mention that you kick like a mule in your sleep?" Gwyn said.

And back they came to earth again. "I do not."

"My bruised shins beg to differ." She stepped out while brushing her teeth and winked to show she was teasing a bit.

But Holly couldn't let it end there. Even goddesses had flaws, and if everyone was going to start naming them… "You snore."

"So I've been told," Gwyn called a second later. "But not enough to overshadow my obvious charms. At least, your wandering hand thought so."

Holly's traitorous cheeks burned again. "Please do not share that with Renne. He's going to be smug enough. He's going to assume we slept together."

Gwyn grinned when she emerged. "We did."

"You know what I mean."

"Can you not even say it?" Gwyn asked as she sat on the foot of Holly's bed, her eyes twinkling annoyingly.

"Sex, okay?" Holly got up in a huff and grabbed her things to go to the bathroom. "Sexy sexy sex sex."

"If he hears you yelling that from across the hall, he will be smug," Gwyn called after her.

Holly looked in the mirror and breathed deep. Why did feelings have to be embarrassing as well as incredibly stupid? But her stomach still carried a pleasant buzz, and she felt lighter, freer. If Tiss killed them all, at least she'd die happy.

She continued getting ready even after Gwyn suggested teaching Renne a lesson by making him wait while they had steamy shower sex. The thought made her laugh, and it was still a boost that someone like Gwyn was interested in her. "I'd love to, but I'd be too distracted by visions of him looking at his watch. I only want to give you my best."

"I appreciate your commitment to excellence."

What would they say to Renne? He wouldn't tease Holly that badly, not if she started blushing like crazy, and she did share everything with him, but she wasn't even sure what was happening between her and Gwyn. She either needed time to explore it or time with Renne to discuss it. And not while racing a Fury to Las Vegas and transporting a criminal necromancer.

She knew relationships weren't easy but damn.

When she and Gwyn met Renne and Sunny downstairs, Gwyn said, "Right. We slept in the same bed after a long discussion." She laid her napkin in her lap as she sat. "Nothing more happened," she said quietly. "Well, a bit more did, but we're not up for discussing it, and any nonsense will earn you a swift kick under the table."

Renne went still, his coffee cup halfway to his lips. Sunny stared at them while buttering his toast and now part of his thumb.

"Okay." Renne set his cup down. "Um."

Gwyn held up a hand. "No questions at this time. Coffee?" she asked Holly.

"Please," she managed. Her cheeks were on fire, but a large part of her was relieved. Now she could get all her embarrassment out of the way at once and get on with the task at hand. She fled to get a muffin, timing her return to the table so Gwyn would be with her. She only managed one look at Renne. He gave her a smile that said they *would* be discussing this later, at length, and Sunny and Gwyn had a somewhat forced-sounding discussion about bread until it was time to leave.

Holly smiled on the way to the car. Not only had it been a lovely night, it had been the least awkward morning after, sex or no sex. Maybe this was what it was like seeing a centuries-old fey. Or maybe this chain of budget hotels really was magical.

Or maybe it was just Gwyn.

Shit, she really had feelings. Oh, this could get bad.

It seemed inevitable when Sunny asked if he could ride with Gwyn to the hardware store for the trap supplies. It wasn't that far to the next ley line, and he wanted to be ready when they arrived. Holly had hoped to put off a conversation with Renne, but not everything could be perfect. As she started the Olds and followed Gwyn out of the parking lot, she opened the conversation with, "Please don't go all smug. I know you've been shipping us this entire time."

"Only in a half-hearted way. I'm a little surprised, both that you seemed to have cuddled up and that you didn't take it further. I am happy you seem more relaxed."

She was floored. She couldn't even find it in her to bark back a sarcastic response, not when he sounded so sincere.

"Holls," he said after a few breaths, "you know that if she makes you happy—"

"That makes you happy, yeah, yeah. Thanks and ditto." She smiled, her chest sickeningly warm. "And if she breaks my heart, the authorities will find her body in little pieces?"

He grinned, dentures gleaming. "Oh, hun, they'll never find her at all, you know that. Blue crabs don't leave a trace."

Sweet. And terrifying. And gross. Very them.

When they finally reached their target ley line intersection, Holly thought that several lengths of rebar, some duct tape, red rope, bottled water, and a few wood chips didn't seem like a lot to stop a murderous Fury. Or even slow one down. But as Gwyn had said, they were targeting the bikes more than the riders, though any fey still riding with the Hunt was in for a nasty shock as well.

Sunny was walking around the rocky soil wearing a wide-brimmed hat and the highest SPF sunblock they could find to protect his pale skin. He looked out of place in a field at the border of Texas and New Mexico with a compass and a hastily constructed dowsing rod made of copper. He'd told them that traditionally, dowsing rods were made from tree branches, but they couldn't afford to be too picky.

"I expected more activity on a ley line," Renne said, shielding his eyes from the harsh sun. Even with sunglasses, the glare was incredible. But there was nothing out here.

Holly joined him in looking at nothing. It wasn't the interesting part of the desert with mesas and colorful buttes and multi-armed cacti. It was just mildly hilly, rocky wasteland.

"Many people find ley lines disturbing to be around," Gwyn said.

A shiver went up Holly's spine, and Gwyn hadn't even touched her. She kept having flashes of being pressed up against her, of their lips locking. Maybe this was what her human ancestors had called being elf-shot or fey touched, a fascination with fairies or elves or any fey. Of course, she and Gwyn had enjoyed a little more than just a howdy and a handshake.

And there was still so much more to come.

"Earth to Holly," Renne said.

"Hmm? Oh yeah, sure," she said, her cheeks burning, but a brief thought about what "much more" entailed was worth it.

He sighed and gave her a look. Their conversation in the car hadn't really gotten past the, I'm happy if you're happy, stage. He'd just have to handle that she was mildly distracted. She could pay attention when Tiss arrived.

Renne went to join Sunny, and Gwyn sidled closer to Holly. "You were thinking of me, weren't you?" Gwyn said.

"No smirking," Holly said, but she made sure there was no real bite to her voice.

"I know you don't like the swagger, even if I'm terribly good at it. It's just hard not to be smug when you've kissed a beautiful woman, especially a brave one with a big brain and great legs."

A pleasant tingle passed through Holly, but she couldn't succumb to flattery, not without disappointing the incredibly dignified part of her personality. Even if that part was currently being subdued by other parts. "Were your ancestors a particularly flirty kind of fey?"

"Naturally." Her hand brushed Holly's hip, and she had to force herself not to lean into the touch.

Getting distracted was a far cry from doing anything that might lead to making out in public. "Is it an elf thing?"

"Ha, I doubt it. The elves I remember are mean bastards. Any elf in my blood is well diluted."

Holly looked at her in surprise. "I was kidding. You have elven ancestors?"

"A few. Like I said before, you go back far enough, and we all spring from the same chaotic source."

"You can't claim family connections to get the Vegas elves to help us, right?" She tried not to be too upset that Gwyn hadn't mentioned this, either. After all, Holly wouldn't go to her own family for help, even if they had been good at anything besides taking things that didn't belong to them.

Gwyn was quiet for a few moments before she sighed. "I keep forgetting…" She shook her head.

"How little I know about the fey?" Holly guessed. She forced herself not to get angry, but her temper still seemed the strongest feeling of them all.

"No fault of yours," Gwyn said with a heartfelt smile. "No one knows anything until they're told. To be considered an elf and worthy of elven help, one must be pure of blood, elven all the way back. Of course, they were never too uptight about spreading their seed to the common fey and having some exceptional children." She flipped her hair over her shoulder. "But they never claim any parental responsibilities."

Holly took her hand, understanding how much that hurt with every fiber of her being. "I'm sorry."

Gwyn gave a surprised chuckle but still intertwined their fingers. "No, no, though my father had nothing to do with raising me, I don't think he was a pure elf. Partly, sure, but so was my mother, and she was an excellent parent. I'm sorry yours wasn't." She gave Holly a quick kiss on the knuckles after glancing at Sunny and Renne as if to make sure they weren't looking.

Holly appreciated both gestures immensely and had to restrain herself again. "It's okay. I found my family." Thoughts of Marcus and the SCDA surprised her. She'd thought only Renne would leap to mind.

"They'll be all right," Gwyn said as if reading her mind. "Tiss won't go after them if they're not in her way."

"It makes me feel a little better that I'm keeping them safe." Unless. "She doesn't take hostages, does she?"

"Not her style. Straightforward as a right hook." She flinched, and there was so much Holly wanted to say about how Gwyn wasn't alone anymore, that she couldn't wait until Tiss had been dealt with, and they could explore everything together: their feelings, the world.

It was a bunch of romantic nonsense that turned her stomach. When Sunny waved them over, she barely kept from saying, "Thank God."

CHAPTER SIXTEEN

The rebar had to be laid out in a very precise pattern that Sunny spent way too much time tutting over, then moving a few inches. Or instructing everyone else to move. Gwyn normally would have lost her mind with frustration or would have had to tease him and move things in the wrong direction or find some other way to let her puckish side out.

The fact that she wasn't doing it was all down to Holly.

Hell, the fact that she even considered a mischievous response rather than just an angry one was down to Holly. Lovely, leggy Holly. Gwyn had imagined that making out with her would be angry, passionate, or maybe even timid, a bit of shyness behind those walls.

It had been nothing like she'd imagined, just so much better.

She could not stop thinking about it, keeping her from snapping as Sunny again directed her, "A smidge to the right."

She sighed, her patience waning if his constant tinkering was going to interrupt her erotic daydreams. "What kind of precise ritual uses smidges as measurements?"

Renne chuckled. Holly had stayed by the car, well away from the orderly magic. When Gwyn glanced over, she smiled but only a little, the closest she came to public displays.

Sunny put his hands on his hips. "Would you understand if I used centimeters?"

"Of course. I'm old, but I'm well-traveled." She grinned. "A centimeter is about a smidge and a half."

Renne rolled his eyes this time. "We should get a move on. The wood and string are bound to move the rebar a bit when you lay them down, Sunny. Can we do the smidge-ing afterward?"

He agreed and began instructing them on how and where to lay the bark and string and when to tape it down. It began to look like a giant cat's cradle with the rebar as long, spindly fingers.

Sunny constantly consulted his compass and knots and Renne's phone, shifting and muttering so much that even Renne seemed short on patience, wiping his forehead with the back of his hand. No one had told the desert that it was fall, at least during the day. Last night had been quite chilly.

At least out of bed.

When Sunny called a break, Gwyn went to lean against the car with Holly and sip some water in companionable silence. Somehow, their hands found each other again. Maybe it was the ring on Holly's finger pulling them together. Or maybe this was their new normal. What bliss that would be, even with the danger.

No, don't think of that now.

"Is it weird that I sort of miss our bickering?" Holly asked. "Not that just standing here with you isn't nice."

"Nah, I understand. We can try to add more sexual tension if you don't think we'll combust."

"Renne would argue that we had that all along."

"And he'd be right," his voice said from behind them. He reached inside the car and pulled out two more waters. "I'm taking one to Sunny since you lovebirds didn't offer us any."

"You're both grown-ups," Holly said.

"And not distracted by amore," he added. "Thank goodness or we'd all stand here and flirt until Tiss ran us over."

"Jealous?" Holly called as he took a water to Sunny. He didn't bother to answer.

"Maybe we should try to be a little more present," Gwyn said. When Holly's smile slipped, she added, "At least until after we've kicked Tiss's ass."

That earned her another grin, as she'd known it would. She didn't quite feel that level of confidence, but it was nice to pretend.

Finally, Sunny was ready for the ritual. Holly stayed well back but still rubbed her arms and grimaced as if ants were running over her skin. Orderliness had never affected Gwyn as much. Or maybe it had, but her long life had taught her to ignore it.

"What happens now?" Renne asked. "Chanting? A ritual dance?"

"Now that I'd pay to see," Gwyn said.

"No," Sunny said, the picture of offended gravitas. "But I would like you to stand there, Renne." He pointed. "And slowly pour out the water from the gallon jug. This will add the aspect of running water to the ritual, and your presence will add weight and allow Gwyn's blood to flow more freely."

Great.

Sunny scratched his head and mumbled something that sounded like, "And it shouldn't drain too much life force."

"What was that?" Renne asked.

"Nothing," Sunny said brightly, clapping his hands. "Right. Ready?"

Gwyn got her knife ready. She always kept one in a hidey hole in Faerie, though she wished she had the one she'd cut Tiss with, but it had broken on her rib. She'd thrown it away, not wanting to keep a reminder of her failure to maintain control over the Hunt.

Sunny began to chant, moving around the rebar jumble as he went. Renne dribbled the water into the dirt, coating the rebar, too. When Sunny gestured to Gwyn, she ran the knife along the old scar on her side, wincing through the pain, though this cut didn't hurt nearly as much as the original.

The memory had stayed as sharp: the Hunt watching, wide-eyed as Athena's owls, their silence heavy as a lead sheet. Gwyn had kept her hands from shaking as she and Tiss had circled each other. Tiss's power had lain thick in the air, coating Gwyn's tongue with the tang of copper, like blood and old pennies.

The end had come soon, Tiss darting in, barely any emotion in her black eyes as she'd sunk the knife into Gwyn's side. The pain had the ache of a punch, and she'd imagined the blade going all the way through her and down her whole lifeline.

"I win," Tiss had said in her face, shuddering as if in ecstasy.

But Gwyn's hand had been wet, too, sticky, and hot. Tiss's expression had warped to shock as they'd both looked down to see Gwyn's knife in Tiss's side. "That's right," Gwyn had said through a mouthful of blood. "I got you once, darlin', and I'll get you again."

The feel of the knife leaving her body had hurt more than it had going in, robbing her of breath, leaving her cold. After she'd hit the ground, she'd noticed her knife had broken, and Tiss's blood burned where it touched her.

Like her own blood was doing now.

Sunny was still chanting. Gwyn put a hand below the wound as fire swept through her veins. She didn't seem to be bleeding any faster, but something was being pulled from all the corners of her body.

Tiss's essence.

Did that mean this was working? Somewhere along the road, was Tiss's scar burning too?

Gods, Gwyn hoped so. "Got ya again," she muttered, overcome with a pride she hadn't felt in uncountable years.

She caught Holly's worried gaze, a sight more pleasurable than all her years with the Hunt. "Okay?" Holly mouthed.

"Better," Gwyn whispered back as the last of Tiss's essence left her. She didn't know how much good this would do them, but it felt like a victory.

Sunny's chant began to slow, and even under the harsh sun, the tangle of rebar, wood, and red thread seemed to glow. Gwyn's blood marched over it drop by drop, like an army of ants. Trying to look at the jumble became as difficult as staring at an optical illusion, and she gave up when her eyes kept crossing.

Finally, Sunny fell silent and leaned his hands on his knees like a runner. Gwyn waited. She didn't want to move if they weren't finished, but she also didn't want to stand here and bleed longer than she had to.

"Sunny?" Renne asked.

He waved without looking up, but did that mean to wait, or were they released?

Gwyn was about to ask when the ground pulsed slightly, and a flash blinked from their ritual site to the horizon in four directions. It happened so quickly, she would have thought she'd imagined it if she hadn't just seen the trap being cast.

Sunny straightened. "Now you can move." He beamed and wiped the sweat from his brow, his eyes practically glowing in the shade of his hat.

Holly hurried forward and passed Gwyn a bandage to press to her side. "Are you all right?"

"Better than." It was only Holly's obvious dislike of kissing in public that kept her from doing so, and she hoped her smile said that all her affection would be waiting when Holly was ready.

Holly's cheeks went a little pink, and her smile turned shy, and by all the gods, it was hard not to love her.

"Everything all right?" Renne asked, breaking the moment very untactfully, but they did have a job to do.

"Did it work?" Gwyn asked.

Sunny nodded, then shrugged as he took a drink. "Well, something happened. We won't know it was the right thing until later."

"Not very helpful," Holly said.

He flinched. "I've never done a ritual like this before."

Before anyone else could speak, Holly held up a hand. "I know, I know. It's the frustration talking. I'm sure it's all…" She waved around. "Fine."

Not exactly the highest praise, but it didn't dampen Gwyn's affection one bit. Sunny's ego would have to look after itself.

"When will we know it worked?" Renne asked, his soothing tone never doubting that their efforts would be successful.

Sunny seemed to take heart in that, but he still shrugged. "Since we used the connection between you and Tiss"—he nodded at Gwyn—"you may feel it when the trap is sprung. But since we also cleansed you of her blood, who knows?"

She crossed to him and shook his hand. "I know we weren't doing this to rid me of her blood, but I still feel a million times lighter. Thank you, Sunny." A little drunk on feelings, she pulled him into a hug. He stammered, and she let him go before things could get really awkward. "Sorry."

He shook his head and mumbled and smiled like a lad with an A in school.

Gwyn couldn't wait to see if their efforts bore fruit. Even if it didn't, she'd count today's work as a success, new scar and all.

Gwyn's testimony about the glow aside, this whole side trip seemed to Holly like an enormous waste of time.

Apart from where she had woken up cuddled with Gwyn.

Except now she had to deal with this distracting *need* that kept popping up at the worst moments. She kept finding excuses to put her hands on Gwyn. She kept *smiling*. When she read lust in Gwyn's eyes, she kept hoping they would act on it.

In *public*.

Not that there was much of anyone around, not in the patch of desert where they'd been and not on the highway now.

But still.

Gwyn was riding ahead in the scout position, helmet on since Sunny was back in the car. Her thick braid fluttered slightly over her black tank top that showcased her muscular arms to perfection. And her ass in those jeans? Mm. Holly was certain they could be careful of the bandages if they made another stop before Vegas.

"Do you want me to drive, or should I just stay quiet as you swerve into oncoming traffic and kill us all?" Renne asked.

Holly sighed. She was never this distracted, yet one more reason she hadn't wanted to get involved with Gwyn.

The ring on her right hand winked in the sun as if mocking her. "Sorry," she said, and that wasn't like her, either. She tried to think of a sarcastic comeback, but they'd all abandoned her.

Renne was looking at her as if she was an Edwardian heroine who'd been walking the moors and caught her death. "Are you—"

"I'm fine. Don't need the fainting couch just yet."

That seemed to mollify him a little, but he'd seemed a little spikey since the morning, even after their, I'm okay if you're okay, talk.

She glanced in the rearview mirror. Sunny was slumped against the headrest, mouth open. The ritual had clearly taken it out of him. "Are you all right?" she asked Renne.

"Why wouldn't I be?" He turned to look out the window as he said it, a dead giveaway.

"I was kidding when I asked if you were jealous before, but are you?"

No response.

"You wanted Gwyn for yourself?"

"No." He turned his head before terror could consume her at her next thought. "And, no, I don't want you for myself, either."

Relief flooded her.

"Egomaniac," he said.

And there went all her sympathy. "Then, what? You feel left out?"

He sighed long and loud. "I know it's childish. I'll get over it."

She fidgeted and gnawed her lip. "I'll always be your partner, and um, care and stuff."

"Holly." He turned to stare, even lowering his sunglasses. "Before you die of embarrassment and I follow close behind in sympathy, abandon the role of caregiver. Please. It suits you as well as a pair of rubber pants."

She barked a laugh, then clamped her mouth shut when Sunny stirred before settling again. "Thanks. That *was* painful."

"Anytime."

But she had to do something to signal that their relationship would never change no matter who else came along. "You know that by, 'left out,' I wasn't gonna invite you to a threesome, right?"

"Perish the thought." But he had more of a smile in his voice.

"I mean, I couldn't have you two fighting over me."

"She may have muscles, but my teeth are bigger."

"Thought you were quite clear about not wanting me, and now I have to ask, why the hell not?"

Another sigh but one she heard on the daily.

"Am I not hot?"

"Lord, give me strength."

"Am I not what some generations have labeled, a snack?"

"Biting the shit out of you does sound tempting." And his little smile said he appreciated this conversation all the same. She wished she could high-five herself. She might not be the best at reading random people, but she had those she knew down pat.

When they stopped to eat near Albuquerque, they decided it was time for the vision tea again, but some quick scans of the news told them exactly where Tiss was.

"'Five dead in tanker explosion near Amarillo,'" Renne read from his phone. Before anyone could ask how he knew it was Tiss, he read more of the story about how the tanker was driving on the freeway with no trouble before witnesses reported it blowing up. They mentioned an unseasonably strong wind that blew through, guessing it must have jiggled or tripped something on the truck, as it hadn't even tipped over before exploding. The wind had torn through, and then, boom.

"Sounds right," Holly said, her appetite gone. She squeezed Gwyn's ring between her fingers for comfort.

"At least we know she sensed the direction change before she reached Houston," Renne said. "She's coming after us."

Yes, at least they could be grateful for that, but it was hard in the face of actual deaths.

They consulted a map, and Sunny tapped where Tiss was most likely to encounter their ley line trap. It crossed several freeways at an angle, but there was no telling which she would take, even if they knew where she'd been several hours ago.

"And she's been known to take a back road or two when one of the Hunt feels drawn to a certain area," Gwyn said.

Like Dodge City.

Renne was frowning at his phone, swiping and clicking.

"Messaging someone?" Holly asked. But who? Like her, he didn't socialize outside of the office much. Unlike her, he still spoke to his family, but since he couldn't discuss what he did, they'd more or less lost touch.

"Doing math," he said.

She blinked. "For fun?"

He gave her a flat look. "I'm trying to calculate Tiss's speed. She seems to be going faster than before."

"I warned you that might happen," Gwyn said. "She senses her target is on the move away from her. And she can set a brutal pace and cheat by taking shortcuts through Faerie, but she'll still have to stop from time to time."

Holly set her napkin down. "Let's head out anyway."

"Wait." Renne shook his head. "The timing of that tanker explosion seems to match with our ritual. Could Tiss feel it somehow?"

Everyone looked at Sunny. He stammered a bit and finally shrugged.

Gwyn rubbed her chin. "I suppose she could be going faster than I've seen, but she'll risk draining some of the Hunt's power."

"Making her weaker?" Holly asked. Maybe they should switch to luring her in rather than outrunning her.

But Gwyn shook her head. "The connection is still there." She threw a tip down on the table. "Come on."

When they stepped out the door, the sky had gone overcast, throwing shadows over the parking lot and lending a chill to the October air. Gwyn slung on a black leather jacket, looking particularly yummy even in their current situation. She turned her head and grinned, her braid tucked beneath her collar.

Her eyes went wide as she froze.

Holly turned to see what had alarmed her, but there was nothing. Sunny cried out, and Holly spun back to see Gwyn clutch her bandaged side and fall. Blood spread into the dust under her unmoving body. Holly staggered, dizzy. She'd seen this before. And just like with every vision, she hadn't been able to prevent it, could only feel her heart stop twice.

CHAPTER SEVENTEEN

Agony careened from Gwyn's hair to her toes as a bolt of lightning cracked into her side and stampeded through her body. Had she been shot? Stabbed? She hit something hard, barely felt it. Too much pain to note the difference. She had to move, speak, defend herself. From what? Zeus? No, too much had happened in her life to make that funny.

Move, she told herself. An arm, a leg, a finger.

Nothing. Her body had become a cage, and if the pain binding her limbs went on much longer, her thoughts could become lost like her breath. *Move, move, oh gods, it hurts, move!*

A light, felt if not seen, gave life to her body. She tried to bend toward it, and the spasms in her arms and legs turned to numbness and needles, the better to focus on the hot poker in her side where Tiss had once struck her.

The scar she'd just reopened.

The trap? Was Tiss feeling this right now too?

Please the gods, yes.

Even if that meant she was closer than they'd thought.

Voices floated through the roaring in her ears, sharpening like the pain in her side:

"No, no, ma'am, she doesn't need an ambulance. Thank you for asking."

"Fuck, Renne, maybe she does."

"If this is because of the ritual, a doctor won't be able to help her."

Renne, Holly, and Sunny. Gwyn wished she could vote for the ambulance. Human painkillers would work for a little while.

"We'll help her. We can't involve more humans, Holly."

"To hell with this secrecy bullshit."

"It must be the ritual, but how…ah, the bleeding seems to have stopped."

Could have fooled Gwyn. The throbbing was enough for gallons of blood. As more of her senses returned, she moved to show them she was alive and listening.

"Shut up," Holly said. "She moved her hand. Gwyn, can you hear me?"

Chattering went on in the background, Renne shooing away passersby, and soft hands fiddled near the wound in Gwyn's side. She tried to speak but could only manage to wet her lips.

"There," Sunny said. "The new bandage seems to be holding."

"Should we get her some water?" Holly asked, her tone thick with worry.

"I don't know much about first aid. All of my anatomy knowledge comes from, well…"

"Zombies," Gwyn managed.

He made a grunt of protest, but he couldn't seem to argue with her.

"Gwyn?" Holly asked, the hope in her voice enough to crack the stoniest of hearts.

"Yeah. It just hurts." She opened her eyes to two anxious faces and a swath of cloudy sky. "The trap went off, I think." She glared at Sunny, needing a target.

"I didn't know this would happen," he said but still fidgeted, clearly guilty. "As I keep saying—"

"You've never done this before," Gwyn said. "Yeah, yeah, I'm not really mad at you, lad." She waved her hand, and Holly helped her sit up. "Otherwise, I'd be punching you for this." While he sputtered, she pressed her side. The pain was fading, but the memory would live on for a long time to come. "That hurt more than the original wound."

"Really?" Sunny asked, transformed by curiosity. "I'll have to make some notes."

"As long as my painful experience will help future generations slow down murderous Furies, it's all worth it."

Renne moved to stand behind them, his jaw set. "If you can grouse, you can stand. We need to leave before the cops show up. I think my insistence that you don't need an ambulance just made people more suspicious." He jerked his head toward where several people stood near the entrance to the diner on their phones.

Gwyn tried to give them a reassuring smile. Several shrugged and went inside, but a few hung around, frowning, maybe even filming, hoping for future clicks.

Renne helped Gwyn to her feet, and his look softened with his voice. "Will your bike accept a rider who's not part of the Hunt? You don't seem in any condition to drive."

She handed him her keys. "If I say so. And I do."

"Good, let's regroup down the road at the first gas station we find."

As Gwyn rode shotgun in the car, her body came fully back under her control, and the pain faded in fits and starts that prompted her to take some of the aspirin in Holly's glove compartment. "Gods, I hope Tiss felt this," she said as they pulled into a gas station in a strip mall.

"Me too." Holly rested a hand on her shoulder as Sunny got out to pump the gas. "Are you okay?"

"The thought of Tiss writhing on the ground in agony is making me feel better all the time."

Renne pulled up next to them, killing the moment as surely as he killed the engine, but he had a big smile on his face. "I could get used to this. I haven't ridden a bike in ages and nothing as smooth as yours."

"Told ya," Gwyn said, leaning out the window, "it's just disguised as a bike. I could almost ride it in my sleep, but who knows where I'd end up."

"If Tiss hit the trap," Sunny said from where he leaned on the roof, "she's closer than we thought before the math, yes?"

"We have to assume so," Renne said.

Holly shook her head. "It's not enough to assume. We have to know." She grimaced and laid her head on the steering wheel. "I'm going to have to drink the stupid tea again. At least my useless gift can act as a GPS tag."

"That's helpful," Gwyn said. "Very much so."

"And just think," Renne said, "once you get the hang of slipping into a trance whenever you want, you'll never have to hunt for your car keys again."

The look she gave him could've prompted a cold day in hell. "Oh, thank goodness. Holly to the rescue," she said flatly.

Gwyn patted her knee, onlookers be damned. "Just think of it this way, you might get to see Tiss lying in the road in a pain-ridden heap."

That got her a smile, at least.

They secured a cup of hot coffee—the closest the gas station came to just hot water—and Holly mixed her magic leaves in to create something that smelled truly awful. While she and Gwyn waited in the car for it to cool, Sunny and Renne finished filling the tank and perused the small store.

"I really appreciate you going through this over and over," Gwyn said, nodding at the cup.

Holly shrugged, clearly pleased even as she tried to downplay it. "I just hate seeing things I have to worry about." She took Gwyn's hand. "Like someone I care about lying on the ground."

Gwyn squeezed back. "There's one worrying thing down. Anything else you're desperate to check off the list of disturbing visions?"

A strange mix of longing and fear passed over her face. "Not that I can make sense of yet."

A half truth if ever she'd heard one, but she didn't push. "I care about you, too."

Holly's smile was so shy and cute, Gwyn had to give her a kiss on the cheek. After making sure Sunny and Renne weren't on their way back, of course. Holly seemed to appreciate both gestures.

When everyone was present, they pulled into the alley behind the strip mall between a pizza place and a nail salon. Everyone piled in the car, Holly in the passenger seat so she wouldn't be behind the wheel, and Gwyn hopping into the back with Sunny. Hopefully, no curious gawkers or patrolling police would question what they were doing anxiously staring at an unconscious person who was babbling in her sleep.

Holly gulped down the coffee-tea mixture as quickly as she could, and after she'd done little more than pull a few faces, she slumped, her head down. Gwyn reached over and pulled it back against the headrest so she wouldn't get a crick in her neck, earning her a smile from Renne. Sunny pointedly looked away, still obviously writing fan fiction about them.

"Shoes," Holly said loudly, her speech slightly drunk. Renne dutifully started writing on a scrap of paper. "Legs. Boots. She's down, everyone's lying around." She seemed to be getting better about describing her visions as she saw them. Their last try had only been staccato bursts of words.

"Motorcycles twisted into half a horse. Someone asking for Kara. She's gone."

"One of the Valkyrie," Gwyn whispered.

"Dead eyes," Holly said, shivering. "She's bloody. Doesn't care. Pissed off."

Tiss. So they'd made her bleed and stoked her anger, a red letter day.

"Kara's gone and…two other names I can't pronounce. Everyone's freaked."

Sunny hummed, a triumphant noise. "We separated them."

"And seems like the bikes are incapacitated," Renne added. "If that's what 'half a horse' means." He frowned and shook his head as if banishing an image.

Gwyn would have to remind him again that they weren't real horses or bikes, weren't even alive, so there'd be no mess. It sounded like the trap had made the mounts lose all cohesiveness, even the most basic that kept them in one form.

A win all around.

"Holly?" Renne prompted her as she began to squirm.

"She's…lookin' at me." Holly shook her head. "Talkin' to the host but lookin' at *me*." Her voice went higher, terrified. "She knows, sees me. Gwyn!"

Gwyn leaned around the seat and stroked her cheek. "I'm here, Holly, come back to me. You're not there. She can't hurt you. Just open your eyes."

"She sees, knows." Holly tried to shrink away.

Gwyn held fast, trying to believe her own assurances. "Open your eyes, darlin'. She can't hurt you from there. Open your eyes." If Tiss could somehow reach Holly like this, Gwyn was going to kill her five times over. "I won't let her hurt you. Open your eyes." She gave her a little shake. "Open them."

Holly's eyes popped open, wide and scared as she gasped. She pressed back hard into the headrest until she seemed to focus. "Gwyn." Tears swam in her eyes before she hugged Gwyn awkwardly around the seat.

Gwyn only got to hold her a moment before Holly pulled away with a last squeeze. She also patted the hand that Renne had rested on her arm and nodded at Sunny as if reassuring them and herself that everyone was safe.

"I think we got most of that," Renne said, sounding a little breathless. "I'm glad you're all right." He cleared his throat before reading from his notes. "Tiss is hurt, some of the riders seem to be missing, and the bikes are out of commission. For a little while, at least."

Holly sipped some water. "No. I mean, yeah, I saw all that, and…looked Tiss in the eye." She took another drink, dribbling a little and wiping it on the back of her hand. "I wasn't…I don't think I was in one of the Hunt. It was someone who stopped to help. She, Tiss, when she saw them, she stalked over, and her eyes…"

She shook her head as if trying to banish an image that would no doubt star in quite a few nightmares. "She knew I was there. She said, 'What prying eyes are these?' She looked right at me." Another shaky drink as Gwyn patted her shoulder and Renne her hand. "She never saw me in the glimpses I had of the future or when I saw her at Dodge City. Why now?"

"She must be able to sense you in the real-time visions," Gwyn said.

Renne nodded. "In the Dodge City one, she seemed distracted by the camera. Maybe that was what she thought any prying eyes were."

"This was worse than watching that video," Holly said.

Gwyn bit her lip, fighting the urge to argue once again that she could handle this alone.

Holly glanced at her, then pinned her with a stare. "Don't you dare tell me to go home."

Gwyn hoped her expression didn't betray her guilt. "Wouldn't dream of it."

With a nod, Holly took another sip of water.

"Well, we don't know exactly where she is now, but we can get farther ahead," Renne said. "Maybe trap another ley line if we have to."

Sunny shook his head. "I believe the trap destroyed the link between Gwyn and Tiss when it detonated. We have nothing more of hers."

Just as well. Gwyn did not want to go through that again.

She grabbed her helmet and opened the door, loath to leave Holly but anxious to get going.

With a terrifying shriek of twisting metal, a dumpster at the end of the alley flew against the wall as if slapped by a giant hand.

Everyone flinched or cried out, and Gwyn stood slowly from where she'd crouched, peering into the haze of dust in the dumpster's wake. There, her leather-clad shoulders heaving, stood the missing Kara, blood on her cheek and murder in her eyes.

Chapter Eighteen

Gwyn cried, "It's Kara," but Holly had already guessed it was one of the Hunt based on the leather, the furious expression, and the fact that she'd thrown a dumpster into a wall.

Holly climbed out of the car as fast as she could, still a bit woozy from her vision. Gwyn was halfway down the alley, facing off with Kara.

Alone.

Fuck.

"Wait for backup," Holly said as she flicked open her telescoping baton, but she knew Gwyn wouldn't back off.

"Now you know how I feel when you go off half-cocked," Renne said as he joined her and drew his gun. "Sunny, get in the driver's seat and be ready to floor it."

They advanced together to flank Gwyn. She had her hands out in a pleading gesture. "It's okay, Kara, you're safe. We're not going to hurt you. You don't have to do what Tiss says anymore. I'll be taking back the Hunt soon."

If Kara even recognized Gwyn, she gave no indication. She was a beauty, her skin softly tanned and her pale yellow hair drawn back in a crown of braids. Her cornflower blue eyes narrowed at Renne and Holly, and her full lips parted in a snarl.

Gwyn waved at Renne and Holly without taking her eyes from Kara. "Put the weapons away. They'll only make her angry."

Holly glanced at Renne to find him looking at her, too. "What are we supposed to do?" he asked as he pointed his gun off to the side. "Ask her nicely to surrender?"

Kara spat something in a language Holly had never heard.

"No, no," Gwyn said. "It's all right. No one's in your way. And you don't have to do as Tiss tells you because—"

Behind them, the Oldsmobile started, and Kara glanced that way.

And smiled.

Oh shit. Sunny.

The Hunt always recognized the target.

Kara dashed at Holly as if to bowl her over. She ducked, used to fast opponents, and launched upward again when Kara was almost on top of her, lifting Kara off her feet and flipping her. She landed hard on her back, but before Holly could advance, Kara leapt to her feet seamlessly, like someone in a kung fu movie.

Renne's gun cracked, and Kara staggered but only glanced at the hole in the arm of her jacket before sneering again. Holly swung for her head with the baton, but she ducked, her arm shooting up to grab Holly's wrist.

"Shit." Holly sagged, hoping to drag Kara down and kick her.

Kara lifted her with ease and swung her around, the world going sideways as she flew through the air. She braced herself to hit the ground only to crash into Renne, her head bouncing off his bony shoulder as they went down in a tangle.

Gwyn barked something, and Kara made a satisfying *oof*. By the time Holly disentangled from Renne, Gwyn and Kara were locked together like Sumo wrestlers. When Kara fell back a step, Holly got to her feet, ready to dive in and help, but Kara whipped a hand into her jacket and came back with a butterfly knife. She flipped it open quicker than Holly could blink and sliced at Gwyn's arm.

Holly shouted a warning, but Gwyn had already blocked and given Kara a shove, using the momentum to slide past her. Kara came on like a Cuisinart brought to life, seeming as comfortable with a knife as she'd no doubt been with a sword.

"Fucking gun's under the dumpster," Renne said. He had his own baton out now and nodded toward Kara's back.

Holly charged with him, but Kara pivoted like a dancer, knife flashing toward them. They pulled up short on either side. When Gwyn rushed forward, Kara kicked back and knocked her off her feet.

Kara didn't take her eyes off Holly and Renne, slashing at one and then the other. Renne cried out, falling back to cradle his arm. Holly blocked a hit with her baton and stepped in front of him, but Kara was too fast, striking like a bushel of snakes. Holly blocked again but got a shallow cut across her knuckles. She tried to breathe through the pain, but Kara took the opening and punched her in the stomach with her free hand.

The air rushed out of her in a blossom of pain, and she collapsed, waiting for the end. Gwyn dove for Kara's ankles, but she dodged easily.

And turned as if to run for Sunny.

"No," Holly cried. "Watch—"

The Olds collided with Kara's body in a sickening *thunk*, and she bounced across the alley without a sound.

"Get in," Sunny yelled through the window.

Kara was already stirring like the goddamned Terminator.

Renne hooked an arm around Holly's elbow and lifted her. She tried to get her breath back as she walked. Gwyn yanked the door open for them, and they all piled in the back seat, sitting atop one another.

"Back up," Gwyn said. "Don't try to run her down again. She'll be ready for it."

Holly jerked forward as the car reversed quickly, and banged her aching head on the seat. "What the fuck are we gonna do?"

"Run like hell," Gwyn said. "I don't know how the ritual transported her here, but hopefully, her mount is as fucked as the rest of them. Stop here," she said to Sunny when they reached her bike. She leapt out before Holly could tell her to be careful. Kara was running toward them, but they'd given her a limp, and she faded from view as Sunny turned quickly in the parking lot and drove away, the roar of Gwyn's bike at their side.

Gwyn rode with one arm pressed against her side. Not much blood, but she ached like she'd been kicked by a mule. It seemed they'd dealt Tiss a blow only to hit themselves on the follow-through.

If Kara was here, did that mean the other missing members of the Hunt were nearby, too? Or were they going to be scattered throughout the rest of the journey like hideous surprises?

Miles later, no one appeared to be following as they pulled off at a rest stop. Gwyn's side had stopped bleeding, but between her wound and the shallow slices on Renne's arm and Holly's hand, they were running short on bandages. And the Olds had a very suspicious dent in the hood as well as a torn grill and bumper. Kara was lucky to have such a hard body.

Gwyn winced. She hadn't wanted the other members of the Hunt to get hurt. She hadn't seen Kara in years, but she'd expected some recognition in her face. The fact that there had been none seemed like proof that the Hunt had been warped by Tiss into her personal killing machines and nothing else.

"We didn't have a choice," Holly said as she joined her.

"I know. It's all on Tiss. I just hope that we left Kara and any other Hunt members in that town."

"And that they don't take their anger out on innocent people." Holly clenched her wounded hand and frowned.

Gwyn laid a hand on her wrist. "Don't. You'll make it bleed." She caressed Holly's arm until her fist relaxed. "I'm sorry we had to retreat. I don't think she'll hurt anyone who isn't in her way. She didn't even attack us until she saw Sunny."

"And what if she decides someone *is* in her way? Or carjacks someone and kills them?"

"So let's go back," Renne said from where he leaned on the car. He had his sleeves rolled up, the gauze bandage like a warning he seemed inclined to ignore. "I can't leave my gun lying in that alley anyway."

Holly nodded, but Gwyn shook her head. "The sooner we get Sunny to Signal, the sooner we defeat Tiss. Then, Kara and the rest will be free of her influence."

"You're guessing about that," Holly said softly.

"And how many people will they hurt in the meantime?" Renne added.

Holly nodded again, her gaze as soft as her tone. "Take Sunny and keep riding toward Vegas. Renne and I will take care of Kara and meet you—"

"By 'take care of,' you mean kill?" Gwyn shook her head. "No, no, this isn't her fault."

"Not kill necessarily."

"Then, what? Put her in the supernatural prison you're carrying around in your pocket? Cuff her and take her with you to be banished? She knocked all three of us down and was only defeated by our fifth member, the fucking car."

"We'll be better prepared now that we know what we're dealing with," Renne said, all his soothing charm gone.

"A Valkyrie is what you're dealing with, chum. What are you gonna do, buy a bazooka from the corner shop?"

Holly was rubbing her wounded knuckles and staring into space. "We do still have the car."

And she seemed serious, even though every word was absurd. "The same trick won't work twice."

"Only if she sees it coming," Renne said.

"You don't even know where she is right now!"

Holly winced. "I can find her."

"Great, so you'll be bombed out of your socks when you meet her, and Renne will run her over, right? Oh, if she doesn't spot you first. And if she's still on foot."

"Gwyn." Holly's eyes went soft, pleading, while Renne's were still cold and angry. The world had gone topsy-turvy. "We have to do something."

"We are doing something." Gwyn stabbed her finger toward where the sun was sinking in the west. "We just need to saddle back up and do it." When they both spoke at once, she waved her arms to stop them. "You don't want to leave guns lying around? Fine. Let one of your SCDA contacts know where it is, and they can go collect it. Kara will be long gone by then. Dealing with her can wait until she won't be an issue."

"And whoever she kills in the meantime?" Holly asked, still infuriatingly patient.

"You don't know that she'll kill anyone."

"You don't know that she won't," Renne said.

"Yeah, she'll kill you," Gwyn shouted. "You and Holly, and I'll…I'll…" All the air went out of her, washed away on a tide of grief along with her anger.

"Come on, Sunny," Renne said with a sigh, leading him away.

Well, at least two people wouldn't see the tears she couldn't stop. She hadn't completely broken down in…she couldn't remember. And it was damned inconvenient now.

"Gwyn," Holly said again.

"No." She opened the driver's door of the Olds and parked herself behind the wheel. "I'm not gonna let you."

Holly got in on the other side. "Gwyn—"

She turned. So many of her emotions felt as foreign as a third arm. It had been so long since anything had affected her like this. That had to mean something. Maybe if she let Holly know how badly the thought of losing her ached? "I think I'm falling for you."

Holly sucked in a breath as if she'd been sucker punched again.

Gwyn remembered the same noise from the alley, but it didn't scare her this time. She took Holly's unwounded hand. "I haven't felt this way in, hell, I can't remember. I can't lose you before I see where these feelings can go."

Holly's mouth worked before she said, "I want to see where they go, too."

Gwyn pulled her in for a kiss, her soul singing, but it fell quiet when Holly's lips stayed still under hers. She drew back slowly. "I kissed you before you got to the 'but,' didn't I?" She tried to make light, but Holly didn't lose her heartbreaking expression of caring sadness.

"But neither of us can keep the other from her duty."

Gwyn snorted and crossed her arms. "You've been helping me keep myself from my duty all this time."

Holly's caress on her cheek would have had her purring like a kitten any other time. "Your duty isn't to be the herald of the Hunt. It's to stop Tiss."

Damn it. "I can't lose—" Tears choked her again, only slowing when Holly kissed them away.

"I promise, I won't die."

"As if I can hold you to that."

"There are people who can communicate with the spirit world. You could give me an earful whenever you want."

"Huh, like a reverse haunting."

"Except I'm not going to die."

Gwyn rolled her eyes but uncrossed her arms. "Yeah, well, I'm not going to die better than you're not going to."

"You're cute when you don't make sense."

Gwyn pointed at her. "Stop winning me over." An idea struck her, a way to guarantee that Holly lived. "I'm coming with you. Renne can ride on with Sunny."

Holly's mouth fell open, but before she could object, Gwyn pointed at her again. "Can't keep each other from our duty, yeah? It's either me and you or none of us since I think we agree that Sunny can't go looking for Kara."

Holly's lips set in a firm line. "Renne is not going to like this."

"We'll put him on the planning committee, and he'll have to be satisfied with that. Because we do need a better plan than running her over if we want everyone, including the car, to survive."

Holly pulled at her wig and tried not to smear the thick makeup that was making her nose itch.

"Stop fiddling," Gwyn said from the driver's seat of the Olds where they sat in the parking lot of a Spirit Halloween in the town they'd left Kara in. "You look great."

Holly took another look in the vanity mirror. "I look like a reject from a kabuki theater."

"You don't."

"Like I failed out of geisha school."

"No."

"Like Sunny's goth younger sister."

"That's more like it."

At the rest stop, Gwyn had explained that unlike the fey, Valkyrie didn't seem to have many weaknesses. They were sort of like demigods, responsible for escorting the honored dead to Valhalla, but they could also kick butt in a fight. When Odin had lost power, they'd lost the ability to shift planes, except through the power of the Hunt, which let them go back and forth to Faerie with Tiss.

It had been getting dark and chilly, so everyone had urged Gwyn to hurry from the history lesson to how they were supposed to fight Kara. She hadn't seemed to mind being shot, and Gwyn had told them that the bullet probably hadn't penetrated as far into her as it would into a human. So guns were out. They attracted too much attention anyway.

"I say we distract her," Gwyn had said, "and I'll pounce and hit her with a jolt of chaos energy."

"If she's traveled to Faerie, won't she be used to that?" Renne had asked.

"Not all the voltage I can muster." She'd pointed at Holly. "And you should stay mad as hell the entire time. Your personal chaos field will act like a bit of armor and might even spoil her aim after I've walloped her."

Holly had grinned. Finally, something she could guarantee.

"How will you distract her?" Sunny had asked.

And Gwyn had stared at him for a long time. And had grinned.

"This will never work," Holly said now, sneering at her white wig and makeup in the mirror. "Can't she feel the target? She'll know I'm not him."

"Yes, but she didn't go after Sunny last time until she saw him. The Hunt must have a picture of him in their minds. She'll still sense him since he's not too far away. All we're trying to do is get her to slow down enough for me to get the drop on her." She leaned over and gave the wig a tug. "We're lucky it's so close to Halloween, or we might not have found all this so easily."

"Wouldn't that have been a tragedy." Holly wouldn't have any trouble staying irked while looking like an extra from *Village of the Damned*. "Why aren't you the one dressing up like the world's saddest clown? Then she'd come running up to you, and you could blast her."

"She might not know me anymore, but she'll be able to feel that I'm fey."

"Won't she feel my chaos field?"

"Trust me, darlin'. There is a difference."

Holly snorted. "Is the difference that you don't want to look like a Morlock?"

"Come on now," Gwyn said. "You'd look cute in a paper bag, and now's no different." She gave Holly a charming smile that was hard to stay angry at. "Thank goodness Sunny isn't here while you're mocking his style."

"He can keep it." She sighed and flipped the visor up. "I'm gonna owe Renne a thousand favors for missing this fight."

"I'll help you pay them all." Gwyn laid her head on Holly's shoulder. "Or I could just take a pic of you now and share it with him. That would make you even."

Holly shoved her. "Don't you dare."

"I won't, I won't," Gwyn said, chuckling. She was smart enough to drop it, but she also handed Holly the tea they'd already mixed so they could find out just where Kara had gone. This was their last dose, but neutralizing Kara was worth it, even if it meant they couldn't spy on Tiss anymore. Hell, the last vision hadn't even given them a location for her.

Fuck, it had better work now.

Holly sighed. At least she was getting the hang of this seer nonsense as a person locator. "Don't let me flop my head around too much and get makeup all over the headrest."

"Right. Wouldn't want it to look like any sad clowns were fooling around in here."

Holly glared before downing the tepid tea as quickly as she could. The world went hazy in a way that was becoming disturbingly familiar. Last time, she'd commanded her power to find Tiss right away, but she hesitated now. She'd seen Gwyn make her declaration of pre-love, and she could have watched that a few more times, but she'd never seen the past. Who knew what other awesome things she might see, maybe even the moment she fell in love, too.

Or she could see everyone's bloody deaths at Tiss's hands.

As colors began to take shape, she thought, no! She didn't care whose death that was going to be, she was going to skip it.

Kara.

Holly pictured her in all her angry glory. The swirl of colors hesitated as if to say, are you sure you don't want the grisly deaths?

No, damn it, Kara.

A group of motorcycles and cars came into focus, the windows all down, music blaring. Light from above glinted off the white stripes of parking spaces and the beer bottle in her hand.

A parking lot party?

Laughter came from her right, and the host's head turned. "She was a six at best," one guy said, snickering into his drink.

"Fuck you, man," another guy answered, banging his bottle on the hood of a car.

Three or four more voices erupted with, "hey," and "whoa," and "take it easy," Holly's host included. She saw several closed storefronts behind them but couldn't read the signs.

And where was Kara? Since Holly didn't seem able to look through the eyes of the Hunt members, she supposed these were the closest people to where Kara was now. Hopefully, she wasn't going to pass over this crew in a ball of fire like in Dallas.

"Who's that?" one of the guys said.

The host turned as a walking figure passed from the circular glow cast by one light pole and back into shadow. Holly didn't need to wait for the next light. She knew who it had to be. And she was heading toward a group with transportation.

Fuck, look around, let me know where you are.

The host seemed fixated on Kara as she crossed back into the light, limping slightly, her stare like a laser even at this distance.

"It's a chick." That sounded like the "six at best" guy, and the amused excitement in his voice made Holly want to sit back and watch Kara trounce them, at least that one.

No one responded, but finally, her host's head turned. "Maybe she needs help."

That gave Holly some hope for the future. Better still, she caught a glimpse of a green sign just behind them, one she knew well, the same kind of organic grocery store down the street from her apartment. She always meant to shop there and never had.

"Come back, Holly," someone said, and she tried to turn the host's head to look but couldn't. And she knew that voice. Gwyn.

"You told me the store, and I looked it up. We're on our way. Come back before you see us arrive."

Holly tore herself from the vision of Kara stalking her prey and opened her eyes to see headlights rushing past as Gwyn weaved through traffic. The engine of the Olds whined in protest as she pushed it.

"We're close," Gwyn said, the streetlights and shadows strobing across her face. "You back with me?"

"Yeah." Holly sat up, shaking off her lethargy and remembering at the last moment not to rub her face.

Gwyn exited quickly, a horn blaring behind them as they cut someone off. She flew through a U-turn lane, and then they bounced into a parking lot.

The group of guys still stood, waiting, but Kara was nearly to them. Gwyn screeched to a halt a few lanes behind Kara, no way to run into her without taking out the guys, too.

She turned right as Holly got out of the car. Her eyes widened, and she took a step toward the Olds. Was this stupid disguise actually going to work? Holly had even borrowed Sunny's hoodie in case the Hunt partly operated on scent.

Holly stepped back as if she might run. All they needed was Kara to get close, and Gwyn could get out and zap her.

"What's goin' on?" one of the guys yelled, and Kara half turned.

"Shut up," Holly muttered. If she yelled, it might give the game away, but she didn't know how much Kara knew about Sunny. She had to make herself a more enticing target.

She ran.

Someone in the lot party yelled again, and Holly heard pounding footfalls over her own. She risked a look back and saw a shadow closing fast. With her uninjured hand, she fumbled for her baton. She couldn't believe this was actually going to work. If she could just stay far enough ahead—

Her foot connected with something hard. She cried out as pain vibrated up her leg, and she flew forward, glimpsing the handicap wheel block that had attacked her as she plummeted to the ground.

Chapter Nineteen

When Holly took off running, Gwyn nearly leapt up in surprise. She grabbed hold of the steering wheel from where she slumped in the seat and pulled up enough to see Kara race past in pursuit.

"Shit." Gwyn clawed for the door handle and tumbled out. One of the partying lads had called out again, and Gwyn cursed his name. Holly had no doubt run to protect them, and now—

Holly took flight before crashing to the ground in a clatter, her baton bouncing across the asphalt.

Kara leapt on her.

Gwyn broke into a sprint. Kara and Holly rolled into shadow, who was who lost in a tangle of limbs. With a prayer that a jolt of chaos would hurt one more than the other, Gwyn dove into the pile. She grabbed hold of whatever she could reach and sent her energy out in a burst.

Two voices cried out, and Holly's chaos field roared to life as Gwyn had hoped it would. Kara screamed in pain again, but Gwyn lost her grip as Holly's chaos field sent her rolling into a fucking parking block.

She struggled up, grateful she hadn't hit her wounded side. A chorus of voices approached, the party lads, and Gwyn rounded on them, baring her teeth to summon the memory of when she'd been a thing that went bump in the night.

They stumbled all over each other trying to stop and turn and flee, at least one making a keen of terror she knew from long ago, an animal in fear for its life.

Gwyn kept hold of that feeling as she turned back. By the gods, it was past time to remember that she was dangerous.

She leapt on Kara's back, punching, kicking, gouging, throwing chaos energy like sparks. Kara's knife glinted as the glow of headlights passed over them. Gwyn grabbed that hand and wrenched. A human wrist would have broken. Kara only grunted, but the knife still fell to the ground.

Gwyn dashed it away and left herself open to Kara's fist. Stars burst in her vision as it caught her cheek. *Fight through.* Ears ringing, she brought her knee up into something soft as a hand smacked her in the shoulder. She lurched sideways, bringing her own fist up, but Kara got a knee between them and flipped them over, sitting astride Gwyn and making the wound in her side burn in agony.

Another set of headlights washed over them, highlighting Kara as she brought her hands down in a double-fisted blow.

Gwyn put her arms up, blocking, but the force sent shockwaves through her arms and smacked her aching head into the ground. She pooled her power in her hands again and slapped Kara's stomach, earning another cry of pain. Her power was ebbing with her stamina; she'd not fought this hard in years. Fucking hell, if she lost, she was going to let everyone down.

Kara brought her hands up again. Her face was bloody, one eye already swelling. At least Gwyn had done that much.

Something connected with the side of Kara's head, a thump even Gwyn could feel where they touched each other. Kara half turned, arms up, but the long line of Holly's baton came for her again.

And again.

And again.

When Kara finally slumped to the side, it seemed a mercy.

Holly fell to her knees, breathing hard. "You all right?"

Gwyn pushed Kara's legs off and sat up, groaning, all her aches and pains singing now that she was no longer in a rage. "Yep. You?"

Holly nodded. "Whatever you did felt like fire ants all over my body. And when I reached for my baton, it kept rolling away from me."

"Your chaos field. My fault. Sorry."

"Don't apologize. We did it." She glanced at the headlights still pointed at them. "Sorry it took me so long. I got the car because I couldn't tell which of you was which and—"

Gwyn put a hand on the back of Holly's neck and brought their foreheads together. "You don't apologize, either. We did it."

"You're getting clown makeup on your face," Holly said softly.

"In for a penny." Gwyn pressed a quick kiss to Holly's lips before they helped each other up.

Holly nudged Kara with her foot. "I don't think she's dead."

"No, probably not."

"What do we do with her?"

Gwyn almost snapped that she'd asked that very question at the rest stop, but Holly's points from before had also been proven: Kara had certainly been on her way to fuck those lads up for their transport. Holly and Gwyn had done a good thing even if it now lumbered them with a problem.

She looked around the now empty lot, hoping for inspiration, and focused on a closed bakery before moving on and coming back, something tickling her mind.

Cinnamon rolls baked daily? That would make anyone take a second look, but it wasn't the answer. Specialty cakes? No. Doughnuts served until two p.m.? No. Pretzel twists?

She grinned.

"What?" Holly said, looking where Gwyn pointed.

"Have you ever heard of the Gordian Knot?"

Holly wasn't quite sure what she was looking at as Gwyn mixed a seemingly random bunch of ingredients in a big bucket.

After they'd dumped the unconscious Kara in the trunk of the Olds and Holly had washed off her disguise, they'd raced through a big box store that was open late. As they'd shopped for a seemingly random bunch of ingredients, Gwyn had explained the Gordian Knot

"The legend that humans know says Alexander the Great came to a city in what's now called Turkey. They had this ox cart with a rope tied to it in a very complicated knot, and whoever undid it would be king."

Holly had questions, but Gwyn had steamed ahead.

"Now, I don't remember why, but legend has it that he tried to untie it and couldn't, so he either cut it or took off part of the cart to get it loose."

"But that's cheating."

Gwyn gave her a wink. "If you'd been there, that's just what you would have said, but it's a metaphor about thinking boldly or how some situations require force, I'm not sure. But the knot itself is important because it's based on a fey recipe for a rope that can't be untied."

So now they were in the back edge of the parking lot mixing water and some dried herbs with a handful of gold-plated jewelry, some copper plumbing doodads, honey, and lemons. Gwyn added a drop of blood—"for the chaos"—and put in a coil of nylon rope. "That should do it."

Holly frowned. "Won't she be able to break the rope like you did my handcuffs?"

"Not while she's injured." But she didn't seem entirely convinced. "The magic should help with that too."

Holly studied the limp form in the trunk, feeling a little bad that they were restraining her without any medical attention, but Gwyn had assured her that not only would Kara recover, she'd heal faster than a human.

"She shouldn't fully heal before we get to Vegas. This is just a precaution. And a damn good one, if I do say so myself." She seemed a little put out that Holly wasn't more impressed.

Though she had her doubts, Holly gave Gwyn a sideways hug and a kiss on the temple. "I'm so impressed that my girlfriend knows how to restrain women in my trunk after we've bludgeoned them into unconsciousness."

She didn't realize she'd said girlfriend until it was out there like a missile, and nothing she could do would recall it.

Gwyn's mouth was open, and it might have been the dim lighting, but there seemed to be tears in her eyes. It was beyond adorable.

Holly had to hug her again, mindful of all their sore spots. "Yeah, I said girlfriend," she whispered in Gwyn's ear. "And I meant it. Don't make it weird."

With a breathless laugh, Gwyn hugged her back. "Well, we girlfriends better get to tying before the Valkyrie in our trunk wakes up." She bent but froze. "It's not too soon to say 'our' car, right?" She winked.

Holly gave her a little push. "I told you not to make it weird." She rolled her eyes. "But everything about this is already weird." She waited until they were busy tying to say, "And it's a no on the car. It belongs to the SCDA, so you'll have to fight Marcus for it."

"I won't lie," Gwyn said as she looped the rope around Kara's wrists and ankles. "I thought about it. Just wondered if I could take the big man."

A pang of sadness shot through Holly. After everything, she didn't know if Marcus would ever speak to her or Renne again, even to reclaim the car. "Well, if he decides to kick our asses after this, you may get your chance."

Gwyn snorted as she tied.

Holly looked over the knot and frowned. The pattern looked a little complicated, but not enough to hold a woman who fought like a tiger. "Are you sure that's gonna work?"

"The magic is in the rope, not the knot, though the pattern does make a difference. That's what the legend got wrong, or so I've heard."

"You've never actually tried this before?"

"Nah, but it's fine." She sounded confident but wasn't making eye contact.

"So we might get a crazed Valkyrie busting through the back seat?"

With a weary sigh, Gwyn looked at her. "Love, and I say that with all respect, we're all the way out on a limb here. It's shrugs and dunnos and having to wait and see from here on out."

Holly could understand that. This whole adventure had a seat-of-the-pants vibe. Very chaotic. Very fey. Her personal chaos field was probably the only reason it hadn't driven her insane.

They threw a bottle of water and a protein bar in the trunk where Kara could reach them and shut the lid. Gwyn was adamant that she'd recover her wits as soon as Tiss was dead, and Holly supposed they'd just have to wait and see if that was the case.

As soon as Tiss was dead. Holly wondered when she'd gotten used to thinking of that as their endgame. She didn't do rough justice, had always known this about herself. Even though she worked outside the human law, she still worked within a system that had rules, even though those rules made her skin itch. Planning to kill someone was so far outside her regular life, she didn't even know how to sort her feelings.

Holly clenched the wheel as she pulled out of the parking lot. Gwyn put a hand on hers. They were now driving west as fast as they dared. They'd keep in touch with Renne by phone, and Gwyn could sense her bike. It was already dark, and they were still about eight hours from Las Vegas.

"What's bothering you?" Gwyn asked. "Besides the demigoddess in the trunk and the murder Fury."

Holly breathed through a laugh. "We have to kill Tiss, don't we?"

Gwyn cocked her head. "Sorry, love, but you're just realizing that now?"

"I just…I haven't accepted it until now. I keep hoping, well, I don't know."

"You'd have to keep her tied up in your trunk forever."

"I know."

"She'd get out eventually."

"I know, I know."

Gwyn rubbed Holly's knuckles. "She's a Fury. Down to the bones of her. She can't be anything else. It's like that with a lot of old…legendary creatures, I guess you'd call them."

"But you're not the same as you used to be."

"True, but I wasn't born into a role as strict as Tiss's. Entities like Furies or gods, they're shaped by human belief, powered by human consciousness. Except for now, Tiss is powered by the Hunt. They can't be other than what they are. That's why you don't see many gods around fucking up the landscape. Their power has waned with humanity's belief."

"So she can't change."

"Except to get worse, no. You'll never find her minding a garden or working in an animal shelter. She's like a serial killer, won't stop until she's stopped."

Humanity had places to put people like that, facilities they'd never leave where they'd be studied like lab rats for the rest of their lives. None of those facilities would hold Tiss.

Maybe Holly should be comparing her to those killers who were executed. She and Gwyn and Renne were executioners. Not appointed by the SCDA, but new laws had to be written all the time for new situations, and new positions had to be created.

"I'll say this," Holly said, "I'm not becoming the new SCDA executioner if they decide we need one after this."

Gwyn gave her one last pat. "I don't blame you. As much as I'm looking forward to the Hunt being free, I am not looking forward to the actual killing."

Thank God or this relationship was over right now.

And it was on the tip of her tongue to ask what Gwyn's plans were once the Hunt was free, if she was still determined to lead them or if certain other developments had changed her mind. Before she could, Gwyn grumbled something. "What is it?"

"Sunny. He texted that they were pulling over near Gallup and was praising the fact that Renne drives the speed limit—which is a dig at me, I'm sure—but he's gone incommunicado."

Holly sighed. She could think of a thousand reasons someone would stop texting out of the blue, and nine hundred and ninety-nine of them were bad, especially on this trip.

She put her foot down harder.

CHAPTER TWENTY

Renne had taught Gwyn how to share their phone locations for when they were separated, showing a level of foresight she wished she had. She had the tracker open now, directing Holly to a Waffle Hut in Gallup, New Mexico.

The strobing red and blue lights of cop cars were also a handy beacon.

"Fuck," Holly said as she slowed, easing into the parking lot.

"I'm sure it's nothing," Gwyn said, certain it was something, but that felt like the right thing to say.

Holly didn't reply as they slipped into a parking space. The doors of the police cruiser were open, no one inside. The Waffle Hut looked empty, one overhead light fixture swinging in the middle, turning the plastic booths and chairs into a sad disco.

Gwyn exchanged a look with Holly, and without a word, they walked toward where the double doors stood open, letting the scent of fried food loose into the chilly night air. It wasn't until she was halfway through the vestibule that Gwyn caught sight of a hand lying limply behind the hostess's podium. She pointed to get Holly's attention.

Holly's mouth slipped open, but she nodded as she drew her baton.

Deep inside the restaurant, something crashed to the ground, and someone shouted, the words muffled by walls.

Gwyn and Holly stepped in together, and as they neared the half wall that separated the waiting and dining areas, Gwyn saw that the place was anything but empty.

She counted three people at first. One was slumped on a table, their arms dangling. Another lay in one of the booths. One more had the brown uniform of a server and lay in a crumpled heap on the floor, legs spattered crimson. Well, one leg was spattered. The other was… gone.

The hand was just as alone.

Holly put the back of her hand to her mouth but still moved to check the pulses of the server and one of the slumpers. Gwyn checked the other. No signs of life. Just bits of gore and other horrors. More unmoving forms waited deeper in.

No Sunny or Renne.

Yet.

Gwyn held her bile back and kept her hope up.

Near the swinging doors to the kitchen, someone in a tan police uniform lay against a row of cabinets, eyes shut. Through the blood on their clothes, Gwyn was able to spot a patch with…*County Sherif... partment*. More law enforcement would doubtless be on their way.

"Let's go," Holly whispered, ready to burst past the swinging doors. Gwyn took the exit side, and they went as one into a room packed with deep fryers and griddles and microwaves. Something moved near the back, then someone came stumbling backward around a corner. They righted themselves on a counter before thumping back the way they'd come. Shambling, almost.

"Stop," Holly yelled at them, but before she could run forward, Gwyn gripped her arm. Their shambly friend was lacking a hand, the stump not bleeding, and they seemed decidedly on the gray side.

"How does a necromancer defend themselves?" she muttered.

Holly looked at her in horror, then yanked out of her grip. "Renne?" She dashed between the counters.

With a curse, Gwyn followed. She hadn't thought the zombie might be fighting Renne, not after everything they'd been through together with Sunny, but—

With a shrill war cry, a woman wearing a leather jacket, her black hair in a topknot, pushed the zombie back, hacking at it with a meat cleaver. She had a cut across her forehead that had cemented one eye closed, and her left arm hung limply at her side, but she swung her chopper wildly with the other.

Aella, one of the Amazons.

Before Holly could rush to help, Gwyn called, “Aella!”

She glanced up, but like Kara, her face held no recognition. She wasn’t a Valkyrie, but she still had godly blood in her veins, and she wouldn’t give up her chase unless forced.

Holly blinked at her and the zombie in confusion. They stood alone in the kitchen, but instead of advancing on her, the zombie paused outside a narrow door marked, *Office*.

“Renne?” Holly called.

“Holly?” he yelled behind the office door.

Aella cried out again and went for the door, but the zombie blocked her path. She sliced with the cleaver, and it took the deep cut blithely across the inside of one elbow. That arm now hung crookedly, twitching on the end of tendons and a sliver of bone.

Gods, what a sight.

Gwyn picked up a cutting board and held it like a shield at Holly’s side. Parts of other bodies were strewn across the floor, including another in a tan uniform. Aella had cut all of them to ribbons, but there wasn’t nearly as much blood as there had been in the dining room. Sunny must have been summoning one zombie after another to defend him and Renne.

“Watch out for the woman with the knife,” Renne yelled, his voice almost lost through the door. “Don’t try to come in past the zombie.”

“It’s a risen,” Sunny called.

“Thanks for the warning,” Gwyn said as she and Holly advanced.

Aella swung the cleaver. Gwyn darted forward, blocking with the cutting board. Holly tried to lean around her and swing her baton, but the corridor was narrow here between the office and what seemed like a staff bathroom. Aella was pinned in but could also hold the ground easily.

Time wasn’t on their side.

As if to echo her thoughts, the kitchen doors *thwocked* open behind them. Gwyn glanced back, expecting an army of officers with shoulder mounted missile launchers, but it was the cop from just outside the door. Their head tilted oddly, glassy eyes staring at nothing, huge hole in their chest that wasn’t bleeding anymore.

"The next zombie just reported for duty," Gwyn called.

"Risen!"

"Shut up and run for it, Renne," Holly yelled. "We'll cover you."

The office door banged open into the back of the first zombie, but it didn't seem to mind.

Aella growled as Renne appeared with her quarry. She lunged in a series of wild chops, the knife whirling like mad. Holly fell back with a swear. Gwyn tried to cover until her cutting board snapped in half from the force.

"Fucking hell!" She threw the pieces, but Aella blocked them, her arm like a paper shredder gone mad. She managed to knock Gwyn and Holly to the side before she pushed forward.

Her cleaver going for Sunny.

Renne opened his mouth far wider than it should have been able to go and sank his teeth into her arm, the sharp triangles disappearing all the way up to his gums.

Aella screamed and kicked him in the chest before he could rip her arm off. Holly scored a hit on her forearm, but she barely seemed to feel it, not stopping until the first zombie wrapped an arm around her waist.

She brought the cleaver down on its wrist, and it wouldn't be long until that arm was as useless as the other. Thankfully, the other zombie was nearly there. Gwyn grabbed Holly's waist and dragged her to the right as the second zombie shambled by. It wrapped its arms around Aella, too, no doubt wrenching her wounded arm and hindering her chopping one. But by the way she gave that war cry again and went wild, she wouldn't be pinned for long.

They couldn't leave her here to cut up anyone else.

Gwyn gathered her chaotic energy until her hair felt as if it was standing on end. She mixed it with her anger, ducked between four zombie legs, and grabbed Aella's knees. With a snarl, she unloaded every ounce of power she could muster.

Oh, the screams.

Aella's nearly brought the roof down, and even the zombies managed a whining shriek or two. They blew backward, their bodies singed. That whistling sound might have been their organs flash-frying instead.

Aella swayed for a moment, her mouth open, before her eyes rolled back, and she crumpled with a thump.

It took a moment before anyone moved. The zombies seemed dead. Again. Gwyn felt for Aella's pulse, remembering the times they'd shared a drink or two right before Tiss had joined the Hunt. They hadn't known each other long then, but the memories were still good.

"I shouldn't have hit you as hard as I did a Valkyrie," Gwyn whispered, guilt choking her.

"Gwyn?" Holly asked. She was back near the kitchen doors helping Renne hold up Sunny. "Are you okay?"

"Right as rain." Gwyn couldn't sit here wallowing. All of this was yet another crime to lay at Tiss's feet. She scooped Aella over her shoulder and stood. "Don't dawdle. We've got to go before more police come."

Holly was loath to separate again, but Gwyn didn't want to leave her bike behind. She wouldn't ride far from the Olds, she said, not with two Hunt members tied up in the trunk. They'd managed to tie Aella to a barely conscious Kara on the next hill over from the Waffle Hut. Flashing lights had turned the sky red and blue as more police cars had descended on the place. God knew what they'd make of all that mess.

Now they were on the road again, Gwyn riding point as Renne told his story in the car. He and Sunny had stopped for a bite to eat, and Aella had arrived not long after and killed everyone who got in her way. "With a freaking sword," Renne said. "Probably worth a lot as an antique until she broke it on a zombie."

"Risen," Sunny said sullenly from the back. "The people weren't even truly in the way. She could have stepped around them, but she went through everyone, even those who were just trying to get away from her."

"Some folks got out," Renne said, "but all along the row we were sitting on…"

"I saw," Holly said softly. She put a hand on his knee and squeezed.

He patted it gently, then put it back on the wheel. “Safety first.”

She didn’t know whether to laugh or cry. The sight of that place, the bodies, the…parts would stay with her for a long time. She couldn’t imagine what it had been like to be there when it happened.

“We ran for the back and barricaded ourselves in the office, but we knew it wouldn’t be long until she burst in.”

“I raised them hastily,” Sunny said. “Sloppily. I didn’t do it justice, but I don’t have everything I need for the perfect risen. I didn’t even have time to give them a name.”

It seemed a very odd thing to be sad about, given the circumstances, but Holly didn’t have the heart to reprimand him for being sorry about the sloppy zombies and not the lives lost. There was plenty of sadness to go around.

As if to redeem himself, he added, “I’m sorry for the people, too, of course. None of this would be happening but for me.”

“Don’t go borrowing guilt,” Renne said. “You did your crime, and you’re paying for it. The crimes of the Hunt are on them.”

“But if I hadn’t—”

“Listen to Renne,” Holly said, though she had to grit her teeth. It would have felt so good to have someone to yell at. “If Tiss hadn’t turned the Hunt into a pack of murderers, this wouldn’t be happening, either.”

He fell quiet, and Holly let him stew.

“The rest I’m sure you’ve already pieced together.” Renne winced as if aware of the tastelessness of that statement in light of events. “God.”

“I know,” she said. “It sucks.” What more was there to say, really?

“It’s still about six hours to Vegas. Question is, why are we finding Hunt members ahead of us all of a sudden?”

“Ah,” Sunny said, the single sound carrying its own share of guilt. “I’ve been thinking about that. I think the running water in the ritual might have been a mistake, as little as we had. I think it might have…dispersed the Hunt along an east-west ley line.”

Holly tightened her grip on the wheel and ground her teeth until she could almost hear the crack. She replayed Gwyn’s earlier words in her head: they were all out on a limb here. Right. Uncharted territory. “I remember three missing from when the trap went off. We’ve got two. One more isn't that bad." Except that the rest of the Hunt had probably recovered by now and were charging up behind them.

"I think we need to stop," Renne said. He'd reported some bruised ribs from that kick by Aella. The cut on his arm had reopened, maybe even a little wider, and Sunny had stumbled on the way to the office and wrenched his ankle. Holly and Gwyn hadn't fared much better against Kara, and Holly knew those blasts of chaos Gwyn kept throwing around had to be taking a toll on her along with the wound on her side.

"And risk meeting the third Hunt member?" Holly asked. She hadn't been able to pronounce the name and couldn't quite remember it now.

"We might get lucky."

"And pigs might fly." But she sighed as she said it.

They made it to just outside Flagstaff before Holly couldn't keep her eyes open anymore. Sunny had already passed out in the back seat, and even Renne was drooping. Holly did all the talking at a motel they found just off the freeway. They got one room this time, wanting to stay together in case of any more misfortune, but Holly and Gwyn took one bed and Renne and Sunny the other.

Holly stared at the ceiling in the dark after everyone had showered and lay down. The nearby freeway rumbled with the occasional passing truck, and the halogen lights in the parking lot shone around the cheap blackout curtains. They'd shut the AC off, but the unit under the window still emitted the occasional whine as the fan kicked on and off with no direction, and the whole place smelled faintly of cigarette smoke and feet.

It was the kind of place her parents would have made her stay as a child when they were on one of their "road trips," aka running from the cops. They loved the chaotic nature of some places, but Holly thought they might have been confusing chaotic with unsanitary and depressing.

Sunny snorted in his sleep before turning over. Renne didn't make a sound, something to be grateful for. When he ground his teeth, people in the next county heard him.

Gwyn mumbled something and shifted, her arm flopping across Holly's midsection. She gave it a reassuring pat and turned toward her, snuggling into what quickly became an embrace. She wished they were alone so she could kiss Gwyn awake and forget her anxiety in a round of passionate lovemaking, but everything in her rebelled at the thought of even kissing someone in Renne's presence, let alone Sunny's.

She and Gwyn *would* get caught if they tried. That was just Holly's luck.

But you're winning, she tried to tell herself. They had two members of the Hunt tied up in their trunk. As well as the Gordian Knot to keep them quiet, Sunny had performed some kind of ritual that he hoped would keep them asleep. He said it made someone appear dead, slowing their heart rate and such but not actually killing them.

He'd never done that one before, either, as out on a limb as they always seemed to be. As they might be for the rest of their lives. Even if they got Sunny to Signal and beat Tiss, the long line of Holly's life stretched in front of her sleepless eyes. She'd realized just after they'd stopped that they'd never retrieved Renne's gun, had forgotten all about it, and Renne had to call the SCDA and report it. He hadn't been able to get anyone on the phone, and no one had replied to his texts. Holly had said they were probably busy, but even she didn't believe that. It was clear that she and Renne were persona non grata now.

Maybe Gwyn would give them a space in the new and improved Wild Hunt.

She thought of what that would look like, riding at Gwyn's side on a horse or a Harley. It might not be so bad. The thought mutated into sexy fantasies that carried her into sleep.

When next she opened her eyes, everyone was stirring as Renne's alarm went off. Holly joined them in grumbling and stretching and inhaling sharply at various aches and pains and too little sleep on an uncomfortable bed.

Sunny sat up in his boxers and tank top and put his head in his hands. "I'm starting to think death might be preferable to this trip." They'd wrapped his ankle in an elastic bandage, but some of the purple bruise peeked out, stark against his fair skin. As he rubbed his temples, Holly handed him a bottle of water from their dwindling supplies.

"All this magic taking it out of you?" she asked.

He nodded weakly and gave her a grateful smile. He fiddled with the cap after drinking. "Thank you all."

Everyone paused in getting dressed or making coffee, Gwyn turning in the doorway to the bathroom.

"For everything," Sunny said. "I know you consider escorting me and keeping me alive to be doing your duty," he said to Holly and Renne. "And I know you hope to defeat Tiss," he added to Gwyn. "But treating me so kindly? Making me a participant and not just luggage to haul around? You didn't have to do that, and I'm grateful." He made a noise halfway between a laugh and a sigh. "I'm sorry I don't have any rings to give you as a pledge, but if I survive in this Signal place, and you ever need my help, come find me, no matter what."

"Well, shit, Sunny," Renne drawled. "Don't make me cry this early in the morning."

Now everyone laughed breathily, the tender moment acknowledged but prevented from overwhelming everyone. Still, they mumbled their thanks before they continued getting ready and hit the road once again.

As she took a turn in the passenger seat of the Olds, Holly considered the mostly empty packet of tea leaves. A few dotted the bottom. "Maybe I should try to bring on a vision with just these?" she asked Renne. "It might work."

He opened and closed his mouth a few times before shrugging. His dentures were back in place. Luckily, he'd remembered to slip them into his pocket at the Waffle Hut. "Like with everything else that has happened on this trip, I have no idea." He gave her a wan smile.

She couldn't even be mad. She felt the same way.

It would be nice to know exactly where Tiss was, but there was no guarantee the vision would show that. No, better to leave the last few leaves for a Hail Mary if they needed one. Or to find Tiss right when they put Sunny through the portal to Signal so they could meet and fight her just after her failure.

That seemed a much more reasonable plan.

CHAPTER TWENTY-ONE

Holly rejoiced when they hit Kingman, only an hour and a half from Las Vegas, and they stopped to refill the Olds. God, they were going to pull this off. She didn't say that out loud; no sense in tempting fate. Still, it felt good just to think it.

"Hey there, darlin'," Gwyn said from where she leaned against her bike while Renne filled the car. "Wanna ride?"

Holly rolled her eyes but still smiled, enjoying the surprise on Gwyn's face when she said, "Sure, why not?" She was the only one who hadn't been on the bike and the only one dying to get her arms around Gwyn.

"Really?" Gwyn straightened so fast, it was a wonder she didn't knock her ride over.

"What? Were you not serious?"

"Completely serious!" Gwyn passed her the helmet and threw her leg over the bike as if in a hurry to leave before Holly changed her mind.

With a grin, Holly waved to Renne to let him know what she was doing, put the helmet on, and climbed up, wrapping Gwyn in her arms.

"Ooo," Gwyn said over the purr of the bike. "I like the way you hold on."

When they took off, Holly couldn't hold in a squeal. She'd never been on a motorcycle before. Renne had mentioned that the ride was smooth, much more so than any bike he'd ridden, and had made him pine for his misspent youth. Holly had nothing to compare this to, but they seemed to glide over the blacktop and slipped smoothly around cars.

The soothing vibration was a nice bonus. As was having her arms around a beautiful fey whom she hoped to know a lot better. As they rumbled down a long stretch of highway, she was tempted to re-create a scene from a movie she couldn't recall the name of: the passenger on a bike lifted her arms like someone on a roller coaster, a devil-may-care salute to life.

But riding a motorcycle had rules for a reason.

And Gwyn was hard to let go of.

Holly wished the helmet wasn't in the way so she could lay her head on Gwyn's shoulder, but again, rules. She settled for leaning the helmet there, hoping Gwyn got what she was trying to say, that this experience was another bit of happiness in a trip that'd had far too few of those.

It couldn't last, but she'd enjoy it while—

The sharp pain exploding in her side seemed almost inevitable, especially after that thought.

She screamed, the helmet drowning her cry even in her own ears.

Don't let go, don't let go.

Shaking, she kept her arms around Gwyn but wanted to clutch her burning side as the bike swerved. She was on fire, the pain radiating through her. She had to have been shot. By an arrow, a bullet, or a bazooka, she didn't know, but the pain washed out everything else, turning the world gray around the edges.

Gwyn looked around wildly, saying something.

"I'm hit," Holly said, her breath coming in gasps, but Gwyn would never hear her that way. She fumbled the visor open and gathered all her strength. "I'm hit!"

Gwyn tried to look at her, the bike swerving again. She pulled to the side of the road, the Olds squealing behind them. As a truck whizzed past, the strength went out of Holly's arms, and she toppled into the sandy dirt of the shoulder.

❖

Gwyn leapt off the bike and eased the helmet off Holly's head. "Love, where are you hit?" She looked her over, running her hands under Holly's jacket, her T-shirt, up and down her jeans' clad legs.

"Side…my side."

Renne ran up, falling to his knees beside them. "What happened?"

"I don't know." Gwyn tried to cast her mind back as she examined Holly's side, but there was no blood, no tears, nothing to indicate she'd been hit as she'd said. "The bike shuddered a bit, and her hands dug into me, and she said she's hit."

"My side!" It was a cry this time, Holly's face pinched in pain.

Renne jerked her shirt up, but there was nothing. They turned her onto each side, apologizing as she moaned, but there was—

Gwyn spotted the purplish dot just as Renne was reaching for it. She dashed his hand away.

"What the hell?"

She ignored him and bent close, inhaling the scent of cloves and the tang of magic. "She's been elf-shot." She glanced around wildly, looking for the assassin, but there were rocks and gulleys and thousands of places to hide, a lot more than someone would have pictured from the word desert.

"What?"

"The last missing member of the Hunt is fey." That meant Gwyn knew her, had known her before Tiss had ever come along. She ran through a list of names in her mind, thinking of three or four who could fire the invisible arrows that were really spells. "Don't touch it. It'll spread to you."

His eyes went wide. "It's getting bigger. How do we fix her?"

We don't, she wanted to scream. There were few things that could reverse elf-shot. That was what made it so dangerous.

A drop of pure elven blood would do it.

"We get her to Vegas as quickly as we can and convince the elves to help her." She slipped her arms under Holly, ready to lift, when a *ping* sounded from the bike, and it rocked a little where it stood.

Gwyn leaned over Holly while pulling Renne down. Like Holly, he'd collapse right away, but Gwyn would survive longer, could maybe even fight it off. "Do you see the shooter?" she whispered.

"Not from underneath you, no," he said from under her arm.

She ignored him and tried to peek through the bike. They seemed to be on opposite sides of the road from the shooter, at least. Whoever it was, she'd be gathering her energy for another shot. They had a little time.

Gwyn gathered Holly under one arm and pulled Renne with the other as she made a shambling dash for the Olds. "Elf-shot can't penetrate anything but fabric or flesh, so you should be safe in here." Sunny opened the rear door, and they put Holly inside before Renne climbed in the passenger seat and clambered over the console to get behind the wheel.

When Gwyn hesitated to follow, he waved her in. "Come on. She can't shoot us in here, right?"

"No, but…" Her bike, her faithful steed. They'd been together for millennia. She couldn't just leave it.

"Gwyn," Renne said, glaring at her.

"Gwyn!" Holly cried.

That did it. Gwyn got in the car. No one could ride her bike without her permission, so all anyone could do was tow it away. She promised to find it again one day and focused her attention on Holly.

Whoever shot her was going to fucking pay.

Gwyn held Holly's hand between the seats as she writhed. The spot was spreading quickly, powerful magic. Renne put his foot down, rattling down the highway as fast as the Olds could manage. They were only a few miles down the road when a shudder passed down Gwyn's spine. Someone was trying to start her bike. Ha, they'd get no luck there, a paltry satisfaction but one she'd take in the moment.

She gasped when the tingle turned into a muted hum. "Oh. Oh no. For fuck's sake, no!"

"What is it?" Renne said, twisting to look at Holly.

"No, she's as fine as she was. Someone's riding my bike."

"I thought no one could do that without your permission."

A few had her permission, especially someone she'd ridden with in the Hunt for a thousand years, a fey she'd once trusted as a sister. "It's Etain," she whispered, countless memories passing through her mind. "Oh gods, Etain." She hadn't let herself think much about the people in the Hunt she'd left behind. She preferred to think of them more as the crew Tiss had assembled, but a few had stuck around from before. "She's one of the Hunt. We've ridden each other's mounts many times."

He glared again. "You should have mentioned that."

"What good would it have done? I couldn't ride with her shooting at us, and there is no way to scuttle my bike. She doesn't need the keys to start it. They're mostly for show." She jingled them at him.

He turned his attention back to the road, swearing under his breath.

Gwyn held Holly's hand tighter as she felt her own bike roaring after them. Etain hunting her, shooting the woman she was falling for? Gods, it hurt. One more fact drifted through her mind. Killing the shooter was one way to slow down elf-shot.

Gwyn pressed Holly's knuckles to her forehead. If it came to it, yes, she would. She'd have to mention it to Renne as an option.

Sunny patted Holly's hair and talked soothingly to her in German. Well, the tone was soothing; the sound of the German? Not so much. But it sounded like the right things to say, "It's going to be all right," and so on. He kept his hands well away from where she'd been shot and cast continual worried glances behind them and ahead, as if afraid of Etain following and also afraid that Vegas would appear magically, and he'd miss it.

"What's happening?" Holly said, shivering. She seemed to be recovering some of her wits, but that wasn't the good sign it seemed. Gwyn had seen too many people get elf-shot to be hopeful. Regaining their senses meant the spell had burrowed into the bodies past the nerves. The pain would still linger but wouldn't be as sharp.

"You were elf-shot," Gwyn said, still twisted around the seat. "It's a magic spell, but it hurts like being hit with an arrow. Humans used to blame it for arthritis and such, but it's really…this." When Holly reached for her side, Gwyn stopped her. "Don't touch it. I don't think it can spread through the same body that way, but let's not tempt fate."

Holly's face was nearly as pale as Sunny's, and sweat beaded on her forehead. "Hospital?"

"They wouldn't be able to help, love." She kissed Holly's hand. Renne leaned past her and handed a bottle of aspirin over the seat. Sunny helped Holly take a couple. Gwyn didn't know if it would help, but it couldn't hurt. It wasn't like they could break into a hospital for some morphine.

Just stay alive, Gwyn thought, trying to keep her face hopeful while her heart felt anything but.

❖

Holly's mind came back to her slowly, and she'd never been so happy to be conscious. Her side was even less achy, though her ribs still burned like she'd been laid on a grill.

She was lying in the back seat of the Olds, and Sunny was patting her hair. She could only recall one other time someone had done that, the only time she'd gotten the flu. She'd been left with the neighbors, Willow McCarthy and her wife, while her parents had been out doing crimes, and she'd gotten sicker than she ever had. In between bouts of vomiting, she'd lain on the couch and watched cartoons while Willow had stroked her hair.

It had been amazing then. Now, not so much.

She patted his hand, then waved it away to say thanks for trying, but no thanks. She didn't need the distraction of memories right now. "How do we fix me?"

Gwyn turned in her seat, her face that mix of sympathy and fear that said whatever she was about to say, the situation was worse. "Get you to Vegas and you'll be right as rain."

Holly wanted to snap at her to be realistic, but she felt too weak for real anger. "The cure is neon lights?"

"No."

"Roulette?"

"Holly—"

"The smell of stale cigarettes and desperation?"

Gwyn closed her eyes as if counting to ten. "Elven blood."

Holly blinked. That couldn't be right. "Pardon?"

"A few drops is all."

Oh, was that all? The elves who couldn't be bothered to get off their asses and save countless humans and fey were going to shed blood for her? "Sure."

"We may have a way to slow the elf-shot down," Renne said, his voice tense.

Gwyn winced. "Yeah, we may."

"If it's one of you dying or something, the answer is no."

Gwyn hesitated a little too long.

Holly's stomach dropped. "Oh God, it's not, is it?"

"Not any of us dying, no," Gwyn said, still with that trembling sadness.

"The person who shot you," Sunny whispered.

Holly drew breath to say the answer was still no, that the thought of anyone dying to save her turned her stomach, especially a member of the Hunt who might have been acting solely under Tiss's influence. She'd argued for going up against Kara and had hoped they wouldn't have to kill, but someone being killed in *Holly's* name? No way.

"It's not up for debate," Renne said before Holly could muster the energy.

"Oh really?" Maybe she could scrape together a little anger after all. "You're right because the answer is no."

"No one asked you," he said.

"It's my life."

"Gently," Gwyn said, easing her back down. She glanced at Renne before smiling at Holly again. "Darlin', none of us wants to lose you."

"And I don't want to live at the cost of someone else, especially someone like the two still in the trunk. You didn't want them to die, either."

Gwyn's falling expression agreed, but she said, "For you?"

Holly managed to shake her head. "No."

"You don't get a say," Renne said.

"I get the only say."

"Keeping calm during illness is important," Sunny said loudly. He wore a fake smile, looking like a kid trying to stop his parents from fighting.

Gwyn met Holly's eyes, and no one had ever looked at her so deeply before. She'd thought of Gwyn's great age as something dangerous once, glimpsing the reason why humans stayed out of the forest at night. But there was something else in the weight of all those years: understanding. Gwyn might not have had certain feelings in centuries, but she'd had them before and understood the reasons behind them, respected them. To be seen and remembered by such a creature was truly an honor.

"Okay," Gwyn said softly. "We'll respect your wishes, love."

The car swerved a little. "Are you serious?" Renne said.

Gwyn fixed Holly with a different stare. "But in the heat of a fight, I can't promise I won't kill to defend you. And Tiss dies no matter what."

Holly could agree to both of those. Lots of things happened in the midst of combat, and she'd begun to think of Tiss as a virus. Countless people would suffer if she wasn't eradicated. After all, she'd caused the deaths of all those people at the diner, and she hadn't even been there.

Renne was muttering under his breath.

"Etain was no doubt planning on your reaction when she fired the shot," Gwyn said to him. "She knew shooting me wouldn't be effective, so she shot the one person in our party she could target at the time. She wants us to slow down and fight her or put Sunny in her reach." She sighed. "Only now, she can catch up to us, too."

"What?" Holly said, confused but glad things seemed to have turned in her favor.

"She's taken my bike."

"But I thought—"

Gwyn waved vaguely. "It's a long story."

When Renne continued to grumble, Holly said, "It's all right, Renne."

"It's not, you selfish asshole."

She'd never heard him this angry with her. It was touching in a disturbing way. "Suck it up, buttercup."

"*Pfft.*" He shook his head. "If she catches us, I'm running her over."

She knew bluster when she heard it, but she still tried to sit up again.

"If you will not let others help you, at least help yourself," Sunny said, urging her to keep still.

She couldn't argue with that. "Fine." She took Gwyn's hands. "I'm sorry it falls on you to—" She finally realized what her being wounded meant. "I…won't be able to help you with Tiss. No, I have to. Dying is no excuse."

"Don't worry. Renne is going to use his charm to convince the elves to help you, and I'm going to get Sunny to the portal," Gwyn said. "By the time Tiss shows up, you'll be ready to fight by my side." She glanced at Renne. "We'll figure out something else to do with Etain."

Holly wanted to ask what but had to let the others work on it. The desire to close her eyes washed over her, and she had to go where it led.

Chapter Twenty-two

Gwyn patted Holly's arm one last time as her eyes closed. Her head was in Sunny's lap, but he didn't seem to mind, staring at her with a look of mild concern and occasionally glancing out the rear window. Gwyn couldn't blame him. She could feel her bike getting closer even at the speeds Renne was pushing the Olds to.

He rooted around in his mouth and pulled out a set of dentures, tossing them onto the center console.

Gwyn eyed them with a frown. "Um." She'd seen his real teeth, but she'd never seen him take the dentures out.

He glanced at her and opened his mouth, and she stared, fascinated as his real pointed teeth grew in along the top and bottom. "They come in every time the plates aren't in the way."

"How do you fit the plates back in?"

"He snaps them off," Sunny said from the back seat. "It's quite riveting. They come right out at the root."

Gwyn swallowed, fighting down bile. Snapping off teeth sounded par for the course for a man who'd once put a zombie toe in his pocket. "Doesn't that hurt?"

He shrugged. "You get used to it."

She would never, but she didn't say that, eyeing the dentures on the console, wondering how long it would be before they bounced over into her lap.

With a sigh, Renne picked them up, reached across her, and put the teeth in the glovebox. "I'll just have to wash them later." He gave her a bright smile that she knew was meant to unnerve her.

Mission accomplished. Oh well, he had to be angry at someone. She tried to shake the image away. "It's a good move. The elves might sympathize more readily with someone who shows fey characteristics."

He only hummed, grinding his teeth so the whole car sounded like a rock tumbler. He kept glancing in the rearview mirror, too. "If we're not going to kill this Etain, what the hell are we going to do with her? The trunk is full."

They were well into the towns that had grown up around Las Vegas, and it was daytime. Anymore piling of captives into the trunk was bound to be noticed. She put raising zombies and casting rituals into the "will definitely attract attention" category, too. "If we can stay ahead of her, I say we skid to a stop in front of the Avalon and all pile inside. The elves won't let Etain go wild in their casino."

She hoped.

Renne raised an eyebrow. "You've never been here, have you?"

"No, but Holly showed me some films and television." The memory made her stomach lurch. If Holly died, they couldn't share more film nights, ones that could end in passion instead of awkwardness.

She shook the thought away. That was not going to happen.

"No one races down Las Vegas Boulevard. The Strip is always congested, day or night, and it's got so many streetlights that even if it was clear, you'd stop and start over and over. There will be no thundering in and skidding to a stop."

She hadn't thought of that. "What about a back door?"

"How would we get in? Casinos are built like fortresses. Even if we found an employee exit or something, we'd set off an alarm."

"That could be just what we need," Gwyn said, thinking fast. "It would attract the elves' attention. Or at least whoever they have working for them."

"And might bring the human authorities down on us, too."

She shook her head. "Holly and I already talked about how humans don't seem to notice the Avalon." Another lurch. "It never gets mentioned in films and such, even though it has to be there in the overhead shots of this Strip. It's probably covered in some next-level glamour, and the patrons will be fey or at least of the paranormal variety. They no doubt have their own security, and the human police wouldn't be called."

"And you think the employees will take us directly to their bosses if we make a ruckus?"

Gods, she didn't know. "How do you normally turn someone over who has been sentenced to exile?"

He shrugged. "I've never done it. Marcus usually sets up the transportation, and the Las Vegas office takes it from here."

They were so far out on a limb, Gwyn couldn't even see the trunk of the tree. "Can you contact them, the Vegas branch of the SCDA? They'll at least know the protocol, and once they get us inside the Avalon, that's half the job done. We'll fight our way to the top if we have to."

He gave her a look that said the idea was stupid, but he appreciated the attitude. "I do not have the contact information for the Vegas branch, and so far, no one at the Houston office has taken my calls."

"Time to try again."

He handed her his phone, and she tried messaging all the contacts he steered her toward. She stared at the phone, willing someone to respond.

Please.

Please.

When three little dots appeared next to the name Finn, she sucked in a breath. "Wait, wait, I've got one. He's given me an address." She looked it up. Google said it was a dry cleaners, but the SCDA couldn't actually advertise their real business. And it was off the Strip, so maybe they could get to it more quickly.

"Try calling," Renne said.

No one answered, just a recorded voice asking her to leave a message.

Gwyn stared at the phone, torn with indecision. "I don't like delaying getting Holly to the Avalon, but it would be nice to have more firepower at our side. Maybe some of them can keep Etain busy while the rest escorts us to the casino."

His lips were one thin line. "Unless they decide to arrest us."

"They can't!" She glanced back at where Holly slept and lowered her voice. "They won't just let her die."

"Not all members of the SCDA are as virtuous as Holly and myself."

Gwyn seethed. "If I have to, I will fight my way out of there."

He nodded. "Oh, me too, no doubt. If I have to leap in their way while you take Holly and go, I'm all in there, too."

"You *are* virtuous."

He gave her a rather grim smile. "Each option has plenty of unknowns, but the SCDA office seems like the best of the bunch."

And a rotten bunch it was.

She tried texting Finn again at Renne's request, but no more messages came through. She vaguely recalled Finn from the Houston office. A good-looking lad with pink hair. She wondered if he'd had to sneak out of the room to text one of the SCDA's black sheep and didn't dare do it twice. "He must be a good friend, this Finn."

Renne fidgeted slightly. "He's all right. I don't really know him. I mean, I know him, but we haven't…we don't hang out."

Gwyn watched him for a moment and had to grin. "Don't be tempted to play any poker while you're here, lad."

He went a little pink in the cheeks. "Like we have time for gambling."

"I was referring to how bad of a liar you are."

He rolled his eyes but didn't comment. She wished she could tease him more, at least take her mind off things a little, but it didn't feel right in the circumstances. She was tempted to watch their progress on the map app, but she didn't want to run either of their phone batteries down, either. There was no telling how much they'd need them.

When they reached Vegas, Gwyn sensed her bike still following at the same pace, and it remained out of sight. Etain must have been planning to ambush them when she had Sunny in her sights. That or she still expected them to slow down and deal with her. She was going to stay disappointed there. Even if that was Gwyn's and Renne's preference, Holly had been adamant, and Gwyn had to respect that, even if it made their task harder.

Renne sped through the back streets of Las Vegas as quickly as he could. The slowdown around Hoover Dam had made Gwyn gnaw her fingernails, something she hadn't indulged in for over a hundred years, though she had taken the occasional nibble, especially on this trip. Now she feared stripping each finger to the bone.

"There." She pointed down a dingy street that seemed far removed from the glamor of the Strip. The "dry cleaners" sat next to a U-Store It and a bare gravel lot surrounded by chain link and barbed wire. Across the street, an old body shop sat closed, even though it was the middle of the day.

Holly's breathing rattled in the quiet car, invading Gwyn's calm like a ticking clock. They pulled up to the cleaners, and Gwyn didn't hesitate to jump out and try the door.

Locked.

She knocked and pressed the button on an ancient-looking intercom, a white box with enough crud in the grooves of the speakers to put someone with OCD in a coma.

The speaker crackled as if someone was listening.

"Hello?" Gwyn tried. "We're from the Houston SCDA office. We need help."

Nothing.

Renne joined her and rattled off a few numbers, undoubtedly a code. "We have a prisoner for transfer to the Signal portal and a wounded agent."

Nothing.

"Contact Marcus Aurkin from Houston. He'll vouch for us."

Still, nothing.

Renne slapped the door. "We don't have much time, goddamn it. We are being pursued by a hostile pack of demigods, and one of us is dying. Let us the fuck in!"

Silence.

Gwyn nearly punched the front window out, but it was clear they'd get no help here.

Sunny stared at them worriedly. He'd shifted closer to the open back door, leaving Holly to lie on the seat. "What now?"

Renne scrubbed a hand through his hair and swore. Finally, he shrugged. "Plan B. Let's head to the Avalon and—"

"Wait," the speaker said, the voice scratchy with static.

Renne leapt back to it. "Hello?"

"Wait," it said again.

"We can't fucking wait," Gwyn yelled. "Your agent has been elf-shot. Someone in your office should recognize what that means. We don't have time to piss about."

"Renne, please," the speaker said, a different voice. One softer, pleading.

"Finn?" Renne asked, staring at the speaker.

"Wait," the first voice said again.

"Fuck it." Gwyn didn't care what game they were playing. She grabbed Holly's baton from the car, ready to smash the cleaner's windows.

At the end of the street, a motorcycle revved.

Etain.

Shit. Gwyn had been so angry, she hadn't realized how close her own bloody ride had gotten.

The crackle from the intercom died as Etain rode closer, her pearlescent skin shining against her dark T-shirt and leather pants.

"Back in the car," Gwyn said to Renne. "Get them to the Avalon. I'll—"

Etain lifted a hand, long fingers curled to fire an invisible elf-shot.

Renne was already halfway around the car when Gwyn shouted, "Duck!" She got ready to charge Etain, tackle her.

The huge metal doors of the body shop rattled upward, revealing Marcus holding the largest pistol Gwyn had ever seen, longer than a rifle but fitted to his massive hand.

And pointed at Etain.

Clearly, someone hadn't gotten the memo about not killing anyone for Holly's sake.

Etain shifted her aim to him, a look of surprise in her bright green eyes, and her perfect bow lips forming a little O.

Marcus's gun roared louder than any bike, the bullet screaming through the air like a missile. Etain didn't have time to shriek before she was blown clear off the bike by a hurricane of force and thrown through the chain link fence. She rolled through the gravel lot and lay still in a heap of dust.

Gwyn's bike glided a few more feet in the silence before stopping right in front of her, idling gently as if purring at the sight of her. She could barely hear it through the ringing in her ears.

Shaking her head to clear the surprise, she ran to the fence. She couldn't see Etain clearly, but something lay beside her, and Gwyn realized with a start that it must have been the projectile from Marcus's gun. If it had been a bullet, it might have blown a hole straight through her chest or cut her in half, but it had only knocked her for six.

Gwyn let out a breath, relieved. She should have realized that Holly wouldn't work for someone who killed as casually as breathing.

Etain stirred slightly. Gwyn tensed, but the side door of the dry cleaner's opened, and SCDA agents swarmed over Etain. With another relieved sigh, Gwyn turned back to the car. Marcus was already there talking to Renne, and Gwyn had the strangest regret that she hadn't gotten to see him move so fast.

"We told the Avalon you're coming," Marcus said to Renne. "They insisted we neutralize the Hunt rider first."

By the sounds coming from the lot, they were having a hell of a time, but Gwyn had to leave them to it. "Watch out for elf-shot," she said.

Marcus gave her a level stare. "We sprang from the same source," he said calmly. She'd said something similar many times and supposed it was his way of telling her to stay in her lane, that he knew as much about the old ways as she did.

It was really annoying, and she pledged not to say it again.

"Whatever," she mumbled. She slipped the baton through her belt and reached for the passenger door of the Olds, but Marcus stepped in front of her.

"Renne will handle this." He waved, and another agent came from the dry cleaner's, the lad with pink hair, Finn.

"No, I have to see her right." Gwyn gestured to Holly. "Sunny too. I can't—"

"You're under arrest."

Arrest. Banishment. She'd never see Holly again. "No."

"I place you under the geas of the SCDA…"

Renne started for the driver's door with a guilty look in Gwyn's direction.

"Entered into with the elves who rule the plane of chaos…"

"What's happening?" Sunny asked through the open back door. Finn moved as if to shut it, not looking Gwyn in the eye.

"Wait," she breathed, desperation roaring in her as her last look at Holly shrank with the closing door

"In the human year of 2015…"

A snatch of thunder rolled over them on the wind.

On a cloudless day?

Everyone froze, looking up.

Marcus glanced around as the thunder grew to a steady growl, the sound echoing unnaturally, as if traveling for their ears alone.

No, not for everyone. This was for Gwyn. And it wasn't thunder or even the roar of motorcycles, not really. This was a pack of hunters with the scent of prey in their nostrils.

Tiss was here.

Sooner than anyone could have expected, faster than should have been possible. Gwyn could nearly taste her anger on the wind. It told her one thing:

One of them wasn't coming home from this.

No more scars.

Marcus began barking orders, the geas unfinished.

"No," Gwyn said, feeling strangely calm. "You'll all be killed. I have to fight her."

He ignored her.

She would have loved to remind him of his own words. This was her house, he was just a visitor, but he wouldn't listen, someone too used to being in charge. She still couldn't let Tiss catch him. His death would make Holly sad.

As much as Tiss wanted Gwyn, she'd do her duty first and take out Sunny. So there was only one way to keep her from slaughtering all of Holly's friends.

Gwyn caught Sunny's eye through the still-open door and jerked her head at her bike.

With a show of trust that made her pity him, he slid his legs out the door, pushing it open all the way.

You're going to live, she tried to tell him psychically. She gathered all her energy for a burst of speed, summoning everything she used to be when she was little more than a predator in the dark.

Everyone else seemed to be moving through sap as Gwyn jerked Sunny from the car and leapt for her bike. She would just have to find a way to get Sunny to the Avalon *after* she'd distracted Tiss. In a blink, she was astride the bike, Sunny held tightly to her back with one hand. As she roared down the street, the SCDA agents were just turning as if to see what the commotion was.

Sprang from the same source indeed, she wanted to yell at Marcus. Some sources were clearly faster than others.

CHAPTER TWENTY-THREE

Holly opened her eyes to the most expensive-looking ceiling she'd ever seen. The intricate molding was gilded, sparkling in the warm light from a crystal chandelier. The spaces between each golden line were painted in woodland scenes with unicorns and white deer. As she stared, trying to remember where she was and what the hell had brought her here, she noticed that all the forest pictures had hidden eyes in the depths of the leaves that glowed with a sinister light.

She sat up slowly, shivering. She lay on a couch in a huge office. Every surface screamed luxe, from the butter-soft leather beneath her to the green carpet to the gleaming wooden desk that was easily the size of a rowboat. When she put her bare feet on the carpet, it felt like sinking into soft moss, and she couldn't help a sigh.

The past few hours came back in a rush, the elf-shot, the agony. Gwyn, Renne, and Sunny were no doubt still being pursued by the Hunt. Holly stood, looking for her boots. They sat next to the couch and had been polished to a high shine. Her socks peeked from the tops. She lifted her shirt, and the skin of her side was unblemished except for a single Band-Aid.

With a shaking hand, she lifted the edge to find a tiny cut where the elf-shot had been. What had Gwyn said? The cure was elven blood? So they'd cut her and then…

She shuddered, thoughts of blood-borne illnesses running through her mind. Maybe elves never had to deal with such things, but the thought of someone else's blood being inside her gave her the willies. She took a deep breath, supposing she *had* consented when she hadn't objected to this plan. Her various aches and pains felt better, too. Maybe if she met whoever had been the donor, she'd feel better.

And it wouldn't hurt to thank them.

After putting on her boots, she turned, looking for the door, but there was so much decoration all over everything, it was hard to see the way out. Bookshelves lined one wall, and glass cabinets lined the opposite one. The cabinets stood packed with curios, all lit by tasteful, recessed lighting, though the placement of each object was chaotic, no rhyme or reason, no symmetry. The wall behind the desk was covered with long plush drapes, and when she peeked, she looked out on the bustling Strip from high above the ground.

"Holy shit." She was in the Avalon.

She took another look around, never thinking she'd be here. When her gaze fell on a cat now standing on the desk, she nearly jumped out of her skin. "Oh, hello," she said.

It blinked calm green eyes. It had long hair, pure white, save for one black paw.

"Where did you come from?" She felt stupid as soon as she said it. As if a cat could answer. "Hello?" she said to the rest of the room instead. Maybe someone had opened a door and let it in.

The cat stood, stretched, and crossed the desk to a single pale card sitting near an old-fashioned inkwell and blotter.

Holly stepped closer. *Welcome*, the card said in elegant script. *Make yourself comfortable*. Each word had a slightly different slant, as if they'd been written by four different people.

"Comfortable?" she asked the cat. "I don't have time for comfortable. My friends are in trouble."

It blinked sedately.

"What the hell is going on?" she asked the room, pacing. "I have to help fight Tiss or…" She trailed off halfway across the room, ready to look for another door, when a thought occurred to her. "Are the elves going to help me?" she asked the cat.

It had turned its head to watch her but had no response save for the flick of a light pink ear.

Elves. Right, what did she know about them? Tricks and deals. "What do they want?" she asked, suspecting this was much more than a simple cat. The elves of old could change their shape. Who knew if any still could? "What do you want?"

If this cat-elf was impressed that she'd figured out its ruse, it gave no sign.

"Not money, clearly," she said, gesturing around. "I don't own anything you couldn't buy. And you probably have plenty of servants." She couldn't help a sneer and covered her mouth with one hand, trying to hide it. She no doubt had to suck up to elves a little. "Do you want me to beg? Would you get off on that?"

She took a deep breath. That was not sucking up. The cat simply regarded her with the same bored expression.

"Look," she tried. "My friends are going to fight a Fury. I trust you know what that is? In your town. Lots of people might die. Tourists, even fey ones. You're going to lose business." If they didn't care about lives, maybe they cared about that.

The cat tilted its head as if to say, go on.

Holly gritted her teeth. "Some of your property might be destroyed, too. I bet you own more than just this casino. Well, a Fury could cost you millions of dollars in—"

The cat began washing its face, obviously bored.

With a clench of her fists, Holly seethed. Some of the cabinets held daggers and a sword or two. She wouldn't consider using them on an ordinary cat, but this elf in disguise was pissing her off. And there had to be something in here that would wound an immortal being with a heart of stone.

"One of the people who might be hurt is my best friend," she said, unable to keep a growl out of her voice. "And another is the woman I am rapidly falling in love with. They're both fey. She's a full-blooded one. You might even have an ancestor in common. Hell, she could be your granddaughter or something. Don't you care?"

The cat looked up, its pink tongue sticking out just a bit before it disappeared into its mouth. She had its full attention.

"Her name is Gwyn. She rode with Odin in the first days of the Wild Hunt, then she led it for a long time, but it was peaceful, keeping to themselves. Then, Tiss, the Fury, got ahold of it and made it into the murdering horde its become. Gwyn is going to take it back and tame it again. She's a good person. She deserves to be saved."

The cat stared, its paw still half raised, waiting.

But for what?

"I'll do whatever it takes," Holly said, meaning every word. "Whatever you ask. No," she added before the cat could take that to heart. "I won't kill for you. And I won't sacrifice my friends. Gwyn wouldn't want me to do that, and I have to respect her like she respects me." She took another pleading step. "I could love her, might already love her, and it won't be like regular love. I think we'd hold on to each other forever. That's so rare, it has to mean something."

The cat only stared while Holly's heartbeat hammered in her ears.

She straightened, nodding. Well, she, Gwyn, Renne, and Sunny had spent this entire adventure relying solely on one another. Why should now be any different? "Then just point me to the way out."

The cat leapt down from the desk and walked to the row of bookcases. It pawed gently at where two stood side-by-side. Holly rushed over and examined the crack, finding it large enough to put her fingers in.

A hidden door.

When it wouldn't open to her tugging at it, she began to push and pull books at random. That was always the way it worked in movies. An ancient-looking book—the spine covered in unfamiliar letters that seemed to shift before her eyes—gave way under her hand, and the door opened with a little pop.

She nearly cried out in triumph at the sight of an elevator car. The cat sauntered in and sat, again looking at her expectantly.

She stepped into a brightly lit space just big enough for two people. Or one and a cat. The metal walls were polished to a mirror shine that reflected her and the cat into infinity, and the control panel had a row of buttons, all with strange glyphs.

No, near the bottom, one just said, *Down*.

She supposed that would have to do.

❖

Gwyn could feel the Hunt closing in as a kind of creeping dread. She couldn't lead them out of town. They'd catch her quickly in the wilderness. She turned down roads at random, looking for a place to pull over so she could google how to get to the Avalon, though she didn't think she'd have that hard of a time finding it. The strong glamour pounded against her senses nearly as hard as Tiss. She only had to give everyone else enough time to get Holly there, only had to distract Tiss for a moment, then she could shove Sunny off the bike at the Avalon's door. That couldn't be too hard.

A turn through a parking lot brought her face-to-face with a wall of traffic.

She skidded to a halt just in time to avoid hitting a BMW. Sunny gave a little cry as his hold tightened on her. There'd been no time for helmets. "Where are we going?" he asked.

She had no idea. She turned to see if they could reverse, but someone else was behind them now, honking for them to go as the BMW moved out of the way. There was barely a gap in the traffic, but she supposed that didn't matter. She dashed into the snarl of congestion that she'd already guessed was Las Vegas Boulevard.

The Strip.

It looked much bigger than on TV. The hotels were larger than any apartment block and overtook the skyline for what felt like miles. The lights weren't on in the day, but the sight of the huge buildings and fountains and gardens screamed, *be impressed*. There had to be more money here than people in the world.

And they were trapped in it.

This mess wouldn't hold Tiss back. Gwyn imagined the great fireball that had rolled over a Dallas traffic jam happening here. All these lives would be lost, and the decimation wouldn't stop with the cars. The fire would eat through all this opulence like a tax audit. Thousands would die.

Holly would never forgive her.

A flash from one of the films came to mind. There were underground passages that connected some of the hotels, and a few led to parking garages. There'd be fewer people there, and if no one stood in Tiss's path, no one could get hurt.

Gwyn passed her phone back to Sunny. "Find us an underground parking garage."

He muttered something but took the phone.

"And hold on." She edged the bike through the middle of traffic, ignoring the honks and the cries from other drivers. She pushed an electric car away with a big kick and weaved around others until she could cut across the median, her tires ripping through flowers and bushes.

A siren sounded down the road, but it wouldn't catch her. Everyone was in a jumble, some now trying to get out of the way of the cops and throwing everything into chaos.

Gwyn grinned at the perfect feel of it.

"Right turn," Sunny cried.

Gwyn didn't wait for the next street but turned into an alley. The quicker she could get to whatever he'd found, the better. The rumble of Tiss's pack was now a drumbeat in her mind. She only prayed that not too many people wandered into her path.

The elevator car opened on darkness, and Holly wondered if she'd stumbled into the depths of hell. From around the corner, someone laughed. That was no comfort. Plenty of demons would be laughing in hell.

She stepped out gingerly, one foot still inside the car and saw a tunnel stretching in both directions. LCD screens hung on the walls, their advertisements providing some dim light. She was in one of the tunnels that connected some of the casinos on the Strip. Some had shops scattered here and there, but many stretches were mostly empty, just routes between hotels that stayed out of the brutal desert sun.

The cat put two paws out and looked at her. The elevator dinged as if telling her to make up her mind.

The walls next to the doors held only a key-card detector, no call button. If she got off here, she'd be out for good. She chewed her lip. She had no phone. How the hell was she going to find everyone?

A sign down the corridor grabbed her attention simply by the fact that its content didn't shift like the other screens. Arrows directed tourists to the casinos in either direction, but the lowest arrow made her stomach do flips.

Parking garage.

One of her visions came back to her, Gwyn facing down Tiss in some vast, underground space.

And someone had been there to hold her hand.

"Thanks," Holly muttered to the cat as she took off at a fast walk that quickly turned into a jog. She risked one look back to see the cat following at a sedate pace. Well, that answered that. It was clearly an elf. At least they were interested. "Enjoy the show, you bastards," she muttered as she ran.

Chapter Twenty-four

Gwyn could sense Tiss moving above her the way computers tracked storm clouds. And she could predict this scenario just as accurately. Tiss was no doubt searching for a way down, and Gwyn closed her eyes and willed her onward.

She waited in the open beside her bike on the garage's deepest level. Sunny was hidden in the scattering of cars in the back, closer to the stairs. Gwyn had put together a hasty plan of distraction, and she only hoped it would hold. He had instructions to flee if the fight seemed to be turning against Gwyn, but he couldn't leave yet, or Tiss would simply chase him.

With a pit of lead in her stomach, Gwyn walked in a circle. Tiss wouldn't be as weak as Gwyn wanted for their showdown, but she was still missing three of her riders and wouldn't be able to draw on their full power. Hopefully, the SCDA had already sent them all to Signal, and Tiss wouldn't be able to access their power at all.

Gwyn should be so lucky.

She took a few jabs at the air with the same knife she'd used to cut herself for the trap. She still had Holly's baton, too. Maybe it would make her feel less alone. Wasn't working so far, but at least part of Holly was involved in this.

Movement above. Tiss was closer, slithering down the garage ramp. The roar of the Hunt in Gwyn's mind was joined by the growl of motorcycles that echoed through the concrete layers and all the way to Gwyn's bones.

She faced the ramp, wanting her eyes on Tiss from the very moment she appeared.

The Hunt filled the ramp in a vee, Tiss at the head, but the sight of the riders made Gwyn's jaw drop. Some were barely awake, gripping the handlebars while their bikes followed Tiss's like obedient dogs. Others slumped completely, lashed to the saddle. Seemed like Tiss had drained some of their power just to get here more quickly.

Sickening. Shameful. But also a reason to rejoice. Tiss had weakened her power base and wasted it all on herself, on revenge.

Gwyn bared her teeth.

As Tiss slowed to a halt, she revved her engine one more time before dismounting, and all the bikes fell quiet at once. She didn't seem weak as she straightened, all six and a half feet of her, though she seemed even taller now, crackling with anger.

Her eyes were as dead as ever.

"So," she said, mouth twisting as if saying even one word to Gwyn tasted foul on her tongue.

"Right, enough small talk," Gwyn said. She flicked the baton to its full length, held the knife in her other hand, and stood ready. "Come on."

Tiss sneered and flexed, and everyone in the Hunt groaned, their eyes opening. Just like all those years ago, they were meant to watch Gwyn get beaten. No more warnings. A death was at hand.

Well, she'd give them a show all right.

"Tisiphone of the Furies," Gwyn said loudly, doing this by the book, "I challenge you for leadership of the Wild Hunt."

Tiss's eyes went wide, a minor blip in the anger that hung about her like a cloud. "I accept." Her voice was deep with the weight of her ancient life, the voice of a daughter of Titans.

Gwyn's heart shuddered. She was going to lose.

She tried to think, oh well, Holly will live, and maybe she wouldn't be too hurt by the geas breaking when Tiss killed Sunny, too. Holly was young, tough. Her heart would mend as well as her flesh.

I wish we had more time.

She put the thought away. Win or lose, Gwyn was still going to give the Hunt one hell of a spectacle.

Tiss glanced over her shoulder at one of the more alert Hunt members, Aisling, one of the fey. "Find the target."

With a weary nod, Aisling stumbled into the dark. Gwyn fought the urge to grin. She'd hoped it would be one of the fey who went looking for him. The twisted bits of iron waiting about the place would be particularly useful, especially if Aisling stepped on one. And the fact that Sunny's clothes were strewn all over—he was wearing some Gwyn had yanked out of Faerie—should throw her off the scent for a while.

If you can't beat 'em, you can inconvenience the fuck out of 'em.

❖

Somewhere in the distance, someone shouted, and Holly paused.

She'd searched every level in the parking garage, or at least listened, but this was the only time she'd heard something that sounded like a fight. She turned right out of the stairwell and heard someone cry out from much closer. Rounding an old van, Holly spotted a woman dressed in the leather of the Hunt hopping around trying to pull what looked like a metal sea anemone from the sole of her boot.

She couldn't seem to touch it without yelping.

Fey.

Holly rushed her, a burst of speed she wasn't expecting. She crashed into the fey woman, and they went down in a heap. Holly leapt up faster than normal and managed to punch the woman in the face, knocking her head against the concrete floor.

She went out like a light.

Holly stared at her fist in wonder. Strength coursed through her limbs. With a deep breath, she realized she wasn't winded at all, either, not even after running down that long hallway and four flights of stairs.

Elven blood.

Ew.

But she couldn't waste it, not when she had a fight on her hands.

"Holly," someone whispered.

Even her eyesight seemed sharper as she glanced around to spot Sunny hiding in a corner. She hurried to him, though she could see movement on the other side of the vast space, too. A fleet of motorcycles, riders watching two people fight.

Gwyn and Tiss.

Holly's heart leapt and shrank in equal measures.

She grabbed Sunny's shoulder and pointed him toward the stairs. "Go up to the tunnel. The signs should direct you toward the Avalon. There's an unmarked elevator near one of the signs. Do you have a phone?"

He showed it to her. "I can't get a signal down here."

"You might be able to at the elevator. Call Renne when you're there. Someone will let you up." God, she hoped so.

He was shaking, directing looks toward Gwyn.

"I'll help her," Holly said. "Go."

With a grateful smile, he ran, limping but determined, staying to the shadows.

Holly raced for Gwyn. "Fuck," she muttered when she saw the sheer size of Tiss. Even visions didn't do her justice; she was like a statue come to life. Gwyn blocked a punch from her only to take a kick that knocked her off her feet. Her knife bounced away. She had a bloody nose and another trickle running from her mouth. With a growl, she swung Holly's baton as Tiss tried to grab her by the hair, and the *thunk* that the baton made as it connected with Tiss's arm sounded like someone hitting steel.

Gwyn managed to skitter away, but Tiss was on her quickly, grabbing her ankle and pulling her back, lifting one big boot to stomp on Gwyn like she had on the leader of the Kansas SCDA.

"Hey," Holly yelled. She'd been hoping to plow into Tiss as she had the fey, but it was more important to keep that foot from coming down.

Tiss looked, frowned, and backed off a bit, eyes squinted curiously as Holly approached.

Whatever she thought, Holly didn't waste this opportunity. She pulled Gwyn to her feet.

"I know you," Tiss said, still frowning like a robot trying to identify a feeling.

"Holly," Gwyn said with tears in her eyes. "You're all right."

Holly wanted to beam at her but not with this monster in front of them. "Of course I am."

"The seer," Tiss said.

With a shiver, Holly remembered being seen by those eyes when she had been sharing another person's head. But even her fear didn't seem as great now. Maybe that was another reason she couldn't smile at Gwyn. The elves just didn't feel as strongly as everyone else. Well, her anger seemed to be firing on all cylinders. She'd worry about the rest later.

"Are you joining the challenge?" Tiss asked.

"Yep," Holly said, not knowing what that was about and not caring, but Gwyn wasn't facing this fight alone.

"You can't win," Tiss said, reading from the vision script.

"It's enough that I'm still fighting," Gwyn answered.

Holly took her hand and not because any damn vision told her to. And no amount of elven blood was going to stop her.

Tiss looked upward as if searching the ceiling. "What did you do to Aisling?"

"She's not dead, just down for the count."

Tiss sneered as if that was just as bad. All she probably cared about was whether she could draw on Aisling's power. She flexed a fist and looked at it, then glanced at the riders. "I expected to kill you by now, Gwyn."

Several of the riders were giving Tiss glares of their own.

"They're sick of your bullshit," Gwyn shouted. "And it's about godsdamn time. Shame it took draining their energy for them to turn on you." Her voice shook with a fury all its own, and there were tears in her eyes. "You weren't meant to be murderers."

One of the riders blinked as if coming to her senses. Her mouth worked a few times before she managed, "We haven't…willingly…" She broke off in a mutter, her eyes fluttering as if those few words had sapped her strength.

Gwyn had been right. They were bewitched or something. Or had been. Tiss was losing her grip.

"You're weak, Tiss," Holly said. "And you're only gonna get weaker. Surrender. This is your only chance."

Tiss's head cocked as if Holly was a complex math problem. She drew in a deep breath as if to shout, and the wind rushed past like she was sucking all the air out of the huge room. She stomped so quickly, Holly nearly missed it before the resulting boom threw her off her feet.

She managed to curl into a ball before she hit the ground, but the impact still cracked across her shoulder as she rolled. The pain was dull, but she had a feeling it wouldn't stay that way. The strength from the elven blood seemed to be waning. She had to act fast, and Tiss had just proven she wasn't exactly a pushover.

A few spaces over, Tiss threw Gwyn into a concrete pillar.

"Stop!" Holly ran, scooping up her baton where it had fallen from Gwyn's hands. Holly slid to her knees and cracked Tiss across her right leg with a backhanded strike.

Tiss grunted, falling back slightly. When Holly tried to hit the other leg, Tiss blocked with the bottom of her boot. A mortal's knee would have broken in Holly's first strike, but Tiss didn't even limp.

Holly leapt to her feet, pushing her advantage, trying hit after hit, but Tiss blocked them all with her bare hands, her muscular shoulders flexing. When Holly tried to swing for her neck, Tiss leaned far to the side and jabbed Holly in the stomach.

The air in her lungs abandoned her with a painful rush, and she felt like her eyes were popping out of her skull. She barely managed to get her baton up to block another punch, but the force sent her staggering back to fall flat on her ass.

Tiss loomed over her.

With a primal cry, Gwyn leapt onto Tiss's back, her eyes glowing, energy crackling. She dug her fingers into Tiss's scalp, and chaotic energy poured from her like the sea. Tiss grunted in pain and growled. Holly's chaos field rose like a dust devil and drove Tiss back.

Tiss grabbed Gwyn off her shoulders and threw her forward. Holly did her best to roll and catch her, but the borrowed strength was leaking from her like water through a colander.

"You…okay?" she managed.

Cradled in Holly's arms, Gwyn managed a weak thumbs-up. "Peachy." She looked like she'd been in a marathon where the runners were also beaten with sticks.

"Renounce her," Tiss yelled at the Hunt where they sat watching everything unfold. "All of you who are wishing for her victory, renounce her or join her in death."

What was this? More mutiny from the Hunt? Holly nudged Gwyn. "We have to get up."

"Five more minutes."

Holly swallowed a weary chuckle. If she let herself laugh, hysteria could only follow. It seemed like her fear was rushing back as quickly as her strength was flowing away.

A flash of white caught her eye. The damn cat-elf had followed her all the way here and now sat primly on a white line, watching them.

"Was this what you wanted?" she asked it as some of the Hunt answered Tiss in a variety of languages. "Enjoying the show?"

It blinked slowly, a cat smile.

The same rider who'd argued with Tiss before managed to stand, swaying slightly. "Too many deaths," she said, straightening as if her strength was returning, too. A few of the others nodded, many finding their feet.

Holly helped Gwyn up. If they had allies, maybe they could win this.

As Tiss punched one of the dissenters to the ground, Holly had to rethink. The rider went down like a sack of bricks, her bike falling on top of her as if it was also too tired to stand.

"Do something," Holly said to the cat.

It ignored her, something so catlike, she wondered if it really was an elf.

No, it had to be.

More of the Hunt members advanced on Tiss, some of them armed with knives. With a growl, Gwyn leapt to join them. Holly wanted to follow, but all her old aches and pains returned in force, and she knew that whatever strength she'd borrowed had left her. Against someone like Tiss, what could she do?

"Gwyn," she shouted and tossed her the baton.

The Hunt began to brawl, the other members still moving like Sunny's risen, but they were shaking off their malaise.

"Yes!" Holly watched for an opening, somewhere she could do some good.

Tiss inhaled again, and when she brought her foot down, everyone fell, and the parking garage shook to its foundation. That was as good as a declaration. If Tiss went down, she was taking everyone with her.

"Well?" Holly shouted at where the cat now looked faintly alarmed. "You want her to bring the garage down on all of us?"

The Hunt got to their feet, but the cries and sounds of combat faded in Holly's ears.

"A pact must be made," she heard from just behind her.

She spun. No one there. The voice was in her mind.

She looked at the cat again. It stared back. "What kind of pact?" she asked.

"A single hair from your head and we will help you." It was a calm voice, neutral in gender and without the trace of an accent or emotion. It sent shivers down her spine.

All the books said never to make deals with the fey, elves in particular. But the SCDA had already made one deal years ago, and that had worked out all right.

And the price was only a single hair.

Tiss stomped again, and dust rained from the ceiling. She hurled another rider away. Four were down already. Only seven left. Gwyn managed another of those energy spikes, but with a roar, Tiss lifted two other riders and slammed them together to lie limp at her feet. She turned on Gwyn.

"I accept," Holly cried.

The cat smiled.

Tiss screamed and fell to her knees, grabbing at where her heart should have been. Gwyn and the others stumbled back, all shaking their heads.

Gwyn staggered back as Tiss howled. What the fuck was going on?

"Thank you, elves," Holly yelled as she ran to join the fight.

Gwyn had to sling an arm around her just to stay on her feet. "What's happening?"

"We did it, you did it, the elves did it."

After another blink, Gwyn shook her head. "What are you talking about?"

Holly gestured to where the Hunt was surrounding Tiss again. Screaming in some ancient language, her black hair in disarray, Tiss couldn't seem to shake them off anymore.

"But we didn't do anything to cause…" Gwyn felt it then, a lightness in the air, her own strength coming back to her even as it flowed out of Tiss. "She failed her mission. Sunny must have gone through the portal to Signal." She grinned so widely, her face ached. They'd fucking done it. After all these years.

"Come on, sisters," one of the Amazons cried. "Rally! We nearly have her."

Holly turned to where a cat was sitting nearby. "You tricky bastards. You didn't do a damn thing apart from what you usually do."

The cat wound its tail around its legs.

Gwyn stared at Holly a moment longer to make sure she didn't do anything even stranger, then joined the Hunt. She pushed through the others and dragged Tiss to her knees. The power of the Hunt had abandoned her, flowing back where it belonged, but Gwyn didn't waste time on speeches or gloating. She dropped Holly's baton and took a knife from one of her sister riders.

With a grunt of effort, Gwyn forced Tiss's head back. "Go find somewhere to rule in hell." Summoning all her strength, the power of the Hunt urging her on, she thrust the knife into Tiss's neck.

Tiss's eyes widened with emotion at last, anger and fear and something like relief. Maybe immortality really was a curse. Gwyn released her, and she fell forward, her body crumbling like sand. When she hit the ground, she was naught but ash.

"It's done," Gwyn said. The words took nearly all the wind from her sails. It was all she could do to face the rest of the Hunt. "You're free. I'm free." There was only one thing she wanted to do with that freedom: spend it all by Holly's side. She looked for her and smiled. Even under these dim lights, Holly was too beautiful for words.

A man in dark clothing stepped from the shadows. Gwyn tensed again. She should have known trouble wouldn't stay away from their door for long. But he smelled mostly human and only cleared his throat with a jovial smile. He wore a crisp black suit and tie. A golden nametag pinned to his jacket read, *Brendan*.

"So you finally changed shape," Holly said.

Gwyn glanced at her. "You know him?"

Brendan squinted. "I beg your pardon?"

"From the cat." Holly swayed as if her adrenaline and wits were abandoning her.

"Oh." Brandon glanced down, bent near one of the pillars, and picked up the white cat Gwyn had glimpsed earlier. "You mean Percival?"

Holly blinked at one and then the other. "But you…"

Gwyn put a hand on her arm, hoping to steady her.

Brendan gave her a kind but condescending smile. "My name is Brendan. I work for the Avalon Hotel and Casino."

"And you're…an elf?"

His eyes went wide. "Heavens no, what a question. I've come to collect two things, one of which is the owners' cat, Percival." The cat purred and rubbed its face on his jacket, but whatever fabric it was made of didn't hold on to a single white hair.

"Percival," Holly said. "Who is an elf?"

Now Brendan stared at her as if she'd gone full Jack Nicholson in *The Shining*. "No, he's a cat," he said slowly.

"He's…he can't…" Holly fought for words.

Gwyn massaged her arm gently. "It's all right, love, we're all punchy. Take a deep breath."

Holly rounded on her. "No! Someone talked in my head. They asked for my hair."

"Your hair?"

Brendan moved quickly and plucked what looked like a single strand of hair from Holly's head.

"Ah!" She turned, and Gwyn had to hold her back from advancing on him.

"What the hell is going on?" Gwyn said. She was tired as hell but more than happy to start punching again if necessary.

"Just getting the second thing I came to collect, what she promised the owners of the Avalon." Brendan leaned close while Gwyn and Holly stood flabbergasted. "You should consider yourself very fortunate that they spoke to you," he said with a quick smile.

"Holly, love," Gwyn said, "what did you do?"

Holly turned back and forth, but Brendan was already walking away, Percival smiling over his shoulder.

Chapter Twenty-five

Gwyn's heart went out to Holly as she adjusted her collar again.

"So I think I work for the elves now," Holly said, fidgeting as she stood in a small room with faux-wood paneling, a single folding table up front, and three uncomfortable church chairs, one behind the table, and the other two in front. Holly hadn't touched hers yet, and Gwyn sat in the other.

Marcus and some higher-up honcho from the Las Vegas SCDA were behind the table, the honcho occupying the chair. Gwyn didn't much care who they were. She was here for one reason, to support the woman she loved.

Loved. She curled her toes just thinking about it.

The honcho cracked the knuckles of her long brown fingers and flipped her hair over one shoulder. She smelled like the sea, at least part selkie, and regarded Holly with liquid brown eyes. She hadn't offered them a name. "Have they given you any orders?"

"No, but Gwyn"—Holly gestured over her shoulder—"said that's probably what the hair is for, so I can be…under their power." The words seemed to get stuck in her throat. If the elves did try to compel her, they'd have a fight on their hands.

"The leader of the Wild Hunt," the honcho said, her gaze traveling quickly over Gwyn, clearly unimpressed.

"For now, your worship," Gwyn said, feeling cheeky under that stare. "I'm ready to pledge my life to Holly and go wherever she goes."

Holly's cheeks went crimson, but the smile she tried to hide under a cough seemed delighted, and the moonstone ring winked on her finger.

"I see," the honcho said, but the overhead lights flickered, maybe from her power, maybe because this place was falling apart.

"Are you quitting the SCDA, Holly?" Marcus asked. He leaned against the wall, arms crossed, his head brushing the acoustic tile of the ceiling.

She blinked. "I…"

The door opening saved her from having to respond. Renne walked in, giving Holly a smile and a nod. They'd all been allowed to clean and rest up before this meeting, though it hadn't been inside the plush-sounding Avalon. They'd slept off their adventure in a shitty motel down the street from the SCDA, the entire Hunt there under guard except for the three who'd been banished.

"The criminals we escorted to Las Vegas are all safe in Signal," Renne said.

Gwyn sighed with relief. Sunny was all right. Too bad the elves had used him to trick Holly into giving them power over her. Bastards.

Renne's presence seemed to give Holly a boost of confidence. "I don't want to quit, but if I do work for the elves in some capacity now, I don't want to compromise the agency, sir."

His smile was slight, but it felt like a cartwheel.

"In the meantime, will you be joining the Wild Hunt?" the honcho asked.

Holly looked at Gwyn. "You'd be welcome," Gwyn said. "We need some direction in life. Why not rounding up criminals as a special branch of the SCDA?"

Holly's smile could have lit up a room. She swallowed it before saying, "What about the elves?"

"If they come calling, you'll have a pack at your side."

Holly turned back to Marcus. "Sir?"

He rumbled, but it was the honcho who spoke up. "We can do a test period, but you'll be reporting to me." She looked at both of them again and stood. "Remotely. I don't want you in my town any longer than necessary." She nodded at Marcus, tugged her suit jacket straight, and glided from the room like a willow tree on a power trip.

Gwyn's sigh echoed Holly's and Renne's. Gwyn would have hated to break up their crime-fighting duo, and it seemed like they felt the same way.

"The shit's not done hitting the fan," Marcus said. He hadn't moved from the wall. "You disobeyed orders, broke ranks. We need all the agents we can get, or you'd be out on your asses, maybe even banished." He finally stood, his anger like a cloud. "You're all on probation. One more fuckup, and I'll bounce you to Signal myself, elves or no elves." He pointed at Holly. "And you're to undergo regular exams with an empath. If the elves are compelling you to do things and lie to me about it, I'm not going to get blindsided." He started from the room, then paused. "It'll be a couple days before we leave. I need to arrange transport." He tossed an envelope on the desk. "At least you didn't trade your hair for nothing, Holly." He ducked through the door, no doubt off to find a cargo plane big enough to hold him.

Holly rubbed her temples, and Gwyn stepped up to pat her back. "You did it, love, faced the firing squad and lived to tell the tale."

Holly sagged into her, and it felt so nice to be trusted to support her. "Thank you for being here, for offering to let me ride with the Hunt. But are you sure you want to work for the SCDA?"

"I haven't signed any contracts," Gwyn said, giving her a squeeze. "We'll see what everyone thinks after our 'probation.' I'm not making any decisions for the riders. They've been pushed around enough." Though she suspected all of them would stay. They were on the authorities' radar now, and none of them had anyplace else to go.

Though there was that intriguing rumor they'd heard about a demigod who ran a sanctuary for folk like them in the Caribbean. Tempting if a bit boring.

Renne whistled from where he was looking through the envelope. He held up three keycards. "We've got a suite at the Avalon waiting for us."

Now that sounded more like it. Still, Gwyn had to roll her eyes. "They couldn't have given that to us straightaway? We had to stay in that rat trap under guard?"

"And the Hunt might have to keep staying there," he said. "This is only addressed to us."

Holly eyed Gwyn. "Are you going to be okay leaving the Hunt here for now?"

Gwyn smiled. "The guilt will eat at me, but I'll try." She sympathized with the other riders, really, but they were mostly sleeping off the effects of Tiss's power. They wouldn't appreciate plush beds, three pools, six restaurants, and five-star service.

She might have done a bit of research in her downtime.

And she and Holly would no longer be secured in separate rooms.

Holly seemed to come to that realization at the same time. Her cheeks went pink again, but that wasn't embarrassment. Desire shone from her eyes, and her lips parted gently.

Renne chuckled and set two keycards on the table. "I'm taking my card and going gambling. I'll meet y'all up there later." He paused halfway through the door. "Oh, and the elves also sent word that in return for his assistance in stopping Tiss, they're giving Sunny's aunt some money for cancer treatment."

Gwyn gawked, shocked out of lust. "Really?"

"So they said."

"Damn," Holly said as if rethinking her opinion of them. Gwyn would have to remind her not to be too charitable with her thoughts. Elves were capricious.

"As for sharing the suite," Renne said, "all I ask is that you keep your activities to one of the bedrooms." He took another step and paused. "And put a sock on the door."

Gwyn would hang an entire hosiery department if it would keep him out of their bedroom. She took Holly's hand. "Shall we, love?"

Holly licked her lips and grinned. "Let's take your bike."

Gwyn nearly carried her out of there.

Holly lifted a hand from the Jacuzzi and watched the drops roll down her arm as she'd once done in a vision. And just like then, arms slipped around her from behind. She'd only seen the water then, never would have guessed that she'd be in a huge whirlpool tub in a giant suite near the top floor of an elven hotel.

They'd taken the larger bedroom, the one with this tub in the corner. Renne would just have to deal with a smaller space. She'd apologize when she and Gwyn emerged in a day.

Holly turned, pressing her naked body to Gwyn's and kissing her deeply. They'd already made good use of the bed, the desk, this tub, and the shower, but by the way Gwyn slipped her tongue into Holly's mouth, she was ready to rechristen at least one of them.

"You are an insatiable ball of energy," Holly said breathlessly when they parted.

"Only for you."

"A perpetual orgasm machine."

"I want you to give my eulogy starting with that exact phrase."

Holly kissed her again. "Don't talk about dying."

"Yes, ma'am."

That earned her another kiss. "Can we just stay here in this wonderful little bubble?"

Gwyn nuzzled her neck. "I'm game for anything with you, but that would mean either forking out the money for this suite or going into debt with the elves."

Holly shivered, both from the idea and the kiss. She was already in the dark about what she owed the elves. She certainly didn't want to add to it. Gwyn squeezed her ass, distracting her, and it wasn't until someone knocked on the door that she came back to her senses.

"Renne?" she called, her arms still around Gwyn.

No answer.

With a grumble, Gwyn got out of the tub. "Honestly, there are about three socks on that fuckin' door."

Holly rested her arms on the side of the tub and enjoyed the sight of Gwyn's muscular body stalking across the carpet. She didn't even bother to put a robe on before she unlocked the bedroom door and threw it open.

Holly waited to hear Renne either cry out in surprise or have some quip ready upon seeing Gwyn's naked body, but there was nothing. Gwyn stepped out into the suite's living room.

"Gwyn," Holly said. She got out, too, snatched up two robes and followed after she had one belted around her. "Don't go around naked when you don't know who's out there."

But Gwyn was alone in front of the huge windows that took up one wall. She glanced in the other bedroom, and turned right back around. "There's no one here."

Holly draped a robe over Gwyn's shoulders, both for the sake of whoever might be in the room and so she didn't get distracted and neglect to "keep their activities in the bedroom."

Gwyn pointed at the large kitchen and dining room that dwarfed the one in Holly's apartment. "Was that there before?"

A large gift basket sat on the dining table. "Maybe room service brought it?"

"And just let themselves in? That knock was on our bedroom door." Gwyn eyed the place as if looking for the invisible. "I don't feel any glamour."

Holly shuddered, imagining eyes all over them. She straightened. If someone was watching, they'd soon see her baton coming for their face. She marched to the gift basket and saw an envelope resting elegantly in the leaves of a pineapple.

Holly, it read.

She recognized that handwriting from the office she'd woken up in, and her stomach clenched in anticipation as she lifted the flap to see that same mismatched script on the inside.

All Hallows' Eve. Be ready.

Gwyn put her arms around her. "Well, that settles that."

Holly frowned and fought the urge to throw the card to the floor. "No, it doesn't. Ready for what? And does that mean we have to be back here in a couple weeks?"

Rising to tiptoe, Gwyn kissed her cheek. "Holly love, for elves, that's positively definitive. You may be on probation with the SCDA, but you're also on the elves' payroll now."

"Great." And what that entailed, who knew?

Gwyn gently took the card from her, grabbed a bottle of champagne and a bag of strawberries from the gift basket, and led Holly back toward the bedroom. "You can rest assured that I'll be by your side for it all, darlin'. Renne, too, probably, but I'm the important one."

Holly had to smile and kiss her softly as they walked. She gestured to the goodies. "Do you have plans for me, perchance?"

"No chance about it. And my plans are *very* definitive."

That sounded perfect for the moment. Everything else could wait.

Epilogue

Gwyn whistled low, thoroughly impressed with the city of Signal on Halloween night.

And that was *after* seeing Las Vegas on Halloween. Sin City had decorations and costumes galore, but all of it paled in comparison to this jumble of lights, people, and chaos in general.

This end of the portal had been a joke. After all the burly guards and locks on the Vegas side, she'd been expecting some well-armed trolls, but all they'd had to contend with was a bored goblin, a blue uniform sagging around its short, thin frame, and its long ears mashed downward under a too-large cap. It had waved her and Holly through a broken turnstile without ever looking at them.

And now they stood in Wonderland at Mardi Gras.

Shiny Halloween decorations covered the buildings at all heights. Even the walls with crumbling brickwork bore the occasional glittery spider and sequined bat. Beings of all shapes and sizes thronged the tight streets, passing bottles and laughing. Gwyn spotted plenty of tinsel wigs and googly-eyed glasses and sparkly hats, but it was still difficult to tell where the costumes ended and the people began.

"Oh my God," Holly said. Her eyes were wide, and Gwyn could see her pulse in her neck.

"Are you all right?"

"I'm…" She blinked and swallowed. "It's like the best and worst place I've ever been. I'm both at home and very uncomfortable."

"Amen." Gwyn winced as a troll lumbered past without a stitch of clothing. Chaos was thick in the air, but she could have done without everything else, like the brownie vomiting in the alley to their side or the couple making out frantically on a doorstep just ahead.

Holly squared her shoulders. "Come on. We have an appointment." She waded into the crowd.

Gwyn stayed on her heels. It would have been a privilege to follow her into hell. And not just because the view was better than anything currently going on around them.

The streets were numerous and narrow, going off at odd angles like in a medieval city. The surfaces changed on a dime, too. Cobbles one moment, asphalt the next, then a patch of gravel, more cobbles, and garden paving stones. The taller buildings tilted slightly, and anything above four stories seemed about to fall over. Some were even propped up by long boards connected to adjacent buildings. The street ahead seemed to dead-end at a squat structure that looked like half of it had come out of the Renaissance, and the other half was '80s pop.

"Who knew neon and white stucco worked so well together?" Gwyn said.

Holly grinned over her shoulder. She stopped in another doorway near where a gangly orange boggart sat chewing gum as they watched the crowd. A tiny gremlin sat on their shoulder, smacking its gum in tandem.

"Okay," Holly said as she pulled their map from her pocket. It was badly drawn on what looked like a paper napkin. Definitely not elven work. They'd gotten it from Brendan, the same young man who'd taken a strand of Holly's hair.

"I do apologize," he'd said as he'd handed it over. "Signal is always changing, so maps are hard to come by. This should be accurate as of"—he'd glanced at a clock in the heavily guarded basement of the Avalon—"two hours ago. Things shouldn't have changed too much since then."

Holly had given him an incredulous smile. "They change the city every few hours?"

"Sometimes." He'd smiled as if that was perfectly normal.

"Very fey," Gwyn had added.

Now, Holly squinted at the map, turning it this way and that. "It says to go to the Ren Pop Disco." She pointed at the monstrosity ahead. "Then go under and turn right at the green living room." She stared a few more moments before shaking her head. "What the hell does that mean?"

"What can we do but go look?" Gwyn asked. She gave Holly a sideways hug. "In the realms of chaos, one must go with the flow. As a reward, we can look up Sunny after we've completed the mission."

Holly nodded, brightening slightly. "Is this what Faerie is like?"

"It's worse."

"Much worse," the gremlin said, now smacking out of time with the boggart. "But not as bad as what's out there." They waved vaguely over their shoulder.

"Yeah, out there," the boggart said.

"The city?" Holly asked.

The gremlin and boggart put on the same dangerous smile, and Gwyn drew back a hair. She'd faced down a Fury, but both of these creatures had disturbingly sharp teeth, as if they were cute, skinny piranha. "In the chaos soup," the gremlin said.

"Yeah, the soup."

Gwyn nodded slowly. Brendan had warned them about the "soup," the morass of wild chaos from which Signal had been formed. It sat between Signal and the realm of Faerie like empty space between galaxies. And it sounded just as dangerous. "Beyond the wall," she said to Holly.

"Right." They'd been warned not to cross the wall no matter what. Gwyn had glimpsed it between the buildings a couple of times, a slab of metal and concrete against a midnight-colored sky. It was the second-largest structure in Signal and the most well-built, circling the entire city. The only thing taller was the lighthouse in the city's center, the beacon that guided anyone who was foolish enough to go outside the wall or those desperate enough to travel here from Faerie.

"Do you know where the green living room is?" Holly asked.

They both pointed toward the Ren Pop Disco, the boggart's iridescent antenna catching the light as they grinned. "Happy Halloween," they said, and for once, the gremlin echoed them.

"Thanks," Gwyn said, their smiles still freaking her out. She urged Holly onward. "Fancy a dance while we're in the disco?"

Holly gave her a flat look, then bumped her with one hip as if to take away the sting. "Maybe later."

Memories of their last stay in Vegas flashed through Gwyn's mind. The non-Tiss parts had been very fun indeed, and she was looking forward to a reenactment. A bit of shopping wouldn't go amiss, either. She still owed Renne a gift to go with the ring she'd given Holly. Maybe they could even find a seer to continue the lessons Holly had begun in Houston.

All thoughts like that flew out of her mind as she saw the disco up close. She'd thought "under" meant they'd have to go inside the building and down, but this was far more chaotic. The building was propped up on stilts that looked hastily erected, assembled from whatever was at hand: wooden beams, concrete pillars, a large lump of twisted car doors, even something that resembled a lot of broom handles lashed together. Chunks of plaster and clods of dirt dribbled from the building above, but people passed under it unconcernedly, and a great many tin shacks, tents, and lean-tos had crowded into both sides of the "street."

"Oh, fuck this," Holly said. "We're supposed to go under there?" She looked at her map again as if it might have changed in the last few minutes.

Gwyn could only shrug. "Fucking elves?" she offered.

"Fucking elves," Holly agreed. Never one to shirk her duty, she marched forward. They went as fast as they could through the crowds on the dirt track until Holly said, "There!"

An eerie green glow filled the dark space ahead. Gwyn broke into a run, using her strength to force a path, though she was hesitant to try that on some of Signal's larger denizens. The glow shone from a tin shack, the wall facing the street completely open to reveal a smattering of furniture and a goblin with a lamp in their hand.

"Is this the green living room?" Holly asked a little breathlessly.

The goblin grinned. "You're in luck. I was just changing the bulb."

The light winked out, only to be replaced with an eerie *orange* glow.

"Ah," Gwyn said. "So that's what Brendan meant."

Holly took a deep breath through her nose, an angry flush creeping up from her collar. "This is no way to run a city. And I'm allergic to order." She stomped down a narrow street to the right, though this one was far smaller, reminding Gwyn of a game path through a crowded forest. They emerged from under the disco into an alley that seemed far older than the trails they'd left behind, but with the way the buildings on either side crowded in, she had no idea how anyone had reached this street before. A dead-end waited about fifty feet in front of them.

"Third door on the left," Holly said, consulting the napkin again.

Gwyn paused beside it.

"What do you think?" Holly asked quietly, chewing her lip as she stared at the maroon door.

"The summons from the elves only asked for you, so it's your mission. You should do the door knocking." Gwyn gave her wrist a squeeze. "You need any heads knocked together, though, I'm your girl."

Holly gave her a grateful smile that promised kisses later. Now they were on duty. "What do you think they want, whoever's in here?"

Gwyn could only shrug. If Holly didn't do as the elves requested, no doubt they could compel her with the hair. But even as Holly seemed nervous and irritated, Gwyn also noted some excitement in the way she leaned forward. Solving mysteries or hunting criminals in this morass of chaos suited her down to the ground. The elves wouldn't squander her talents on anything mundane. Whatever their faults, they weren't wasteful.

With their tools or their toys.

Gwyn still didn't know which she and Holly were, but she was still all in.

"Let's knock together," Holly said.

Gwyn's love welled up in a rush. "Let's." They faced the door together and lifted their hands.

About the Author

Barbara Ann Wright writes fantasy and science fiction novels when not hoarding glitter. She has been a finalist in the *Foreword Review* Book of the Year Awards and the Lambda Literary Awards. She's won three Golden Crown Literary Awards, a Lesfic Bard Award, and five Rainbow Awards. Her novels have made Tor.com's Reviewer's Choice books, BookRiot's 100 Must-Read Sci-Fi Fantasy Novels by Female Authors, and have been recommended on Syfy.com.

Books Available from Bold Strokes Books

An Extraordinary Passion by Kit Meredith. An autistic podcaster must decide whether to take a chance on her polyamorous guest and indulge their shared passion, despite her history. (978-1-63679-679-6)

That's Amore! by Georgia Beers. The romantic city of Rome should inspire Lily's passion for writing, if she can look away from Marina Troiani, her witty, smart, and unassumingly beautiful Italian tour guide. (978-1-63679-841-7)

The Unexpected Heiress by Cassidy Crane. When a cynical opportunist meets a shy but spirited heiress, the last thing she plans is for her heart to get involved. (978-1-63679-833-2)

Through Sky and Stars by Tessa Croft. Can Val and Nicole's love cross space and time to change the fate of humanity? (978-1-63679-862-2)

Uncomplicate It by Kel McCord. When an office attraction threatens her career, Hollis Reed's carefully laid plans demand revision. (978-1-63679-864-6)

Vanguard by Gun Brooke. Beth Kelly, Subterranean freedom fighter, is in the crosshairs when she fights for her people and risks her heart for loving the exacting Celestial dissident leader, LaSierra Delmonte. (978-1-63679-818-9)

Wild Night Rising by Barbara Ann Wright. Riding Harleys instead of horses, the Wild Hunt of myth is once again unleashed upon the world. Their ousted leader and a fey cop must join forces to rein in the ride of terror. (978-1-63679-749-6)

Heart's Appraisal by Jo Hemmingwood. Andy and Hazel can't deny their attraction, but they'll never agree on the place they call home. (978-1-63679-856-1)

Behold My Heart by Ronica Black. Alora Anders is a highly successful artist who's losing her vision. Devastated, she hires Bodie Banks, a young struggling sculptor as a live-in assistant. Can Alora open her mind and her heart to accept Bodie into her life? (978-1-63679-810-3)

Fearless Hearts by Radclyffe. One wounded woman, one determined to protect her—and a summertime of risk, danger, and desire. (978-1-63679-837-0)

Forever Family by L.M. Rose. Two friends come together after tragedy to raise a baby, finding love along the way. (978-1-63679-868-4)

Stranger in the Sand by Renee Roman. Grace Langley is haunted by guilt. Fagan Shaw wishes she could remember her past. Will finding each other bring the closure they're looking for in order to have a brighter future? (978-1-63679-802-8)

The Nursing Home Hoax by Shelley Thrasher and Ann Faulkner. In this fresh take for grown-ups on the classic Nancy Drew series, crime-solving duo Taylor and Marilee investigate suspicious activity at a small East Texas nursing home. (978-1-63679-806-6)

The Rise and Fall of Conner Cody by Chelsey Lynford. A successful yet lonely Hollywood starlet must decide if she can let go of old wounds and accept a chance at family, friendship, and the love of a lifetime. (978-1-63679-739-7)

A Conflict of Interest by Morgan Adams. Tensions rise when a one-night stand becomes a major conflict of interest between an up-and-coming senior associate and a dedicated cardiac surgeon. (978-1-63679-870-7)

A Magnificent Disturbance by Lee Lynch. These everyday dykes and their friends will stop at nothing to see the women's clinic thrive and, in the process, their ideals, their wounds, and a steadfast allegiance to one another make them heroes. (978-1-63679-031-2)

A Marvelous Murder by David S. Pederson. When a hated director is found dead in his locked study, movie star Victor Marvel, his boyfriend Griff, and friend Eve seek to uncover what really happened to Orland Orcott. (978-1-63679-798-4)

Big Corpse on Campus by Karis Walsh. When University Police Officer Cappy Flannery investigates what looks like a clear-cut suicide, she discovers that the case—and her feelings for librarian Jazz—are more complicated than she expected. (978-1-63679-852-3)

Charity Case by Jean Copeland. Bad girl Lindsay Chase came home to Connecticut for a fresh start, but an old, risky habit provides the chance to save the day for her new love, Ellie. (978-1-63679-593-5)

Moments to Treasure by Ali Vali. Levi Montbard and Yasmine Hassani have found a vast Templar treasure, but there is much more to the story—and what is left to be found. (978-1-63679-473-0)

The Stolen Girl by Cari Hunter. Detective Inspector Jo Shaw is determined to prove she's fit for work after an injury that almost killed her, but a new case brings her up against people who will do anything to preserve their own interests, putting Jo—and those closest to her—directly in the line of fire. (978-1-63679-822-6)

Discovering Gold by Sam Ledel. In 1920s Colorado, a single mother and a rowdy cowgirl must set aside their fears and initial reservations about one another if they want to find love in the mining town each of them calls home. (978-1-63679-786-1)

Dream a Little Dream by Melissa Brayden. Savanna can't believe it when Dr. Kyle Remington, the woman who left her feeling like a fool, shows up in Dreamer's Bay. Life is too complicated for second chances. Or is it? (978-1-63679-839-4)

Emma by the Sea by Sarah G. Levine. A delightful modern-day romance inspired by Emma, one of Jane Austen's most beloved novels. (978-1-63679-879-0)

Goodbye, Hello by Heather K O'Malley. With so much time apart and the challenges of a long-distance relationship, Kelly and Teresa's second chance at love may end just as awkwardly as the first. (978-1-63679-790-8)

One Measure of Love by Annie McDonald. Vancouver's hit competitive cooking show Recipe for Success has begun filming its second season and two talented young chefs are desperate for more than a winning dish. (978-1-63679-827-1)

The Smallest Day by J.M. Redmann. The first bullet missed—can Micky Knight stop the second bullet from finding its target? (978-1-63679-854-7)

To Please Her by Elena Abbott. A spilled coffee leads Sabrina into a world of erotic BDSM that may just land her the love of her life. (978-1-63679-849-3)

Two Weddings and a Funeral by Claudia Parr. Stella and Theo have spent the last thirteen years pretending they can be just friends, but surely "just friends" don't make out every chance they get. (978-1-63679-820-2)

BOLDSTROKESBOOKS.COM

Looking for your next great read?

Visit BOLDSTROKESBOOKS.COM
to browse our entire catalog of paperbacks, ebooks, and audiobooks.

Want the first word on what's new?
Visit our website for event info, author interviews, and blogs.

Subscribe to our free newsletter for sneak peeks, new releases, plus first notice of promos and daily bargains.

SIGN UP AT
BOLDSTROKESBOOKS.COM/signup

Bold Strokes Books is an award-winning publisher committed to quality and diversity in LGBTQ fiction.